Praise for
The Crossroads of Grace series

"*With Endless Sight* paints an unforgettable story about the power of love and a young girl's gritty determination to remain true to God. This stunningly beautiful novel is written with an emotional depth that will touch your heart and remain with you forever."

—NANCY JO JENKINS, author of *Coldwater Revival*

"*With Endless Sight* sets a tender story against the harsh frontier landscape. Allison Pittman writes the kind of lush details that pull you into another time and place. She's definitely earned herself a spot on my must-read list!"

—ALLIE PLEITER, author of *My So-Called Love Life*

"Once again Allison Pittman has painted a masterpiece with words. With the deft brushstrokes of a master storyteller, Pittman's canvas is filled with characters and places that will live on long after the last page has been turned. *With Endless Sight* is not to be missed, for to do so would be to miss an opportunity to see the grace and love of God working through the simple yet complicated faith of those who choose to love Him even in the hardest moments."

—KATHLEEN Y'BARBO, best-selling author of *Beloved Castaway*

"In *Speak Through the Wind*, Allison Pittman guides her heroine down the dark alleys of New York and through the bustling streets of San

Francisco on a harrowing journey toward wholeness. Carefully chosen details and realistic dialogue bring the gritty scenes to life as Kassandra spirals downward, even as her day of redemption draws near."

—LIZ CURTIS HIGGS, best-selling author of *Grace in Thine Eyes*

"While *Speak Through the Wind* is beautifully written, wonderfully moving, and a testament to God's love, it suffers from the following: It is highly incompatible with mascara (waterproof or otherwise), getting one's children to school ahead of the tardy bell, and putting dinner on the table. I simply could not put it down."

—TAMARA LEIGH, author of *Perfecting Kate*
and *Splitting Harriet*

"Pittman beautifully articulates the depths of despair and hopelessness that often arrive with disappointment and loss. Her knowledge of history combined with the human component of injustice and suffering is what makes *Speak Through the Wind* so engaging and compelling. The ultimate message of God's love and redemption leaves the reader uplifted and encouraged."

—*Romantic Times* magazine

"*Ten Thousand Charms* is a terrific tale of love and redemption that grabs you and won't let go. It will leave you like it left me, anxious to see this author's future work."

—JAMES SCOTT BELL, best-selling author of *Presumed Guilty*

With Endless
Sight

CROSSROADS OF GRACE

BOOK THREE

With Endless Sight

A NOVEL

ALLISON PITTMAN

MULTNOMAH
BOOKS

WITH ENDLESS SIGHT
PUBLISHED BY MULTNOMAH BOOKS
12265 Oracle Boulevard, Suite 200
Colorado Springs, Colorado 80921
A division of Random House Inc.

Scripture quotations or paraphrases in the main text are taken from the King James Version. Those used in the reader's guide are taken from the Holy Bible, New International Version®. NIV®. Copyright © 1973, 1978, 1984 by International Bible Society. Used by permission of Zondervan Publishing House. All rights reserved.

The characters and events in this book are fictional, and any resemblance to actual persons or events is coincidental.

ISBN: 978-1-60142-012-1

Library of Congress Cataloging-in-Publication Data
Pittman, Allison.
    With endless sight : a novel / Allison Pittman. — 1st ed.
        p. cm. — (Crossroads of grace; bk. 3)
    ISBN: 978-1-60142-012-1
  I. Title.
    PS3616.I885W58 2008
    813'.6—dc22

                                                    2007048152

Printed in the United States of America
2008—First Edition

10 9 8 7 6 5 4 3 2 1

For Brenda—

I think you know which one of us is Phoebe!

We Walk by Faith
and Not by Sight

by Henry Alford (1845)

We walk by faith and not by sight;
No gracious words we hear
From Him who spoke as never man,
But we believe Him near.

We may not touch His hands and side,
Nor follow where He trod;
But in His promise we rejoice,
And cry, "My Lord and God."

Help Thou, O Lord, our unbelief:
And may our faith abound,
To call on Thee when Thou art near,
And seek, where Thou art found:

That when our life of faith is done,
In realms of clearer light,
We may behold Thee as Thou art,
With full and endless sight.

I wasn't asleep—wasn't even pretending to be—when my cousin Phoebe slipped into my room. She settled on the edge of my mattress, creating such an imbalance that I rolled toward her, giggling as our bodies collided.

"Shh!" Phoebe hissed into the shadows. "Do you want to wake the whole house?"

"Sorry," I whispered.

"Do you have everything?"

I nodded. She gripped my hand with her soft, pudgy one and led me across my own bedroom floor. I held my other hand in front of me, gingerly searching out the familiar obstacles, and stopped when my fingers brushed the corner of my bureau.

"Wait." I slipped my hand from her grip and took hold of the brass pulls of the top drawer. It opened smoothly, silently—trademark of a quality piece of furniture, Mama said—and I had to stretch up to my tiptoes to feel inside.

Normally I would be sifting through rolled stockings, cotton chemises, and ruffled pantalets, but all of those things were packed away. Now the drawer was empty, and after just a few searching pats my fingers closed around the stump of a tallow candle and the gilded handle of the mirror I had received as part of a matching set for my twelfth birthday.

"Let's go."

When we came to the top of the stairs, I transferred the stub of candle into the hand that was holding the mirror and used the other to grip the banister. I'd been running up and down these stairs at least twenty times a day for most of my life, but never in the dark. I gripped the varnished wood—slick enough to slide on if Mama wasn't around—and used my toes to search out the edge of each step before moving down. Phoebe was behind me, breathing down my neck, occasionally tapping her knees into my spine to hurry me along.

Once safely on the ground floor, she brushed past me and took the lead, her white gown iridescent in the night shadows of my family home. It never occurred to me at the time to wonder why I was following her, why she took the lead in navigating through our front parlor, our morning room, our receiving hall. I suppose her frequent visits—sometimes lasting for weeks on end—made her feel less like a guest than did my other cousins, who were all gathered in what used to be our formal dining room. Where twelve perfectly carved and upholstered high-backed chairs once stood, a litter of bedrolls and blankets covered the floor. When Phoebe and I walked into the room, the bundles sprang to life, and six girls were on their feet, hair streaming unplaited down their backs. They burst into whispered anticipation, then exchanged even louder admonitions to be quiet until Phoebe had to raise her voice to achieve silence.

"Is everybody ready?" Phoebe said. "Do you have your candles?"

"Yes, yes!" they chorused, first quite loud, then softer in response to Phoebe's scolding finger. They held out little stubs of tallow for Phoebe's approval.

"Come on, then."

The pack of little girls—the youngest, Anne, not quite eight years old—followed us out of the dining room and into the kitchen.

I handed Phoebe the mirror and candle, reached into the box on the shelf above the stove and took out a match, and drew it swiftly across the striking surface attached to the wall. The sulfurous odor lent an additional air of mystery to our little adventure, and the girls let out a collective gasp and shiver at the ordinary spark and light. I touched the flame to the stub of candle Phoebe held, then brought the match to my lips to blow it out.

"No," Phoebe said.

"You can light the other candles off this one." I was not happy about being in a power struggle in front of these younger girls.

"Each candle must have its own flame." Her voice took on a deep, earthy quality, and I could sense the excited shivers of my younger cousins.

"It's going to burn my fingers."

"Only if we waste time arguing about it."

"So we'll stop arguing."

I gave a decisive snap of my wrist, extinguishing the flame. The only light in the kitchen came from the candle Phoebe held close to her face, her pale skin now ghostly, her blond hair transparent.

"You're going to ruin everything." She shouldered in close so the other cousins wouldn't hear.

"We shouldn't be doing this anyway, and you know it," I said, matching her tone. "Mother would skin us all alive if she knew."

"That's why nobody is going to tell her." She slowly turned and faced the group. "Nobody's going to tell anyone."

The cousins took a collective step back, twelve wide eyes nodding in pale faces.

Then she turned directly to me. "Now, what can we use to break the mirror?"

"Isn't that bad luck?"

"Only if you believe it is."

"I got this for my birthday."

Phoebe leaned in close. "Listen, Belinda, you chicken out on me now, and I'll march right upstairs, wake your mother, and tell her this was all your idea."

I snatched the candle out of her hand and used it to light my search for any leftover tea towel and some heavy utensil not yet confiscated by a needy neighbor. I quickly found a scrap of cloth crumpled on top of the counter and a rusty potato masher left to languish in a drawer.

I offered these to Phoebe, who took them with the solemn air of a presiding priestess. As the girls craned to see over her shoulder, she placed the mirror on the kitchen counter, covered it with the cloth, and broke the glass with one decisive *whack* of the potato peeler's handle. We all jumped back at that moment, as if expecting the shards to fly straight into our faces, but surged forward again when Phoebe removed the towel to reveal the broken mirror. She gingerly poked around and handed me the largest piece.

"For your soul and your soul mate," Phoebe said in that eerie voice she had affected just for this evening. She repeated the gift and the incantation until each—even the youngest—held a sharp-sided piece. "Now, whoever goes first will have to be very, very brave. I'm sixteen, the oldest, but I can't go because I'm holding"—she looked at me—"the first flame."

"So Belinda's next," my cousins chorused, pointing at me. "She's thirteen!"

"No! I, um…I gave the sacrifice of the looking glass." I tried to sound as eerily authoritative as Phoebe. "In fact, I can choose not to participate at all."

Before Phoebe could argue, Ida—just a month younger than I—stepped forward, holding out her candle stub. "I'll go."

"Very well." Phoebe squared herself in front of Ida. "But remember, you must follow the instructions exactly. First, light your candle."

Ida touched the black wick of her tallow stub to the flame.

"You must stand on the top step with your back to the cellar and say, 'I descend into the darkness to see the face of my true love.' "

We all shivered at the word *darkness*.

"Then," Phoebe continued, "you walk down the steps backward

to symbolize that you are able to trust yourself. You mustn't try to steady your steps by clinging to the wall or else you will never fall in love. Hold the candle and mirror in front of you. Do not look down or your husband will find an early grave. Do not look into the flame or your true love's eyes will burn for another. You must look only into your own eyes, the reflection you see by the light of the candle. In this way, you are looking into your very soul."

By the time she finished speaking, her voice was a mere whisper, and we all might have stood there in our little semicircle until dawn if Anne hadn't piped up to ask, "Then what?"

"Then," Phoebe said, her voice even deeper, "when you know you are on the cellar floor, without taking your eyes off your reflection, blow the candle out!"

We gasped.

"In that split second, before everything goes completely dark, you will see the face of your true love reflected in the glass."

All of us, Phoebe included, burst into nervous giggles. When we had sufficiently hushed ourselves, Phoebe asked Ida if she was ready to take her journey down the steps.

"Yes," Ida whispered.

She held her lit candle in front of her and walked toward the cellar door. It was closed but not locked, and there was an unspoken understanding that I was the one who should pull it open. Her candle illuminated only the top two steps; after that it was a dark, gaping maw. Ida looked terrified.

"You don't have to do this if you don't want to." I gazed into her wide, staring eyes.

"We all promised we would," Phoebe said in that bossy tone nobody ever seemed to have the will to fight against.

"I'm fine." Ida positioned herself at the edge of the top step against a canvas of black and took a deep breath. "I descend into the darkness to see the face of my true love."

Step by careful step, she drew away from us. We all gathered at the doorway, so close we could each feel the heartbeat of another. Nobody said a word, and Ida's gaze never left its target. She grew smaller and smaller, the darkness seeming to crowd around her, then finally she stopped. We heard the sharp intake of her breath, and at once the tiny flame was gone, and Ida was consumed.

Silence, and then a voice from the abyss. "I saw him!"

The girls nearly threw themselves down the stairs, exhaling the common breath we all held. For the briefest moment, I doubted my own disbelief, wondering if there might be something to this voodoo falderol that Phoebe had roped us all into.

I made my way to the front of the crowd, cupped my hand to my mouth, and said, "Who'd you see?"

"Michael Foster!"

Phoebe caught my eye and sent me a look of smug confirmation, but I was nowhere near convinced. Cousin Ida had been talking about Michael Foster in her letters to me for at least three years. His father owned a textile mill that Michael would surely inherit. I met him once when we went up to visit. His hair stood on end like porcupine spikes and his hands were softer than mine, but Ida had her heart and mind set on marrying him. I would have been more surprised if she *hadn't* seen his face in the glass.

Ida's success infused all the girls with anticipation—except Anne, who insisted she was too little to have a true love.

The honor next went to Lillian, who had just turned thirteen but had the face and figure of a much older girl. She and her family lived twenty miles away, and Mother often said she was glad because Lillian had all the earmarks of a girl who would grow up too fast, and a girl like that could ruin the reputation of an entire family.

As Lillian poised herself at the top of the stairs saying, "I descend into the darkness to see the face of my true love," Phoebe elbowed me in the ribs and muttered something about being certain Lillian had descended into darkness before. I giggled and drew a reproachful glare from the other girls waiting their turn. When Lillian's little light extinguished below, we once again leaned forward, waiting.

"I definitely saw someone," she said, "but I couldn't make out the face clearly. He had curly hair, though."

"Maybe it's someone you haven't met yet," Ida's voice chimed in from the darkness.

"Maybe there's just too many for the fates to choose from," Phoebe said, and all of us upstairs laughed.

Next were the twins—first Violet, then Virginia—twelve years old and identical with the exception of the scars each one sported after an agreed-upon wounding to establish separate identities. Violet swore she saw a distinct face in the glass but refused to divulge a name until Virginia had descended. Nobody was surprised to learn that both girls saw the same face—some boy named Virgil who worked as a day laborer on a neighboring farm. The ensuing squabble might have lasted until dawn if a mysterious scuffle hadn't brought it to an abrupt halt.

Then came Rachel, eleven, a level-headed girl who must have shared my skepticism about the night's events. When she delivered her line about descending into the darkness, she did so in a warbled falsetto, dragging out the word *love* for at least the first three steps. When she hit the bottom and doused her candle, she swore she'd seen the face of Thomas Jefferson.

That left only Phoebe, little Anne, and me at the top of the cellar steps, and when Phoebe tried to maneuver the girl into her starting position, she was met with a swift kick in the shin.

"I said I didn't want to!" Anne stamped her foot and settled her face in a determined pout.

"And I said you have to. Otherwise, you'll be left up here all alone in the kitchen. Is that what you want? To be the only one in here when Uncle Robert comes down to see what all the ruckus is?"

Phoebe's uncle Robert was my father, and the thought of facing him in a dark kitchen in the middle of the night with a bevy of would-be witches tucked away in the cellar was not a soothing one. It was some kind of miracle that he hadn't heard us at all—yet.

"What if we let Anne go down face forward?" I said. "Just let her keep her candle lit, walk down the stairs holding on to the wall, and join everybody else at the bottom."

"Yeah. I don't want no true love anyway. Boys stink."

Phoebe rolled her eyes at the grand concession. "Just go."

I watched Anne make her way down the stairs, feeling guilty for having brought her into this mess. I also knew there was no way that little girl would be able to keep this a secret for long, and I hoped I would be deep into the Great Plains before she cracked.

"All right, Belinda." Phoebe held out her candle to me. "Now it's your turn."

"Ah, Phoebe, you know I don't believe any of this. It's…it's evil; it's witchcraft."

"It's not *witchcraft*," Phoebe said, her voice full of disdain. "It's just, it's—"

"Wrong. It's just wrong. It's sinful."

"So you're perfectly fine with letting the rest of us sin, but you're too good?"

"You're welcome to do what you want, but I can't."

"You promised."

"I didn't know what it would be like. I thought it would just be like the apple peels." That was another of Phoebe's favorites, peeling off a strip of apple skin and seeing what letter it formed when dropped into a dish of sugar. Mine was always a *J;* hers a *C.*

"This isn't any different," Phoebe said. "Besides, if you don't believe, it won't even work for you. It will just be a walk down some stairs."

Compliance seemed to be the only way to bring this wretched night to a close, so I tipped my wick into Phoebe's flame and stood at the mouth of the cellar. "Idescendintothedarknesstoseethefaceofmytruelove."

I could have cheated, could have stumbled into the wall and used it to guide me down, could have cast my eyes down to follow my feet, but once I saw my reflection, illuminated by that small flame, I had an overwhelming desire to know if what the other girls experienced was real. The piece of glass I held was almost a perfect triangle, curved slightly along its longest side, and it afforded me a full view of just one eye obscured by a few strands of long, loose hair. I kept my focus on that eye, seeing not my soul but something completely detached. A tiny flame dancing in a deep, dark orb.

The cellar steps were rough and cool beneath my bare feet—a marked change from the soft carpets of the house and the smooth finish of the kitchen floor. I put one foot gingerly down behind me, fought for balance, then brought down the other. I told myself I was just playing a game, appeasing my cousins, participating in a ritual as harmless as tossing spilled salt over my shoulder.

The whispers petered into silence, and one final toe-reaching behind me confirmed that I was on solid ground. I took a deep breath and extinguished the flame.

And, nothing. Nothing but the darkness wrapped close around me. I kept my eye trained on the shard of mirror until the glowing tip of my candle's wick was swallowed by black.

"Well?" The girls gathered around me, speaking as a chorus.

"I told you this was a bunch of nonsense," I said, not allowing a drop of disappointment to come through.

"Or maybe you're just never going to have a true love," Phoebe said.

"Or maybe God knows the plans He has for me, and He's not going to reveal them through some childish, evil game."

"Aw, save your Scriptures for Sunday school."

Phoebe positioned herself at the top of the stairs and intoned the fateful phrase with more conviction than any of us had mustered. I felt Anne's small hand slip into mine. My failure to see an image hadn't shaken their faith; with the exception of the good-humored Rachel, they were believers.

Phoebe came down the final step, and we took a collective step back. I heard her sharp intake of breath, then a puff into darkness. Nobody broke into the silence that followed, but Anne did squeeze my hand a little tighter.

"Thank you, God," Phoebe whispered.

"You leave God out of this." I dropped Anne's hand and shook my finger in the direction of Phoebe's voice. "There's nothing of God in this. It's just—"

"You know who I saw, don't you?"

"You didn't see anybody. None of us did."

"Who was it?" The eager voices of my cousins overrode my singular voice of reason.

"Chester," Phoebe said.

"*Cousin* Chester?" Rachel said.

"Not by blood," Phoebe said, reminding all of us of her adopted status—the very factor that gave her such mysterious appeal and power. "Now all of you get back upstairs."

The girls shuffled their way back to the stairs, and excited whispers accompanied their ascent. I moved to join them, but was detained by a grip on my sleeve.

"Now do you see?"

"This doesn't mean anything."

"It changes everything." Phoebe jerked me hard against her and stood so close I could feel her lips moving against my ear. "Talk to your father again. Tell him I have to go with you."

2

Nobody can agree about how Phoebe came into our family. Her mother is my mother's older sister—my Aunt Nadine—a plump woman nowhere near matching Mother in beauty or stature. Aunt Nadine married Uncle Silas later in life, after seeing her younger sister happily paired off and producing children, which she, to her great sadness and shame, seemed unable to do.

Then one day, according to Aunt Nadine, an angel simply dropped a beautiful baby girl on their doorstep. Some in our family say that angel was the seventeen-year-old daughter of Nadine and Silas's neighbor who left in the middle of the night to attend a teacher's college in Chicago. Others attribute the gift of Phoebe to a pregnant Norwegian immigrant who stayed in town only a few days before moving on—noticeably slimmer—with her husband and seven children.

Aunt Nadine clings to the image of a child-bearing angel, even though Phoebe's pale complexion and almost white blond hair pays testament to the Norwegian theory. This coloring sets Phoebe apart from the rest of us who tend to have dark hair and eyes and skin that turns deep brown with slightest exposure to the sun. Mother's biggest fear in going out West is that we'll be mistaken for Indians and either shot on sight or invited to some heathen feast.

One morning a few days after the cellar game, when all of our out-of-town family had gone, taking the bulk of our household possessions with them, I awoke to hear Daddy whistling downstairs. It was a happy tune—a drinking song with forbidden lyrics. I climbed out of my bed and followed the sound until I came upon him in the kitchen.

"Careful, Belinda," he said before I'd even crossed the threshold. "There may still be some broken glass on the floor."

I went to my toes and picked a careful path toward him. The table was strewn with papers, but he took off his glasses, pushed his chair back, and held out his arms to hug me.

"Good morning, Daddy." I bent to give him a kiss on his cheek, still soft from shaving. He wore a mustache and whiskers on his chin, but the rest of his face was always clean and smooth. In the mornings it was actually cool to the touch and smelled faintly of peppermint. "What's all of this?"

"Just a bunch of boring old papers, sweetie." He quickly gathered them into a neat pile and dropped them into a leather satchel at his feet. "We're going to the notary today to finalize the turnover to Uncle Silas."

"Mother must be thrilled." I knew full well she wasn't.

Months after marrying my mother, Daddy inherited a small ironworks shop that produced many of the farming tools the emigrants strapped to their wagons as they headed out West. The inheritance came through a distant uncle, and father always joked that Mother must have had some premonition, because at the time he proposed he had only an accountant's salary to offer her. She would smile demurely and say that she would count her life no less blessed if the two of them had lived out their entire life in the two-room flat above the workshop. When he was feeling feisty, Daddy would say he'd like to take her up on her offer, even though the rooms had long ago been turned into his plush office. Mother would laugh just as I imagine she did twenty years ago when he carried her over that threshold for the first time.

Over the years, his three younger brothers were all given shares of the company, though none participated in the daily operations of it. All three had moved to Chicago where Uncle Dan and Uncle Frank were both lawyers. Uncle Edward—the baby of the family—was content to live off his share of the annual profits as what my mother called a listless political bohemian. None were interested in spending their days here in Belleville, Illinois, putting a familial stamp of approval on shovels and plows. So there was no choice but to turn the business over to Uncle Silas, who had been working closely with my father as the foundry manager for at least ten years.

"You're awake awfully early." Daddy turned his full attention to me. "I suppose you weren't up late with secret doings." He cocked one eyebrow up and gave me the mischievous look that Mother said could turn a saint into a sinner.

"Thank you for keeping our secret." I smiled and reached for his coffee cup, took a sip, and grimaced at the bitter taste. "I like Mother's coffee better."

"That's because your mother's coffee is little more than brown milk and sugar. She'll have to get used to something a little stouter on the trail."

"Do you really think the trail is going to change all of us?"

"I don't want you to change." Daddy gave my hand a squeeze. "I want us to grow. To see what we can do with a life without having everything just handed to us. A country doesn't stay new for very long."

"But aren't you going to miss all of this?"

"We must remember—and I tell your mother this every day—that we would have nothing if not for the grace of God who gives it to us for this little while we live on earth. He could take it all away from us like *that*." He snapped his fingers so close to my face I thought the stone in his signet ring might graze my nose.

"I know, Daddy. I'm just worried about Mother."

"You leave her to me."

As if on cue, Mother chose that moment to walk into the kitchen.

"Good morning my darling Ellen." Daddy rose from his chair, sending me a conspiratorial wink. "May I pour you some coffee?"

"I suppose you might as well, seeing we've dismissed the staff." Mother crossed over to the kitchen window, pulled back the curtain, and looked out. "Have you seen Chester yet this morning?"

"I can't recall a time I've seen my son before noon." Daddy took a chipped cup down from the cupboard. It was one we would leave behind.

"He's not in his room." Mother let the curtain fall from her hand. "There are so many ruffians hanging about the streets these days—"

"Those are noble boys come from their farms to register for the army. I think if we were going to accuse any of being 'ruffians' we would have to put our beloved Chester at the top of that list." Father poured a generous amount of milk and sugar into Mother's coffee—turning it into the sweet, lukewarm, tan concoction that she favored—set it on the table, and motioned for her to join us.

"Well that is one thing I shall be glad to see behind me." Mother took a sip and set down the cup without the least acknowledgment or thanks. "All this talk of war and regiments—"

"It's hardly *talk* anymore, Ellen," Daddy said. "We've been at war for nearly two months now."

"Just so. And I will be glad to get away before Chester becomes a part of it."

"I'm sure you are no more grateful than the Union Army is, my dear."

I dared a small smile that was caught short by Mother's disapproving glare, and the three of us sat quietly for a moment before I ventured into a new conversation.

"Have you come to a decision about Phoebe?"

The look they exchanged across the table told me they hadn't.

"I just don't see the point of taking her with us," Daddy said.

"The point is," Mother said, "she would be a great help to me."

"Help with what? We are boarding a train, then a steamboat, then a stagecoach. It's not as though we're joining up with a wagon train."

"She is my sister's child."

"Her only child. Which is all the more reason for her to stay home with her parents."

"I'd like to take a little part of my family with me."

Mother's words hit the air like a strong slap. Daddy and I looked at each other, then quickly down at the table.

"I'd like to know that I have someone to talk with," Mother continued.

I studied the series of nicks in the table. "I think she'd be happier too," I said. "Phoebe, I mean."

"Nonsense," Daddy said. "She has loving parents right here."

"Boys don't like her very much." Until this conversation, I had no intention of arguing Phoebe's case, but it occurred to me that I, too, could benefit from a companion.

"Do you honestly think," Daddy said, "that I would drag her along just so she could find a husband? The town's crawling with men—"

"Those are soldiers, dear, remember? Men set for *la guerre* often have no time for *l'amour*. From what I hear, the men are absolutely desperate for women out on the frontier."

"Desperate enough for Phoebe?"

"Don't be mean." I swatted my father's sleeve. "People are

mean enough to her already. She isn't very pretty, and she isn't very smart."

"Mind how you speak about your cousin," Mother said. "But Belinda does have a point, Robert. In fact, the only thing Phoebe has to offer a man is—the foundry."

A dark look came over Daddy's face. "She's not in line to inherit a bit of that," he said.

"Maybe not. But some man is going to see that her father's in charge of it and assume he'll be able to work his way in."

Even as Mother spoke, the full scenario played out in my mind. Poor, stupid Phoebe duped by some smooth-talking man—maybe one of the ironworkers—seducing her with slick words and empty promises, breaking into Uncle Silas's office to get a look at the books. Or not breaking in at all, rather using the spare key Phoebe would wear on a thin chain around her neck…

"Silas and Nadine would never let her go." Daddy's voice was taking on the edge of defeat.

"Yes, Robert, they would."

"We don't know that for sure."

"Yes we do, darling. I spoke with my sister."

Daddy took a long, measured sip of his coffee before setting the cup down and suggesting that I should leave the room.

"You stay right here, Belinda," Mother said.

"Don't undermine me in front of the children."

"She is hardly a child, Robert. And it would be good for her to have a companion on the journey."

"Companion? This isn't a lake-house holiday!"

"We are all aware of that," Mother said, and the tension at the table made me wish I'd obeyed my father and gone back to my bed. "We know our lives are being uprooted and destroyed with little explanation—"

"I've told you—"

"Oh, yes, of course! The new frontier. New opportunities. Building something of your own without having it handed to you. And I've been the good, dutiful wife, not asking for a thing. But I want this, Robert. I want my niece to come with us, to have a part of one sister with me."

"I can't imagine her parents would approve."

"They give her everything she wants," I said, surprised at my petulance.

"I don't know that *you've* ever lacked for anything, young lady," Daddy said. "And I can't believe she would want to abandon such loving, generous parents."

"Well, she does," Mother said. "She and Belinda are very close, you know."

"That much I know." Daddy looked straight at me. "I'm a bit worried about the mischief the two of them might get into."

"Please don't try to be charming, Robert. This is not the time. Now, I don't know why Phoebe wants to come along. It never occurred to me to ask her, and I don't know that she would be my first choice of traveling companion. But she's a young woman whose mind is set, and frankly, mine is too."

"But there's a matter of finances to consider, Ellen. It would be much less expensive to go by wagon, but I'm trying to make this as easy as—"

"If we had a third child, would we leave it at home in an effort to economize?"

"Of course not."

"Because if money is an issue, we might do well to let you go off on your own—"

"Now, Ellen—"

"Mother, you don't mean that!"

At that moment, all of my loyalty to Phoebe fell away. I wished I'd never participated in her stupid ceremony, wished I'd never agreed to speak to my father on her behalf, never brought up her name at our cozy little table. Despite mother's claim to the contrary, I wasn't keen on having my cousin as a companion, no matter how nice it might be to have her as a buffer between Mother and me. I hadn't anticipated this level of disagreement between my parents over such a silly thing and cringed at the thought of how they would react if they found out that Phoebe's sole motivation was a misguided fantasy involving my indolent brother.

"Do not tell me what I mean." Mother got up from her chair. "Think about what I've said, Robert."

She left without another word, and the silence that settled in the kitchen demanded an apology.

Before either of us could rise to the occasion, though, the back door opened and the object of Phoebe's affection walked in.

I wondered if Phoebe would have been so enamored if she had a chance to see him now. His dark curly hair was dirty and unfashionably long. His red eyes were rimmed with dark circles, and he brought with him the smell of sour cigar smoke, dense as a cloud.

"G'morning, Dad," he said, somehow impressive in his lack of penitence.

"Chester," Daddy's voice was tightly controlled, "are you just getting home?"

"Nothing quite like a saloon full of farm boys in the big city for the first time." A slight smile broke on Chester's scruffy face.

"Belleville is hardly a big city," I said.

"Tell that to these rubes." He rubbed his hands together.

"Never mind about that," Daddy said. "Right now you need to get up to your room before your mother comes down and finds you here like this."

"Let me get some coffee first."

We were long past the days when the relationship between Chester and my parents was characterized by submission and obedience. Daddy and I watched Chester pour a cup of coffee, add a spoonful of sugar from the bowl kept next to the stove, then take an experimental sip before committing himself fully. All the while, Daddy clenched and unclenched his fists, probably wishing Chester's throat were grasped within. He waited to speak until my brother had his hand on the swinging door that led to the dining room.

"We leave in three days you know, Son. That'll be the end to these late-night games."

"That's where you're wrong, Dad," Chester said, sending the smile I imagine he unfolded every time he laid down a winning hand. "It's the biggest gamble of all."

3

The first leg of our journey lacked the romance of any great odyssey. We simply boarded a train headed north to St. Louis. Gathered in a little group at the station, dressed in our best traveling clothes and carrying a bundle of boxed lunches for the trip, we looked like any other family off for a summer holiday. It occurred to me then that nobody had consulted Chester about our decision to bring along Phoebe, as he had an expression of mild surprise when she showed up carrying her small carpet bag—the only additional cargo Daddy would allow her.

The only sign that we were embarking on something grand was the final embrace between Mother and Aunt Nadine, who clung to each other as if doing so would reverse the tide that had swept us up and out with the rest of the country.

Phoebe and I stood by, watching. My heart ached knowing how much Mother loved her sister and her life here; Phoebe wore the same resolved, scowling expression she always did. When Aunt Nadine finally released Mother and held out her arms to her daughter, Phoebe walked into them as if each step were a small battle.

"My precious girl." Aunt Nadine crushed Phoebe's body fully against hers, laying her cheek to the top of Phoebe's head. "Are you certain this is what you want to do? It's not too late to change your mind, you know."

"I have to go, Mama." Phoebe's voice was muffled by the piles of lace at Aunt Nadine's throat.

"That's nonsense. There's absolutely no reason—"

"There's every reason." Phoebe pulled away from Aunt Nadine and looked straight into her eyes. Her hands hung to her sides just as they had throughout the embrace, and now I could see they were balled into fists. "We've talked about this. I don't belong here."

"Of course you do. Papa and I love you so much—"

"This is what I want."

Daddy's head appeared in the train window, and he gestured wildly for us to join him. Mother took one more step toward Aunt Nadine, but Phoebe stayed her ground between them. She took Mother's arm and led her onto the train, leaving me alone to say good-bye to my aunt.

"Are you sure you don't want to come?" I said. "There's plenty of room."

Aunt Nadine laughed, then dabbed at her eyes with her handkerchief. "Take care of your mother. She wasn't born for this."

"I will," I said.

"And watch over Phoebe. I don't know where she got this idea—"

"She'll be fine."

I began inching backward toward the train, eager for the first time to be speeding away on it. But she caught me on my third step and pulled me into her perfumed bosom. Her hand clutched the back of my head, and I felt a succession of kisses in my hair. I remained, not fidgeting, as long as I could, even as I felt the image on Aunt Nadine's cameo etching itself into my cheek. But the thought of being left at the station to become Uncle Silas and Aunt Nadine's newest foundling seemed very real. I wrapped my arms around her thickening waist and squeezed before prying myself out of her embrace.

"Good-bye, Aunt Nadine," I said before turning and heading for the train.

"Belinda?"

I turned around again.

"I'll be praying every day that God will watch over you."

"So will I." I gave her a final wave before boarding.

It took just a minute for my eyes to adjust to the dim interior of the train. Even though we weren't moving, I still felt a little unsteady on my feet as I made my way down the narrow aisle. Mother always insisted on sitting right in the middle—as far from the lavatories as possible. I touched my fingers lightly on a leather-upholstered seat with each step.

When I came upon my family, it occurred to me that no casual observer would ever guess that we shared a common destination. Chester was slouched in his seat, his arms folded across his chest, his hat drawn low over his face. Next to him was Daddy, his tattered copy of *The Emigrant's Guide to Oregon and California* open in his lap, making little notations in the margins with a stub of pencil.

Across the aisle, Mother sat, staring out the window, her face streaming with unchecked tears while her seatmate, Phoebe, stared forward with just a hint of a satisfied grin on her face.

I scanned the car looking for an empty seat and found one just a few rows behind my family.

"I guess I'll be back here," I said. No one said anything, though I thought I detected a slight grunt from under Chester's hat.

I'd spent my fair share of time in cities before, going to Chicago to visit my cousins nearly every summer, but nothing compared to St. Louis. Given the chance, I could have traversed this city without touching the ground by walking across the backs of the horses and shoulders of the people that created a constant sea of movement between the wagons and carts and carriages in the streets. A massive structure—white stone, domed roof, six columns—loomed over all. Daddy told us it was the courthouse, and Mother commented on the appropriateness of St. Louis having such an impressive building, as this city was the last bit of law and order we'd see for perhaps the rest of our lives.

Her spirits revived when we walked into the Rutledge Hotel, where we would stay for nearly a week awaiting the steamboat Daddy had booked our passage on. The lobby was large and bright, with windows that stretched from the rich, carpeted floor to the embossed ceiling. A dozen crystal chandeliers dispersed the sun's rays throughout the room, and I could only imagine how beautiful it all would be when the candles within them were lit. At the center of the room, a fountain surrounded by a dozen potted palms gurgled as if it was a promise of the refreshment to come with a proper bath in the luxurious rooms upstairs.

While Daddy made the arrangements at the front desk, Mother and I sat on one of the brocade sofas near the wide, carpeted staircase. I perched on the edge of the cushion, taking it all in, but Mother collapsed in her seat, her feet extended so far in front of her I feared she might slide right off.

"You can't begin to understand the depths to which travel exhausts me." Mother tugged at the strings of her bonnet, then left them dangling, as if removing the hat was too overwhelming.

"Mother," I said, "we were only on the train for a few hours. At this rate, you'll never survive the journey to Oregon."

"Sometimes I think that is exactly what your father had in mind." She narrowed her eyes at Daddy, who was engaged in a lively conversation with the desk clerk. "At some point his eyes will open and he'll see the folly of this all."

"I don't think that's going to happen, Mother."

"Oh, it will, my darling. You can be sure of that. But there's no use telling him now. No man will ever admit that he is following a fool's route. And he's surely not going to listen to a mere woman." She managed not only to sit up a little straighter, but to pop the bonnet off her head and begin to pick bits of dust and ash out of its impressive arrangement of feathers. "No, I'll just keep quiet, and soon enough he'll wake up, look around, and realize just how ridiculous all of this is, and we'll pack up whatever we have left and head straight back home. The key there is not to gloat, not to give off a superior air."

I don't believe my mother had ever taken so much as a single breath without giving off a superior air, and I couldn't recall five minutes' worth of conversation when she had ever kept quiet. But I didn't want to bog down in detail.

"You know, Mother," I said, "that seems rather dishonest."

"Nonsense, Belinda. It's biblical."

"Biblical?"

" 'Wives, submit yourselves unto your own husbands.' " Mother turned her hat over in her hands as if reading the words in the velvet lining. "So here I am. Submitting."

"But you're rooting for him to fail." I looked over at my father, who was now writing in the little leather-bound journal he carried with him everywhere, and felt my spine stiffen in defense. "I don't think that's the spirit a wife is supposed to have."

"Of course I don't want him to *fail*." She put her hat in her lap and looked at me. "If he *fails,* we'll all be dead. I just want him to come to his senses."

Just then Daddy headed our way, and Mother managed to have a weak and nearly welcoming smile by the time he settled into the chair facing us.

"The rooms are ready." He held up a set of keys triumphantly. "The boy will take our bags and meet us upstairs, and we'll have a little time to refresh ourselves before they serve supper in the dining room."

"That sounds lovely, Robert," Mother said with surprising sweetness.

Daddy turned in his chair and looked around the lobby. "Where's that son of ours? And Phoebe?"

"Find one, find the other," I said, not quite under my breath.

"What's that?" Daddy asked.

"Chester decided to take a quick walking tour of the block." Mother sent me a sidelong glance. "I'm sure he wants to ascertain the nature of the night's entertainment."

"Ah," Daddy said, and for a brief moment he and Mother were united in a breath of disappointment. "And Phoebe?"

"Isn't she here?" Now it was Mother who turned around in her seat. "Did she come in with us? Belinda, do you see her?"

I didn't, and to my shame I couldn't recall if she had even walked into the lobby with us. I could picture her, one-and-a-half steps behind Chester, her pale eyes fixed on his dark head, following him through the crowded streets, ducking into doorways on the off chance that he might turn around and see her. I didn't share this vision with my parents, however. I simply said, "No. I'll look for her," and made my way to the hotel's massive front doors.

I didn't have far to look. She was standing on the sidewalk just outside, leaning against a light post.

"Phoebe?" I had to repeat myself to be heard above the street noise before she would turn and acknowledge me. "Are you going to come inside? Our room is ready."

"In a minute." She turned her gaze back to the street.

"Where'd he go?"

"I'm not sure. I followed for a little while; then I was afraid I'd get lost so I came back here. But I think there's a saloon down there."

"Daddy will be furious."

"He's a grown-up man, Belinda."

"And you'll do well to remember that too, Phoebe."

She smiled. "I know he doesn't love me. Not yet. And back home there were so many other girls. So many distractions."

"And there aren't here?" I drew her attention to a pair of women crossing the street. Their hair was piled high and their bodices were cut low, showing bare shoulders in the middle of the day. Something that would have put my mother in a full swoon.

"We aren't staying here," she said, as if speaking to a child.

"You're right. Then it's off to the steamboat. With a hundred other people. And a saloon. And dozens of women just like them."

Phoebe had a certain smile that I likened to the last vision an unsuspecting baby bird has before it is snatched in the jaws of a cat. She looked like that now, and though we were in the middle of a crowded St. Louis sidewalk, I knew her mind was miles away.

"But after that," she said, her voice dreamy, "it's just us. On a stagecoach for days upon days. Just us. Out in the wilderness. He'll get lonely, Belinda."

"Good heavens, Phoebe, what are you planning to do?"

She sneered at me. "Oh, nothing immoral, so there's no need for you to look at me with your little sanctimonious preacher eyes. I'm just hoping that maybe, if I can have him to myself for just a little while…"

"Be careful, Phoebe. Chester isn't always…kind."

"Neither am I," she said.

The luxury of the lobby didn't quite reach to the rooms. Phoebe and I would share a bed that, while ample enough, was outfitted with bedding of a lesser quality than what I had at home. There was a dressing table, a washstand, and an armoire that made walking about the room difficult. The floor was bare, though a worn rug lay at the foot of the bed, and the curtains were just beginning to yellow at the hem.

"It's lovely." Phoebe walked around the room, lightly touching each furnishing. Her reaction didn't surprise me—Aunt Nadine kept a modest home—and I felt guilty for my initial disappointment.

"It is nice," I conceded.

I knocked on the door that joined our room to my parents', curious to see if any of the downstairs glamour lurked behind it. Daddy opened it, and I could see just over his shoulder that Mother had encountered her first real disappointment of the journey.

"You would think for this money—"

"Oh, stop it." Daddy's voice coming as close to being harsh as it ever did. "You'll feel better once you've had a bath."

Apparently he was right, because when we all gathered in the dining room later that night, Mother seemed rested and genuinely happy. In fact, our entire little party had the air of embarking on a grand adventure as we gathered at the linen-covered table. We had a platter stacked with sliced ham, a large bowl of mashed potatoes with red gravy, a plate of steamed radishes, and a basket of warm biscuits.

Chester joined us midway through the meal, and the young woman who served our table immediately went to the kitchen to fetch him a warm plate.

"Glad you could join us, Son." Daddy speared a slice of ham with his fork. "How did you find the city?"

"Ah, Dad, it's amazing." Chester heaped his plate full, scraping the sides of our serving bowls. "Are there any more biscuits?"

"You can take mine. I haven't touched it."

"Thanks, Phoebe."

They smiled at each other, and I nudged her under the table hoping she could get her face under control.

"I take it you haven't been to your room yet?" Daddy said.

"Not yet." Chester signaled for a fresh glass of water.

"Well, you're up on the third floor." Daddy handed over the key. "I had the porter take your bags up already. Now, about our sojourn here." He dabbed the corners of his mouth with his napkin, set it down, and rubbed his hands together, getting the gleam in his eye that he always did whenever he spelled out the details of our emigration. "I trust we will all find adequate amusements for ourselves."

"Oh, Robert, do you think we might be able to go to the theater?" Mother's voice held more excitement than it had for any other part of our journey.

"I don't see why not, my dear. It might be a fun outing for the girls."

Phoebe and I exchanged excited looks, but only for a brief second before Phoebe turned away. "Will you go with us, Chester?"

My brother had a smile that could make you think you've just said the only kind words he's ever heard. It's warm and wide and gracious, and I could see Phoebe falling under its spell.

"No, thanks, Phoebe. I'm sure I can find other amusements for myself."

"Found a good card game, have you?" Daddy didn't try to disguise his disapproval.

"Now, Robert, he's just a young man," Mother said. "No harm's come of it."

"Not yet. But we're not back in Belleville. You can't stay out till all hours of the night, Chester."

"Or morning," I couldn't help add, immensely proud of the amused expression I brought to my brother's face.

"I promise to be safely tucked in well before dawn." Chester raised his glass in a salute that brought the waitress scurrying over to refill it.

"I'm not joking here," Daddy said. "We don't know this city. Or the people here. They could be a much rougher crowd than what you're used to running with."

"I don't plan on *running* with anybody, Dad. And if it would make you feel any better, I could just bring in a bedroll and bunk on the floor with you and Mother."

"Don't be silly, darling," Mother said in the voice she always used when she was intervening between Daddy and Chester. "We're concerned, that's all. We want you to be careful."

"And I can assure you both that nobody is more dedicated to my self-preservation than I am. Now if you will excuse me, I think I am going to go to my room and get washed up for a night of dirty cards and loose women."

Phoebe and I gasped, then giggled, then slammed our hands over our mouths when we encountered my mother's horrified expression.

"Oh, come now, Ma." Chester got up from his chair and stood behind Mother, planted his hands on her shoulders, and leaned down to kiss her cheek. "You know I always play a clean game."

4

*W*e hadn't packed anything suitable for an evening at the theater since Daddy had been so rigid about the amount of luggage allotted to each of us. Mother's suggestion that we all buy new clothes—nothing too expensive, as they would be worn just once and then abandoned to some St. Louis charity—was not met with his approval, so the next day she picked out the best of what we had brought and sent it out to be laundered and pressed.

"What we lack in *habillement,* we will make up for in *coiffure,*" Mother said as she, Phoebe, and I gathered in her room. Despite the warmth of the summer day, Mother asked that the little stove in her room be lit to heat up the curling tongs, and we spent the afternoon curling, arranging, and pinning each other's hair. Mother's was so thick and glorious, it seemed a shame to trap it inside a snood—even one covered in jet beads and pearls. We curled the front, though, into two long dark coils that we swooped up and fastened with a jeweled comb.

"You look like a queen." Phoebe's eyes filled with something that seemed to be a hunger. "I'd give anything to be as beautiful as you."

Mother looked intensely pleased when she reached over and patted Phoebe's hand. "A woman's beauty is not merely a matter of face and figure." She was sitting on the little stool at the dressing table, but she stood up and gestured for me to take her place. "True beauty comes from a woman's bearing. How she walks into a room. How she commands attention and respect. Look at Belinda here."

She was standing behind me and had gathered all of my hair into her hand. She tugged on it, forcing me to look up at my reflection in the mirror.

"She's a pretty girl, fine featured, sweet disposition, but"—and here would come the lecture I'd heard almost daily for the past year—"she slumps. Mousy. Always walking around looking down. You'd think she'd devoted her life to searching for lost coins in the floor boards."

I heard Phoebe laugh, but Mother held my hair too tightly for me to turn and tell her to stop. So I took one last look at my face, taut and pale, before shifting my eyes to my hands folded ladylike in my lap.

"No man is ever going to think you're beautiful until you think so yourself," Mother continued. "The features we are born with are meant to be enhanced, diminished, or disguised."

I tried to concentrate on the sound of the bristles dragging through my hair as Mother used me as the object of her lesson. Hair that is naturally thick and wavy must not be left to its own devices but rather pulled back and curled into symmetrical spirals. Lackadaisical braids and ponytails do nothing but detract from what may well be the one good feature a woman has. Large eyes can be striking, but again, to severely pull the hair away gives one an almost ratlike appearance. Furthermore, one must learn to lower the lids somewhat, to give the *visage* an air of mystery, rather than bug-eyed intensity. And the skin? Really, how difficult is it to wear a bonnet to protect one's self from irreversible freckles?

"As for the smile," Mother prattled on, wrapping a section of hair around the hot iron, "of course we must do all we can to keep the teeth clean and use our powders, but even so we may be left with the dental imperfections God gave us." I clenched my jaw to keep myself from running my tongue across my teeth, but I could still sense them, one top front tooth slightly overlapping the other. "And yet, one can just as easily express joy with a cultivated, closed-lip smile. There's rarely any occasion that calls for a lady to assume the expression of a hysterical donkey."

I had memorized the litany that would follow. Small frames are not helped by rounded shoulders; rather, standing up straight will make one feel—and look—five inches taller. A small bust is easy to enhance if one will only bother to wear a corset and some batting. There's no need to have the figure of a plank when fashions are resplendent with ruffles and bustles. Storklike legs are unfortunate, but thank goodness for at least one calamity that modesty disguises.

By the time I stood up, my hair wrangled into long sausagelike links, swept to the side and secured at my temple with a burgundy velvet bow, I felt pummeled.

Mother stood next to me. "See? Look what can happen with just a modicum of effort."

I summoned my best closed-lip smile and grandly offered the

throne to Phoebe, feeling somewhat guilty about my eagerness to hear Mother's list of charges against her. But when Phoebe settled herself expectantly on the upholstered stool, Mother merely sighed. "At least you, my girl, are blessed with confidence."

Thirty minutes later Phoebe's hair drooped in limp, pale waves secured loosely at the nape of her neck with a bow identical to mine. Mother had allowed her to have the faintest dab from her rouge pot on her cheeks, and her pale skin took on an appealing glow, although the effect would soon be lost with the red blotches that inevitably crept into her face, her neck, and the soft flesh covering her collarbone from heat and exertion.

When our gowns were delivered, clean and pressed, we donned them with great ceremony and perched carefully on the edge of the bed until it was time to walk to the theater. We waited until the last possible moment, wondering if Chester would join us, but when it was a mere hour before curtain and there was still no sign of him, Daddy led us—his pretty parade—down the crowded street.

I wasn't sure if I would ever get to sleep that night. We'd gone to see Mr. William Shakespeare's *Macbeth,* and my head reeled with the images from the stage. I would never forget Lady Macbeth, pacing in her madness, wringing the invisible blood off her hands. I could still hear the clang of the swords and the awful cries as one after one the actors were slain on stage. Most frightening of all, the severed head of Macbeth, proudly displayed by the triumphant Duncan. I cringed and hid my face even as Daddy assured me that it wasn't a real head. As I lay in bed with Phoebe, the sounds of the city outside seemed to be the sounds of battle and her snores the frightful cackles of the three weird women.

At some point, though, exhaustion took over, and I fell into a deep slumber. So deep, in fact, that I didn't wake up with the knocking on our door but with Phoebe's panicked voice in my ear *telling* me there was a knock on the door.

"Go see who it is, Belinda." She huddled down under our covers, holding the blanket up to her chin.

"Why should I go?"

"Your father paid for the room. It's your responsibility."

I took the top blanket off of our bed and wrapped it around me as I padded barefoot toward the door. I opened it just a crack but enough to see the bloodied and disfigured head of Macbeth floating in the dark hallway. I didn't have a chance to scream. Just as the first squeak of terror formed in my throat, a grimy hand thrust through the opening and clamped over my mouth.

"It's all right, Lindy," Chester said as he shouldered his way into the room. Even in the darkness, lit only by the light coming in from the streetlamps outside, I could see a faint, bluish tint to the left side of his face, with his left eye swollen nearly shut. Blood trickled from the corner of his mouth and crusted at his nose.

"Chester, what happened?"

"Never mind about that now."

He closed the door behind him and walked over to the one to

Mother and Daddy's adjoining room, laid his ear against it, and motioned for me to be quiet. Seeming satisfied, he walked over to me and gripped my shoulders, pulling me in close to hear his whisper. "I need some money."

"You look like you need a doctor."

I think he smiled; it was hard to tell with his swollen mouth.

"Maybe later. For now, I need cash."

There was a stirring from the bed behind me, and I turned to see Phoebe sitting up, holding the blankets clear to her chin.

"Is that you, Chester?" she asked, her voice full of awe.

"Go back to sleep, Phoebe," Chester said.

"What's wrong with you? What happened?" She seemed to be making her way out of the bed but stopped when Chester and I both turned and told her to stay put.

I lowered my voice. "I don't know why you came to me. I don't have any money."

"Dad didn't give you anything? Not even for walking around?"

"I guess I don't walk around as much as you."

He muttered a profanity and paced the two or three steps the small room permitted before coming to a stop in front of me. "Sorry. I must remember to watch my language when I'm in the presence of such young ladies."

"Come, sit down."

I led him to the chair next to the washstand. This close to the window, I could more clearly see the damage done to his face. He offered a slight smile and possibly a wink at my horrified reaction, which eased my fears. I took the washcloth draped on the edge of the basin, soaked it, wrung it out, and dabbed at the drying blood on his lip.

"Will you tell me what happened?"

"I was playing cards—"

"I might have guessed."

"—and got into a bit of a scrape. It was a bigger game than I'm used to. I guess they didn't like the idea of some small-town kid taking their money."

"Ha." I moved the cloth to clean under his nose. "If you took their money, why do you need some now?"

"Because, *little* sister, they insisted on getting a chance to win it back."

"Which they obviously did."

"And then some. When it was time to settle up, it seems my wallet was a little lighter than I thought."

"How much lighter?"

"You have a lot of sass in your pants for such a little girl."

It occurred to me then how much he must hate this, and this mask of cocky bravado was beginning to wear thin. When I rinsed the washcloth out, he took it from me and held it against his swollen eye, wincing a little, and turned away from me before speaking again.

"Sixty-seven dollars."

This time it was my hand that was clapped over my mouth to keep from laughing out loud. "Sixty-seven dollars? Why in the world would you think I had that kind of money? You need to go to Daddy."

He took the washrag from his eye and refolded it into a nice, neat square, which he turned over and over in his hands. "I can't."

"Why not?"

"You know how angry he'd be. I think he'd let me just stay here alone and wait for those guys to kill me."

"Don't be ridiculous. Mother would never allow that."

"And Ma's upset enough about being uprooted and dragged along on this whole adventure. No telling what this would do to her."

"Well," I brushed the hair away from his forehead to look for any other cuts or bruises, "I don't see that you have any choice."

"Maybe you could do it for me."

"How would that help? They would still know the money's for you. I haven't any need for—"

"Actually, I was thinking you could just…" He inclined his head toward the door to our parents' room, then looked back at me, holding my gaze long enough for the meaning to take hold.

"Oh no." I stood up straight and backed away.

"You've been in their room. You know where everything is."

"I can't believe you're saying this."

"You heard how upset Ma was at how much cash Dad brought. Sixty-seven dollars? He'll never miss it."

"But that's stealing, Chester. It's wrong."

He stood up and faced the window, pulling the edge of the curtain aside to look out into the street before turning back to me. "You're right, Belinda. But murder's wrong too. And if you don't help me out here, you might as well just kill me now."

"She can't help you." I think we'd both forgotten about Phoebe, huddled at the headboard, blankets pulled up tight.

"What do you mean?" Chester asked.

"Your father put all his money in the hotel safe," Phoebe said. "And he's the only one who can get it out."

"How do you know this?" I was bothered that she knew something this important and I didn't.

Phoebe shrugged. "I heard them talking about it."

Chester sank down on the bed, seemingly unaware of his impropriety. "I'm dead. They're going to kill me. I am a dead man."

He repeated this phrase over and over, and I was just beginning to imagine how I was going to tell our parents about the last time I saw Chester alive, when Phoebe said, "I have money."

Chester stopped and looked at her. "How much?"

"Enough." She sat up a little higher, brought her knees up, and wrapped her arms around them. "My father gave me a hundred dollars before we left. He wanted me to have the means to get home in case I changed my mind about going with you...or you all changed your mind about taking me."

"Phoebe," I said, "you don't have to—"

"Phoebe, you saved me!" Chester practically lunged across the bed to take Phoebe—knees and all—in an awkward embrace, then bounded up and across the room to once again listen at the door.

I sidled over to the bed and sat next to Phoebe. "Don't do this," I whispered.

But Chester had already touched a match to the lamp on the

dresser, flooding the room with soft light and shadows. I heard Phoebe gasp at the extent of the injury to Chester's face, and I knew she would give him anything he asked.

"I can't tell you how much this means to me." He wrung his hands, as if he couldn't wait to feel the cards back in them. "And I'll pay it back to you. Every cent."

"Oh, don't worry about that," Phoebe said, with a hint of a giggle behind the words.

I felt her scooching away from me to make her way out of the bed. Never mind that she was wearing only a nightgown, that it was the middle of the night, and that the boy she was smitten with was in the room to take her money. The impropriety and scandal of the situation hit me, and I stood up to hustle Chester out of the room.

"You should go." I grabbed his arm and pushed him toward the door. "We'll deal with this in the morning."

"I don't have until the morning," he said, resisting my efforts. "None of us do."

"Are they coming here?" I dropped my voice to the merest whisper. "Did they follow you?"

"I'm not sure." He looked over my head toward the window. "They know I'm from out of town. They might have followed me."

"It's going to be fine." Phoebe had gotten up and opened her small carpet satchel on the bed. She hunched over it and ran her fingers through the lining. "I have the money, and I don't mind.

Really." When she stood up again, she had a handful of notes. "This should do."

I'd dropped my grip on Chester's arm, and he pushed past me. "It's perfect, Phoebe. Thank you."

If I didn't know my brother, I could have sworn I heard a hint of humility in his voice.

✑ 5 ✑

he next morning Daddy sent me to my brother's room to bring him down for breakfast. After knocking for a solid minute, Chester finally came to the door, holding a wet towel to his face as if he'd been caught washing up.

"Relax, Brother. It's just me." I remained in the hallway, casting my eyes up and down its length to see if anyone had followed me. "Will you be joining us in the dining room?"

He lowered the towel, and I saw that the past few hours had done little in the way of healing.

"Maybe you could bring up a tray?" He poked his head out and did his own quick hallway surveillance before tucking it back in. "Just some eggs. Or grits. Nothing that requires chewing."

"And what am I supposed to tell our parents?"

"Tell them I'm not feeling well. That I stayed out too late last night and I'm exhausted. All of which are true, by the way."

I gingerly touched the corner of Chester's still-swollen eye and felt an indulgent amusement when he winced away. "You're going to have to face them sometime, you know."

"I know. But in the meantime I figure I'll hole up here, make a few excuses, and hope that by the time we leave I'm healed enough to come up with a plausible explanation."

"You mean a lie."

"Call it what you want, Miss Sunday School. I'd like to think of myself as sparing Ma's fears."

"At least I learned my commandments. Seems all you've learned how to do is break them. Let's see, you're not honoring your father and mother, you're bearing false witness—and asking me to do the same, might I add. You stole—"

"Gambling is not stealing."

"I'm talking about taking that money from Phoebe. You ought to be ashamed of yourself."

He smiled and unleashed the mischievous glint in his healthy eye. "She offered it to me, Sis. It's not like I twisted her arm."

"You took advantage."

"Of the fact that she's smitten by me? Now, I don't spend as much time in church as you do, but I don't think there's any commandment against that."

I crossed my arms and puffed myself up against his charm, refusing to be suckered into believing he had an ounce of honor in him. "There ought to be."

"Well, since you're so quick to sit in judgment, why don't you write one?"

"Don't joke about this. You know what you did."

We locked eyes, and after a moment he reached out to gently tug my braid. "I got in over my head—a mistake I won't make again. Trust me, Lindy, I'm not leaving this room until it's time to get on the boat."

"I'm not going to lie to Mother and Daddy."

"Leave them to me. Now, will you please fetch me some breakfast before I break another commandment?"

"Which one?"

He grinned. "Murder."

The rest of our stay in St. Louis was uneventful. Chester spent the next two days holed up in his room with claims that alternated between having a headache and dyspepsia. My parents chalked it all up to late-night carousing, and I reported their displeasure to him with every meal I carried up.

Daddy spent the afternoons engaged in some sort of business or another, most of it requiring his best brocade vest and cigars, leaving Mother and Phoebe and me to entertain ourselves.

As chairman of our church's Women's Committee on Charities, Mother had long been envious of the St. Louis hospitals, orphanages, and asylums, which put the philanthropic efforts of any other civilized city to shame. Back in Belleville, she complained, the Catholics held an iron-grip monopoly on public benevolence, leaving the Protestant churches the occasional orphan to place. Why, if Phoebe had fallen into the hands of one of those nuns, who knew where she would be right now?

But here in St. Louis, any person of means could take her pick in doing the Lord's work. If one were unfortunate enough to be parentless, indigent, feeble-minded, foreign, or diseased, there was no other place that held so much promise. The variety of institutions was stunning, and with the help of a map, a list generated by the city's Ladies Aid Society, and an infinitely patient cabbie, we saw them all.

Our first visit was to a foundling home. Phoebe and I were waiting on the stoop outside the front door when Mother emerged with Mrs. Colleen Dewney, the home's director, whom Mother had commissioned to give us a tour. Excited at the prospect of seeing so many babies, I took a step toward the front door, only to be stopped by Mrs. Dewney's surprisingly strong little hand.

"Oh no, child," she said in a voice that seemed tinted in bird song. "Every foundling's story begins out here."

She took us around the corner to the alleyway entrance, which seemed on the outside to be like any other door. Once through it, however, we saw that it led only to a solid wood panel. Mrs. Dewney gave a gentle push on the panel, and to our surprise the entire little wall disappeared—well, spun, actually—to reveal the other side of the panel, which had attached to it a shelf with a six-inch railing on all three sides.

"Imagine," Mrs. Dewney said, "you're alone in the city. All alone. And you've just had a baby, with no husband, no family of any kind. It's a freezing cold night, and you know the child will die in your arms, since you have no home to take it to. When that time comes, you know that your child has a warm, safe place to come to. Just bring it here and place it inside."

"Isn't that wonderful?" Mother enthused. "Before that you

wouldn't believe how many of those babies just froze to death on the front stoop."

"There's no sign," Phoebe said. "How do the women know to come here?"

"They just know," Mrs. Dewney said.

"People like that always do," Mother said.

We followed Mrs. Dewney back around to the front of the building and up the stairs, where I cringed with each step, imagining stepping over hundreds of frozen babies. We walked inside what might have been a stately home at one time, but it was now dark, with curtains closed against the morning light. The front parlor had been converted into an office with an ornate mahogany desk and several upholstered chairs. Above the desk, the sole ornamentation on the wall was a cross-stitch with the verse: "Whosoever shall receive one of such children in my name receiveth me."

I expected the rooms upstairs to be full of fat, gurgling babies piling on top of each other in a happy heap of flannel gowns and little knit booties. Instead, the room we entered was eerily quiet and dark. I changed my step to a tiptoe and walked among the cribs— eight in all—that lined the walls of the room, expecting to see a room full of sleeping babies. To my surprise, they were all awake. As I peered over the bars of each little bed, I was greeted with a pair of staring eyes, blank and blinking, belonging to a nearly motionless child clad only in a diaper and lying flat on a thin blanket.

I clutched the railing of the crib nearest the darkened window and turned to Mrs. Dewney. "Are they sick?"

"No, dear. They are, in fact, in perfect health. They are changed and cleaned every other hour, and fed every fourth hour. The curtains are opened for two hours every afternoon to expose them to the optimum amount of sunlight."

"A regular little schedule," Mother said, her voice full of admiration. "My little Belinda here was always quite the savage—eating, playing, sleeping at will. She nearly drove our housekeeper to tears."

"Well, of course such a thing would never do here," Mrs. Dewney said.

"May I pick him up?" My arms were itching to take up the tiny thing whose legs had begun to twitch a bit as I smiled down at him. "Or her?"

"Him." Mrs. Dewney said. "These are all boys in this room. And no, I would rather you didn't. The children do not get held until it is time for them to be fed," she consulted a little watch clipped to her bodice, "and that's not for at least another hour."

"Please?" My hands were now inching within the crib, and the boy's little kicks took on added glee as I approached. "Just for a minute?"

Mother came up beside me and put her hand on my shoulder. "No, Belinda. It'll make it that much harder to put him back down."

I allowed myself the quickest touch of his little knee before being ushered out the door. Phoebe hadn't come into the room at all, never having had much of a fondness for children too young to boss around. As we walked out of the room, Mother took Phoebe's pale face in her lace-gloved hand. "Imagine, dear, if you'd come to a place like this."

Foundlings who weren't adopted by the age of five were taken to any one of the other orphanages we visited throughout the day. *Visited* might be too generous a term, however, as Mother opted to view most of them through either the window of our cab or the iron gate of the yards. At the home dedicated to orphaned boys, we watched a feisty game of tag in a front courtyard.

"Just think," Mother said, "that little fellow you wanted to hold might be playing in this very yard some day."

There was no outdoor play at the Industrial Home for Girls where, according to the pamphlet, indigent and orphaned girls were brought in to learn a trade. Behind its brick walls, I pictured little girls—they had to leave at the age of twelve—sitting at long tables sewing tiny stitches or painting small toys.

"Might not be a bad idea to drop you off there for a spell," Phoebe whispered to me behind Mother's back. "You could learn to be useful."

The cabbie was ordered to merely slow down as we passed the home for the criminally incorrigible (although even it bore a benign saint's name), and by the time our tour took us to the newly constructed hospital for women with unspeakable diseases, we were too exhausted to even crane our necks out the window. I did, however, find the strength to ask Mother what kind of diseases would be considered unspeakable, but she waved my question away and simply told me that if I lived a good life, I'd never know.

Phoebe leaned over and whispered a promise to tell me when we were back at the hotel.

The next day we limited ourselves to a tour of St. Louis's new hospital, walking its labyrinth of hallways and courtyards to the accompaniment of a solicitous administrator who apparently thought we were inclined to leave a large donation at the end of our tour. I gathered this because he was a good deal friendlier when he met us in the front lobby than he was handing us back into our cab with only two shiny new dollars in his pocket.

Even though the tour had been extensive, we were back at the hotel well before the noonday meal, which Phoebe attacked with unseemly gusto considering some of the sights and smells of the morning. Afterward, we all went to our rooms to lie down and rest—taking one more hour's advantage of feather mattresses and soft quilts. Soon after, the maid brought all my freshly laundered clothes from the previous days, and I carefully folded and packed them away in my little bag.

That evening, I took one last supper up to Chester's room. His face had healed nicely, with nothing more than a bluish tint surrounding his eye—something, he said, that could easily be explained by a bump into an unfamiliar bedpost in the middle of a restless night.

"So you'll be joining us for breakfast?" I asked.

"That depends." He took the tray from me. "How early?"

"Daddy says five o'clock. The boat leaves at eight."

He laughed. "You'd better tell Dad I'll just meet you all at the dock."

I stood there in the hallway, my nose inches from the door he'd just closed, and for the first time wondered if I would ever see him again.

6

When I was nine years old, I spent the greater part of the summer engaged in the daily trials of the tiny residents of a little mound just off the side of our front porch. Every day there was one perfect hour when the anthill would come alive in the afternoon sun, and I could watch from the cool shade of the house with a glass of lemonade and two sugar cookies as my snack. Ants would pour out of the opening and descend in a steady stream, lured by the crumbs I scattered around the perimeter of the mound. It was a straight-minded mission—to the crumb, a sharp turn, then straight back to disappear into what I imagined to be a bustling, homey world.

Once I took a cube of sugar from my drink, set it directly in the path of those marching ants, and watched it disappear, buried under a shifting solid mass of the creatures. Then one day Chester, acting with a level of cruelty reserved for older brothers, came upon me in my reverent observation of this tiny kingdom. With one swift kick, the mound was toppled, and the perfectly ordered, single-file parade was destroyed. The newly flattened earth revealed a chaotic scramble as ants clambered over each other and staggered in hysterical circles.

God must have had the same impression I had that day when

He looked down at the docks in St. Louis. It seemed the line started half a mile away, mules and oxen pulling wagons full of children and barrels and furniture—all families vying for a ferry to take them up the Missouri River to Independence, where the overland journey would begin.

"You'd all better enjoy these next few days." Daddy surveyed the masses with a distaste better suited to Mother. "I've booked us passage on one of the finest boats available. Once we're back on land, it's going to get a lot rougher."

I couldn't imagine anything rougher than this. The closer we got to the river, the less we saw of any semblance of order as wagons and livestock and men became a tangle covered by such a tapestry of unintelligible shouting it was a wonder anybody ever got on board at all.

Added to this frenzy was the fevered pitch of war. St. Louis, Daddy explained, was as divided as the rest of the country, and the unrest seemed especially evident on the docks. Men stood on crates, fists pummeling the air, bellowing the power of secession, urging young men to flee the city and head south to support the Confederate cause. Their pleas soon became muddled as the shifting crowd shouted over the passionate oration, professing heartfelt loyalty to the Union side. All the while, dark-faced slaves wove throughout the crowd, eyes low, backs bent, their loyalty defined by the men who owned them.

Our little family watched all of this from the comfort of our hired cab.

"It'll be good to get away from all this," Daddy said. "There's no telling what amount of blood this war will bring."

"By all means." Mother turned from the window. "We'll all be much safer in the wilderness with hatchets and arrows flying over our heads."

"Don't start with that again, Ellen. You just remember this scene when we're standing on a little patch of land, starting trade with a brand-new civilization. Pure, untouched by all this racket."

"Oh, I'm certain I'll never forget it." Mother launched yet again into her list of complaints that had grown so tiresome.

Was it possible to secede from one's own family? I sank down in my leather-upholstered seat and caught Chester's eye. He gave me a good-natured wink, which quelled the riot inside the carriage and made the one outside seem far less threatening.

"It's a good thing we aren't staying in St. Louis any longer anyway," Chester said, stopping Mother midsentence. "I think it would make it mighty hard to decide which side to join up with—if I was to join, that is."

The noise from the docks fell away as Mother and Daddy took one synchronized breath and glared at my brother.

"Oh, Chester," Mother said, "how could you even entertain the thought of joining up with those…those *sauvages*?"

"Son," Daddy said, "do not forget that no matter where we lay our heads, we are still citizens of Illinois, and your loyalty is owed to Mr. Lincoln and the United States of America, whether you take up arms for the cause or not."

"The only *cause* Chester cares about is himself," I said, earning a glare from Phoebe and a good-natured kick from my brother. The mood was a little lighter, though, as at least one battle had been squelched.

A steward from the steamboat *Felicity* was at my father's elbow the minute we stepped onto the boat. He tipped his cap to Mother, Phoebe, and me, and shook Chester's hand. His pristine white uniform made him an easy target through the maze of decks and corridors, but I soon gave up trying to follow his endless chatter. I didn't care about the height of the stacks or the pressure point of the boiler room, which was a good thing because the man could barely be heard above the piping calliope. The din of the boat's music and the teeming crowd outside receded once we reached our cabin deck. At the click of a massive pair of double doors, we were transported to a level of elegance that made even my mother catch her breath. In an instant, all of the heat and haunting fury of the docks disappeared.

We stood on a balcony, hemmed in by a gilded railing that ran along the walls of a massive room, and looked down at two dozen chandeliers suspended from a vaulted ceiling. The room below was carpeted in a rich red, and the walls picked up the same hue in a gold-leaf and velvet design. Dark young men in blue suits were setting round tables covered in crisp white cloths, and a lone violinist sat on a raised platform playing a slow, haunting tune.

"We will not be serving breakfast this morning because of launch preparations," the steward explained, as if in apology. "But we will begin serving dinner promptly at one o'clock, which should give you ample time to unpack and settle in."

We followed the steward down the suspended walkway until he came to the first of the two rooms booked for our passage. This is where Mother and Daddy would stay; Phoebe, Chester, and I would take the other. At supper the previous evening, Mother had questioned the propriety of Phoebe and Chester sharing a room, but Daddy had dismissed her out of hand. Chances were Chester would spend most of his nights with the rabble bunking down on the cotton deck.

Everything in the cabin was small—miniature, even—and it had more of an air of play than of luxury. Two beds hung suspended from the wall. One seemed barely wide enough to accommodate two people; another, more narrow, hung above it. There was a tiny washstand attached to the wall and a small pewter pitcher chained to the washstand. The cover on the bed was lovely, though, thick and quilted, and intricate lace curtains hung at the window to the outer deck. There was just enough space for a trunk, leaving a narrow walkway down the middle of the room. While Phoebe and I argued over which of us would sleep pinned to the wall, Chester slipped through the outer door without saying a word to either of us.

I'd never been on a boat of any kind, so I half expected some grand, lurching disorientation when we launched, or at the very least a chorus of farewells and best wishes from those gathered on the dock. But neither happened. When the steward arrived with our bags, Phoebe and I stowed our few necessities neatly away, then tossed Chester's bag onto his bunk. When I opened the door and stepped onto the outer deck, I saw the dock and the city smoothly slipping away. No fanfare, no discernible disturbance. Just quiet, irreversible motion.

I could tell that the days spent on the boat were meant to be a lover's gift from my father to my mother. Every conceivable luxury was laid open to us, and she took full advantage of all the niceties the *Felicity* had to offer.

We took our meals in the dining hall, although Mother usually opted to have her breakfast brought to her on a tray. The tables were large, and we often shared ours with different passengers, dining with entrepreneurs and writers and future politicians. I was quite proud of my father during those encounters, as his accomplishments seemed to equal those of any man who joined us. Admittedly, when the conversation turned to the specifics of business, my mind refused to focus on the details. I did gather that several of our meal-time companions admired my father for managing to keep a small, thriving business in the shadowy threat of new factories, though just as many ridiculed him for selling out when war was the shortest route to fortune.

"I don't like the thought of profit coming from the spilling of so much blood," Daddy said, and my pride swelled all the more.

Often the conversation would divide along gender lines. The

men at the table—Chester was rarely accounted for—entered a debate on the necessity of war; the women, the welcome introduction of the hoop skirt. Here I allowed my imagination to run free, amusing myself with visions of gun-toting soldiers capturing enemies and holding them captive within massive silk-lined cages, all accompanied by the lilting waltz played by the six-man orchestra situated at the head of the dining hall.

Between meals, Phoebe and I amused ourselves by prowling around the boat, picking up bits and pieces of strangers' conversations and spinning them into tales of great adventure.

"Do you see that woman there?" Phoebe inclined her head toward a young woman, probably twenty-five and very pretty, standing alone at the railing. "Her name is Esmeralda. Her father owns a cotton plantation in Virginia. She entered into a torrid affair with an abolitionist minister who says he will not marry her until she agrees to move north and renounce her slaveholding family."

I picked up the thread. "So she left everything behind. Her mother was on her knees, pleading, but her father was furious and slammed the door behind her, telling Esmeralda she could never come back again."

"Worse than that." Phoebe leaned closer. "He told her if she ever did come back, he would kill her rather than forgive her disobedience."

"Oh, now Phoebe, no father would ever be that cruel. What happens is, she meets up with her lover only to find that he is gravely ill. Dying, in fact. Esmeralda walks into the darkened room where her beloved lies in bed, pale and feverish."

"And coughing up blood." Phoebe always wanted somebody coughing up blood in her stories.

"All right. Coughing up blood. She can see, in the dim light of the candle, his hand, thin and quivering, reaching for her. She grasps it in her own, and her heart breaks at how very cold it is."

"I thought he had a fever," Phoebe said.

"It didn't reach to his hands," I said. "Everybody knows dying people have cold hands. So with his last breath, he croaks out the name of his one true love."

Phoebe assumed the posture of the romantic, dying abolitionist and reached out a pale, shaking hand. She transformed her voice into a barely audible whisper, saying, "Samanthaaaaa," before slumping back into her deck chair, looking quite dead indeed.

"Samantha? You said her name was Esmeralda."

"It is." Phoebe opened one eye. "Samantha is her sister. The minister was in love with her all along."

We burst into giggles loud enough to capture the attention of the tragic Esmeralda, who sent over a withering gaze before turning and walking further down the deck.

Because of moments such as this, I came to love my cousin as I never had before. True, she was still bossy enough that she always engineered the ending of the story, but it was during these interludes that I first shared with anybody the depths of my imagination. With Phoebe, the boat was full of romance and tragedy and hope. Our stories made our journey together seem utterly normal. Insulated and safe.

On the fourth day of our voyage, I awoke to the sound of my father's voice seeping through the thin cabin walls. At first, I could barely make out the warbled notes, but after some intent listening, my memories filled in what my ears could not hear.

> *O! lady sweetest lady,*
> *Soft slumbers round thee twine,*
> *Sleep on for thou art dreaming*
> *Of music that's divine.*

Then I remembered it was Mother's birthday. She was forty years old. Back home, this day was always celebrated with as much fuss and fanfare as logic would allow, and Daddy was not about to let our present setting stop that tradition. I could see him now, half dressed and barefoot, his hair wet with combing and his face soft and smelling like shaving soap. He swore Mother could sleep through the grooming of an elephant, if such a thing happened before dawn, and most mornings he insisted we all go through our morning ministrations in near silence as she finished her sleep. But on special days he would woo her out of bed with a serenade. That's what I—and probably every person within three cabins—heard now.

> *Thy father's roof protects thee,*
> *O! would that it were mine,*

Sleep on for thou art dreaming
Of music that's divine.

It must have been quite early, because our cabin was still dark, and for just a moment I thought I must still be back home, nestled down in my bed, eager for the special breakfast that Lorna, our housekeeper, would have prepared. But I felt an elbow lodge itself firmly in my side and heard a painful groan from somewhere above me, and there I was, crammed into a too-small bed with my cousin and with my late-night carousing brother thrashing in the upper bunk.

"What is that?" Phoebe's voice was muffled as she spoke into her pillow.

"It's Daddy," I said, full of pride to be a product of such sweetness and romance.

"Well, he needs to stop it." This weak protest came from Chester, who must have climbed into bed wearing his shoes, because there was a definite *clump* to the sound of his kicking the wall that separated our cabin from our parents'.

"Oh, you stop," I said. "You'll make more noise with your kicking than anything."

No sound shall break thy slumbers,
But let my song be thine,
Sleep on for thou art dreaming
Of music that's divine.

The final note was held longer than any composer could have intended, coming to an abrupt halt only, I'm sure, when Mother at last reached out from her slumber and offered Daddy a morning kiss. My parents had never been ones to hide their affection. I could picture this all so perfectly, and the image made me feel infinitely safe. My cabinmates, however, expressed nothing but relief at the silence, and after a time I joined them in a lazy, early morning doze.

The rest of the day was no less special than the morning. Mother and Daddy breakfasted together in their cabin. In fact, they spent most of the morning sequestered in there, and when they finally emerged for dinner, they were holding hands and smiling, often leaning over to whisper in each other's ear.

I hadn't been prepared to give Mother a gift, but she said having all of us gathered together was enough. At some point the previous day, Daddy must have sought out Chester on one of the lower decks and threatened something dire if he didn't make himself available for this little family celebration. So it was that we were all sitting around the same table when a tiny parade of waiters emerged from the kitchen with a tall white cake balanced on a silver platter. This they brought to our table and served it with a flourish of snapping napkins.

"Oh, Robert," Mother said, "so much fuss!"

"My darling Ellen, the day is yet young. Though not so young as my lovely bride."

"Oh, Robert," Mother said again, fanning herself with fluttering fingers.

"I'll see you all at supper." Chester pushed away from the table.

"Wait right there, Son," Daddy said, his tone firm.

He reached for a small box that had been sitting on the table throughout the meal. Mother's eyes grew wider the closer it was brought to her.

"Oh, Robert, you shouldn't have." Her fingers clutched at the pretty ribbon. She untied it with ladylike decorum and lifted the lid gracefully, breaking into a silent smile at what was hidden within.

"Let us see." Phoebe leaned forward in her chair.

Out of the box Mother lifted a bracelet of dark amethyst stones set in gold, interspersed with gleaming jet beads. Daddy made a courtly gesture, offering to help Mother clasp it around her slim wrist.

"Robert, it's beautiful." Mother held her hand aloft as she gave him a soft kiss on his cheek.

"And that's not all." Daddy grinned. "When you go back to the cabin, you'll find a new dress waiting there for you. Tonight's supper will be a party. Champagne, dancing, everything your heart could want."

"Is the champagne for us too?" Phoebe asked.

"Maybe just one glass." Mother smiled warmly at my cousin. "I wouldn't want you to get carried away."

"Am I free to leave now?" Chester was already standing.

"Be back here promptly at seven," Daddy said. "And clean yourself up first."

Without another word, Chester turned and left the dining room. Phoebe excused herself too, saying she wanted to rest up for the party this evening, and I was left alone with my parents. I felt I should say something, but the way Mother and Daddy were looking at each other, I decided any attempt at conversation would be an intrusion. Instead, I used my fork to pick up every last crumb of cake, then reached over to nibble up those that Phoebe had left on her plate.

"Belinda," Mother said, her birthday gift glistening just beyond her admonishing finger, "don't be such a barbarian."

"Let her be, Ellen." Daddy picked up a morsel of cake with his fingers and popped it in his mouth.

Mother set her mouth in disapproval, but I could tell by the glint in her eye that she was no more unhappy with Daddy's manners than she was with mine. Jewels sparkled on her wrist, cake languished on her plate, and tonight there would be dancing.

7

*W*e disembarked the *Felicity* in Independence, Missouri, and all semblance of luxurious travel ended.

It seemed the same people who had crowded the docks in St. Louis were here as well, fiercely bargaining with riggers and merchants as they prepared for their westward migration. Each family looked to be a soiled, grimy replica of our own, with fathers' faces flushed excitedly, and mothers' set in grim resignation.

After one night in a hotel spent listening to drunken brawls that threatened to fly through our very windows, we walked to the station to board the stagecoach that would carry us halfway across the country. It was a magnificent vehicle, painted a deep red with bright yellow wheels. A team of six snorting horses stood impatient to tear into their journey. They were no more impatient than my father, however, who hoisted our baggage into the boot of the stagecoach himself, strapped it down, and handed Mother up to her seat with a gallant, "Your coach is here, m'lady."

There was enough of the steamboat glow left for Mother to giggle in appreciation, and she settled herself grandly in her seat. Chester, Phoebe, and I followed, lining ourselves up on the bench facing her, and Daddy was the last one in, slamming the door behind him. Chester propped his feet up on the upholstered bench in the center of the cab and tilted his head back, intending to make up for many nights' lost sleep. But then we heard the crack of the whip, and the horses took flight, knocking Chester's hat off his head.

"Guess I'll wait till the ride smoothes down a bit," he said.

He'd have a long time to wait.

Riding in the stagecoach was like trading one boat for another that was jarring, cramped, and hot. The graceful strings of the small orchestra were traded for the endless jangling of the traces as we careened across the plains.

"This is what money can get you!" Daddy shouted over the constant noise of our travel. He'd lifted the window shade and gestured toward the blur of green grasses and wildflowers outside. "Only thing faster is a train!"

We had been warned about the discomfort of riding in a stagecoach, and it wasn't the first time any of us had traveled in one. But the well-worn routes between Chicago and Belleville hadn't prepared us for this ever-lurching battle. Mother complained that she couldn't bear the thought of pinning a hat to her throbbing head—which was just as well, because no bonnet had the tenacity to withstand the constant bobbing and occasional collision with the back of the seat. Phoebe, however, never complained, as she spent the better part of each day smashed shoulder to shoulder with Chester, who remained his usual uncommunicative self.

We stopped every fifteen miles to hitch the coach to a fresh pair of horses.

"Think about it," Daddy would say, marking the stop off on the little folded map he kept in his pocket. "That's about how far we'd make in a *day* if we were going by wagon."

"Yes, Robert," Mother would say, rolling her shoulders. "But then we might actually have the capacity to sit in our seat, turn our heads, and observe the world around us."

"Yes, but can you imagine? Some of them have their wagons so loaded, they end up walking for the entire trip."

"I'd like to be able to walk again someday," I'd say.

Most of our stops were just that. Stops. We would unfold our bodies and stumble into the sunlight as the dust settled around us. There would be a little shack—sometimes not more than a pile of sod—and a team of horses held by some wizened old man wearing a dirty shirt and offering a cup of questionable water. We might have enough time to visit an equally dilapidated outhouse, or just a quick trip to the tree line, before the new team was hitched, the driver seated, and we were off. Other times, the stops were actual homes with a man and a wife—sometimes children—where we could pay for a meal and a washup. Here, too, we might be offered a bed—for a price. Otherwise, we camped outside when the weather permitted or slept on our seats when it didn't.

Our driver was a man known only as Whip. I would learn later that was a common nickname for any stagecoach driver, but it thoroughly suited him, as he was tall and thin. He was often accompanied by another man charged with keeping an ever-ready shotgun balanced across his bouncing knees. These shotgunners remained anonymous and faceless, with their hats pulled low over their eyes and wearing leather jacket and gloves. On the occasional leg that we didn't have a man to ride shotgun, Daddy said not to worry, as he always had his trusty derringer at the ready.

"Let me see that thing," Whip had said, narrowing his eyes in suspicion.

Daddy then, mustering all the style of his notion of a gunman, flipped his vest open to pull the weapon from its hidden holster.

Whip just laughed. "Well sir, if nothin' else, you can throw that thing at anyone who comes at ya. It'll leave a nasty bruise on somebody's noggin."

My father had paid for a private coach for the length of the journey, but there were occasions when it was necessary to wedge one or two other passengers in with us for a few miles. When that happened, Chester would often opt to ride on top and take a turn with the gun. Other times we might have huge sacks of mail and packages stuffed under and around our feet. All of this, according to Daddy, was a small inconvenience since we would be in the midst of a whole new life before winter.

We had been traveling on the stagecoach for two weeks. Our trunks were lashed to the boot of the coach, where the driver refused to access them. Here we were, in the middle of Nebraska, wearing the same clothes we'd worn since boarding the stagecoach in Independence. We'd been subjected to the hospitality of a woman named Mrs. Tosh, who lived with her husband in a long, low-ceilinged structure with canvas curtains that separated it into individual rooms. By all appearances, she had been wearing her dress at least as long as I had been wearing mine. After providing two beds for the five of us—Chester and Daddy in one, Phoebe, Mother and I in the other—she prepared a simple breakfast of biscuits, salt pork, and gravy, which under most circumstances I would have stepped away from immediately. Despite its unappetizing appearance, it was the first food we'd seen since breakfast the previous day (which had also been biscuits, salt pork, and gravy), and I found myself forking it into my mouth before I gave it much thought.

I was giving it much consideration now, though, as we lurched and swayed along, mostly in silence, listening to the sound of raindrops pelting the coach. Of course, we weren't limited to just listening to the rain. We felt it too. Daddy had pulled down the leather window shades, which were efficient at blocking out the sunlight, but they proved no defense against any other force of nature. We continued along at a tumultuous pace—the horses' gait unaffected by the inclement weather—and Mrs. Tosh's morning meal began to take on new life within me.

"I think I'm going to be sick," I said into the darkness.

"Don't be silly," Mother said. "You're fine."

"Maybe if I could sit next to the window."

"I'm sitting next to the window," Phoebe said in a tone that gave no indication she intended to move.

"Fine," I said. "I can be sick all over your shoes if you prefer."

"Come here, Lindy."

I felt my brother's hand clasp mine and pull me up from where I had been wedged between my parents. He gently guided me across to the other seat while he slid over, placing himself between Phoebe and me. I felt a little better the instant I sat down and turned my face toward the window. The midmorning breeze was quite cool, and the intermittent spray of raindrops refreshing. For a second I almost forgot about the gravy and salt pork sloshing around inside of me, but only for a second. After that, it all came back to me, then up and out of me as I hung my head out of the window, vomiting Mrs. Tosh's breakfast out into the storm.

"Now really, Belinda," Mother said, and I was grateful that her own dishevelment made her incapable of any more admonition than that.

I felt a tap on my shoulder and the corner of a handkerchief grazed my cheek. I took it and wiped my mouth, but I continued to hang my head out of the window, relishing the rain against my face. I rose up to my knees and leaned further out, feeling the rain on the back of my neck, running down the collar of my dress.

"Belinda! Get back in here!"

Mother's rebuke seemed far away, and it never crossed my mind to heed her. Instead, I rose still higher, and pulled my arms out through the window. I cupped my hands to let them fill with the cooling rain, brought it to my mouth, and let it wash away the breakfast bile.

"Belinda!"

It was a chorus of voices now, my father's deep and authoritative among them, but still I ignored their heeding. I tore the ribbon that tied my hair and let the stringy mass of it fall free. It was soaked through now, and I raked my fingers across my scalp, using them to comb through the wet locks. Suddenly a pair of hands grabbed me around my waist and began to pull me back into the coach. I had no reason to continue hanging out the window, except that the tiny act of rebellion was invigorating in so many ways. It got me away from these people, muted their voices. Out here there was a breeze and cool, clean air. The colors were softened by the gray light, distorted by the rain, but no one behind me would appreciate that. Not even my mother, who refused to see this journey as anything but a means to an end. An inconvenient hurdle.

The hands that held me tightened their grip and pulled again, so I braced my elbows against the bottom of the window and held on. But my sleeves were wet and the side of the coach slick with rain. Despite my resolve, I lost my grip and was toppled inside, knocking one side of my head so hard against the window I feared my ear would be slashed off. Inside was a confusion of skirts and legs and Mother's hysterical screeching. One minute I was on the floor, and the next I wasn't. I don't remember hitting the door's latch, though I very well could have during the mad scramble to put everything back to right. Whatever the cause, I soon found myself back in my beloved rain, tossed down into the mud and rolling down a slick, wet hill.

The shouting never stopped; it just grew faint, and when I finally came to a stop and eased myself up, I saw the coach continuing on at an impressive clip, with my father and brother each hanging out a window, pounding on the sides to get the driver's attention. Before the coach could come to a complete stop, Daddy jumped out of it, somehow keeping his footing as he landed, and ran back to me.

"Belinda! Darling, are you all right?"

I nodded. I was able to stand, able to walk, and though my shoulder was sore from the fall, both arms seemed to be functioning.

"This isn't the time or place for games." Daddy's voice was stern. "You could have been killed."

I nodded again and slowly, hanging onto his strong arm, walked back to the coach. Whip looked down at me and smiled, stopping just short of laughing when my father shot him a threatening glare. He jabbed and shared a laugh with the shotgun guard, though. The harnesses continued to jangle as the horses pranced in place. Daddy opened the door, and I climbed in.

"Oh, Belinda, your dress," Mother said. "It's ruined. Are you hurt?"

"She's fine." Daddy settled in beside me.

"That was a really stupid thing to do," Phoebe said. "You could have been killed."

"Yeah." Chester was leaning back in his seat, his arms folded, looking every bit as if he'd just slept through the near death of his sister. "Next time you jump out of this thing, wait until it's not raining. And take me with you."

"Stop it, all of you." Daddy settled in his seat, reached an arm outside the window, and slapped the side of the coach. The driver called out to the horses, and I braced myself for that first lurch. But nothing happened. There was a crack of the whip and another shouted command, but again, nothing.

"Why aren't we moving?" Phoebe asked. Even though it was still quite dark in the coach, I could tell her eyes were boring straight through me.

"My guess is we're stuck." Chester opened the door and leaned out, holding the side ladder for balance. "Hey, Whip, are you going to need some help?"

Whip must have shouted something affirmative, because Chester sighed and jumped out into the rain.

Mother rolled up the window shade, leaned her own head out, and asked, "What on earth are you doing?" Without waiting for a response, she pulled her head back in. "What is he doing?"

"Wheels are stuck," Daddy said.

"That's silly. We were moving along just fine."

"Yes. Then we stopped."

I heard a hissing sound from Phoebe's corner and slunk down in my seat.

Our driver counted off, "One, two, three...," and a grunting sound came from the men outside. I rolled up the window shade on my side of the coach and looked out to see my brother with his shoulder braced between two spokes of the coach's back wheel. His face, sheathed in rain, was contorted in the effort of pushing. His legs were bent beneath him, quickly losing their traction in the slick mud. After a couple of seconds with no results, he gave up his grip and shouted for the man on the other side to do the same. Standing upright, he saw me through the window.

I'm sorry, I mouthed, but he just smiled, winked, and gave his head a vigorous shake, creating a spray of water in the midst of the pouring rain.

"Hey there," the shotgunner's face appeared at the other window, causing my mother to jump. "We're gonna need a little more help out here. Get these front tires."

"Certainly," Daddy said.

"Gotta have one more," the gunner said. "Gotta keep it all equal." He disappeared, leaving Phoebe, Mother, and me to look at each other.

"Well, Phoebe?" Mother said with a chipperness that had to hurt. "Belinda appears to be injured. Is it going to be you or me?"

"I'll go." Phoebe heaved herself off the seat. "I don't want you to think I'm completely useless."

I held my tongue and drew myself further back in my seat as she made her way past me. Daddy had gone around to the other side, so I could see Phoebe from my window. The wheel itself was almost as tall as she was, and she stood obstinately beside it until Chester left his own place and came over to her.

"Let me help you," he said in that sweet, gentle voice that made you wonder how he could ever be such a snake. He positioned himself behind Phoebe and drew her back to him. Placing one hand on her upper arm and the other on her waist, he bent her body to the angle necessary to maneuver her shoulder between the wheel's spokes. "Then on my count, you're going to push as hard as you can and try to turn the wheel."

He was leaning forward, pushing her, speaking right into the curve of her neck. Her face was just on the other side of the window, flushed red despite the pelting rain. She kept her eyes closed until Chester released his grip and went back to his own wheel. On a three-count, the driver gave the command to push, and Phoebe's face contorted in the effort. It seemed the coach budged a bit, and just as I was about to speak an encouraging word to Phoebe, she slipped in the mud, hitting her face on the wheel's hub as she fell to the ground.

"Hold up!" Chester sloshed to Phoebe's side and took her arm, helping her slowly to her feet. "Hey there, girl—you don't know your own strength."

Phoebe offered a weak smile and made a useless attempt at swiping the mud from her skirt. Her cheek was marked with a long black streak of axle grease, and a slight red trickle below it was the only clue that she'd suffered a cut.

"Here, Phoebe." I leaned out the window. "Come back inside and let me try."

"I'm fine." She turned to the wheel again.

Chester had disappeared behind the coach and was back now with an ax from the toolbox which he wedged through the spokes of the wheel. "This will give you a little more leverage. Just be careful not to fall on it." He took off the kerchief that was tied around his neck and used it to wipe the grease and blood off Phoebe's face. "Don't want anybody thinking you're an Indian."

Once he was back in his own spot, he hollered to the driver, and they tried once again to dislodge the coach from the mud. I heard Chester shouting encouragement to Phoebe, and I joined in his praise, saying, "Good job, Phoebe! You're doing fine!" Bright red blood trickled down her cheek, spreading thin in the spattering rain. Her eyes were squeezed shut, but at the sound of my voice she opened her right one—the one above the cut—and sent me a glare that convinced me of two things: she would single-handedly push this coach clear to Oregon for my brother but she wouldn't move it a single inch for me.

Eventually strength and passion won out, and the coach rolled out of the rut it had been mired in. The driver kept the horses at a walking pace, slow enough to allow Daddy, Chester, and Phoebe to grab the ladder next to the coach's door and swing inside after the shotgunner resumed his place on top. Mother didn't say a word as my father, his shirt soaked through to his skin, settled in the seat beside her. I pressed myself against the wall of the coach to make room for Phoebe, who began to shiver the moment she sat down next to me. Chester pulled the door shut and latched it. When he sat down next to Phoebe, she scooted a little closer to me.

I kept my eyes on the coach's floor and said nothing. The only noise was the faint chattering of Phoebe's teeth and the sound of water dripping onto the puddles forming beneath my gaze. Soon enough the heat inside our coach overtook the refreshing chill of the rain outside, and we became a rumbling soup—soggy, steamy, and silent—until Mother said, "I want to go home."

"The driver assures me that we'll be quite comfortable at our next stop. We might even stay an extra day to really wash up, change clothes—"

"I mean *home*, Robert. *Our* home."

"Don't be ridiculous," Daddy said.

"Don't call me ridiculous or silly or absurd or any of those little words you call up when I assert myself."

"This is not the time—"

"You're right. The time was in Belleville, when I had misgivings about this entire mess."

Out of the corner of my eye, I saw Phoebe press Chester's neckerchief to her cheek, pull it away, examine the blood, and press it back.

"I knew even then," Mother continued, "that first evening you mentioned that cursed place. I knew then that you would lead us into disaster—"

"Ellen—"

"But I assumed at some point logic would ensue and you would realize the folly of it all. So like a good little wife I held my tongue and prayed that God would bring you some shard of enlightenment. But like a stubborn fool—"

"Ma, that's enough," Chester said without much conviction.

"I allowed you to sell off my life piece by piece, uproot our children, take me away from my only family—"

"*We* are your family, Mother." I felt my own chills set in at the shrill tone of her voice.

"I meant my still-living sister. Phoebe's mother. The only blood relative I have left in this world, and you just yank it all out from underneath me. I should have stopped you. I should have put my foot down and refused to take part in this *ridiculous* fiasco."

"Ellen." Daddy's tone discouraged any further discussion. "Darling, you didn't have a choice."

8

*J*ust as our driver promised, our stagecoach rolled to a stop in a little courtyard surrounded by a generous, two-story house, a smaller clapboard cabin, and an impressive barn that must have housed the half-dozen horses trotting around the corral. Not quite five o'clock, it was early to declare this the stop for the night, but Daddy had prevailed in his request that we be allowed to bathe, change our clothes, and recover from the day spent driving through the raging summer storm. I lifted the leather shade and peered through the stagecoach window. The sun was just beginning its afternoon descent, and the land—wet with rain—glistened in its brilliance. Off in the distance, a single spire rose from the ground.

"That's Chimney Rock." Daddy flipped through the pages of *The Emigrant's Guide to Oregon and California.*

"How far away is it?" I asked.

"Not sure from here. But just past it, and we're in Wyoming territory. We'll be halfway there."

Even before the coach came to a halt, a man and a woman emerged from the front door of the bigger house and stood together, waving to us and offering shouts of welcome. The broad smiles on their faces turned to something else—a cross between pity and amusement—as one by one we stomped down the little steps that unfolded from beneath the coach's door.

I can only imagine the sight we made—our clothes still damp and mud covered, Phoebe with a scabbing slash on her face, I with one sleeve nearly torn from my dress. Only Mother appeared, on the surface, to be civilized, and a closer inspection of her would reveal days' worth of little stains and splotches and traces of grime in the grooves around her neck.

"Oh, good heavens, let's have a look at you," the woman said, and as she approached, I noticed that she was much older than she appeared at a distance, but not any bigger. In fact, she was just about my height, but the comforting arm she put around me suggested a strength to match any man's. "We don't get many children coming through this way. It'll be good to have a little one around for a while."

Normally I chafe at being referred to as a child, but after all these days, I could imagine curling up in this little woman's arms and being rocked to sleep. Soon enough, though, she'd left me and was fawning over my mother, insisting that no woman could have endured the journey we had and still emerge looking so fresh and beautiful.

"Well, thank you." Mother pressed her hand to her throat and smiled as if she believed it. "It was a harrowing day, Mrs.—"

"Bledsoe. Myra Bledsoe, and this is my husband, Calvin."

Introductions were made all around, and Mrs. Bledsoe effused over each of us in turn. Chester seemed perfectly suited to play the dashing hero on a theater stage, Daddy was a welcome sight for someone who was so deprived of ever seeing a true gentleman, and poor Phoebe must get a salve put on that cut right away because the last thing she needed was a nasty scar. Under Mrs. Bledsoe's brandishing finger, Whip and the shotgunner, with the grudging help of Calvin Bledsoe, brought down our trunks and bags and took them to the second-floor bedrooms in the big house.

"Now all of you follow those bags up there and get out of those things," Mrs. Bledsoe continued, giving my father a little push. "Calvin will fetch some water to the stove, and we'll see if we can't get you cleaned up."

The four of us—Mother, Daddy, Phoebe, and I—made our way through a modest front room and up a set of narrow stairs to find the rooms we had been assigned. Nobody spoke; in fact, Mother and Daddy hadn't said a word to each other for the last ten miles of our drive. When we found our rooms, Daddy carried Mother's bag inside, tipped his hat like any bellman, and announced that he would join Chester and the other men in the little cabin down by the barn. Mother didn't say a word to stop him. Without any attempt to smile over the tension, she turned to us and told us to go into our room and change out of our filthy clothes.

"Our underthings too?" Phoebe asked.

"I don't care," Mother said, her voice thick with weariness. "I'm not about to declare myself your laundress."

Without another word, she went into her room and seemed to take great care closing the door behind her. We walked into the room next to hers, and the back of my throat swelled with gratitude. The walls were painted a soft butter yellow; lace curtains fluttered in the late summer breeze. The bed was covered with a pale blue calico quilt, and a small dish of wildflowers adorned the bureau. To wear such sullied clothes in here seemed insulting, and with unspoken agreement, Phoebe and I set upon them, tearing at buttons and stepping out of moist, muddy heaps.

Soon after, Mrs. Bledsoe knocked on our door. After peering through a narrow opening to be sure there was no one in the hall, Phoebe opened the door wide enough to allow the little woman and her large wicker basket to come through.

"What a shame, what a shame." Mrs. Bledsoe held up our discarded clothing. "But we'll get these washed up, mended, and hung out tonight so they'll be fresh as a Tuesday in the morning. Now, come on," she made a beckoning gesture with her hand, indicating she wanted our undershirts and pantalets too. "I believe these could use a bit of washing as well."

Phoebe and I looked uneasily at each other.

"Now, now," Mrs. Bledsoe said, "this isn't the time to be shy. I'm a woman, same as you. And I'm keepin' all the men out till you've had a chance at a good long bath. Water's heatin' up now, so off with those, and I'll call you down when it's time."

Phoebe unlaced her corset, pulled her chemise over her head, and plopped on the bed to yank off her stockings. Then she was back on her feet to step out of the pantalets. She wadded all of this up and dropped it in the basket, with the air that she was doing Mrs. Bledsoe a great honor in the donation of her dirty laundry.

It was a complicated awe I felt at Phoebe's brazen nudity. Part of me took on the shame that she seemed to lack, never once folding her arms to cover herself. And yet, it wasn't exactly shame that I felt, but rather embarrassment as I slowly performed the same task. I wasn't so bold as to stare openly at my cousin's body, but I was nonetheless struck by the differences between hers and mine. She was soft and round—everywhere. Her legs curved at her calf, again at her thigh, while mine were like a pair of planks marked at the center by a hard, knobby knee. She didn't have sharp little bones poking out at her pelvis and shoulders. Her ribs were nestled safely behind soft, pink flesh rather than straining through white, veined skin. Chester used to joke, saying that he always wanted a little brother and if he just looked at me from the neck down he could pretend he had one. I took a peek at Phoebe as I gathered my discarded clothes and felt a pang of envy. No one would ever tell her she had the figure of a twelve-year-old boy. The mouth of one, maybe, but not the body.

"Oh, my dear!" Mrs. Bledsoe said as I dropped my clothes in the basket. At first I took the shock in her voice to be her reaction to my emaciated appearance, but she put her hand on my shoulder and turned me around, saying, "Just look how you've hurt yourself."

With one hand still holding her basket, she steered me toward the bureau, which had a mirror mounted on the wall above it. After some twisting, I could see what she was concerned about. Nearly a quarter of my back was black and blue.

"Does it hurt?" Phoebe asked, disinterested.

"Not much."

And it didn't, but I could feel the prologue of true pain to come.

Mrs. Bledsoe called us down one by one to bathe in the large galvanized tub in her kitchen. By the time it was my turn, my scalp felt like it was crawling under the dried mud in my hair. So before getting in, I knelt down and bent over the side of the tub, soaking my hair and running handfuls of Mrs. Bledsoe's good-smelling soap through it. While I bathed, she buzzed around the kitchen, humming half-songs under her breath and tapping out little rhythms as she sliced potatoes to boil. The modesty I felt upstairs with Phoebe was not so powerful here. Mother would have been shocked at my sitting stark naked in a room with a stranger. She, no doubt, had tossed Mrs. Bledsoe out of the kitchen in order to have some privacy. But there was something comforting about this woman, like Saturday nights at home with Lorna slathering butter and sugar on bread for my after-bath treat.

Once we had bathed, Mrs. Bledsoe instructed Mother, Phoebe, and me to put on our nightgowns and stay in our rooms to rest; she would have our supper sent up on a tray. "You deserve some pampering, poor things," she said, and we heartily agreed.

Aside from Mr. Bledsoe's forays into the kitchen to put more water on the stove or dump out what we'd used, the men—even my father—had been banned from the house all this time, forced to take their baths in the nearby creek. Now, though, the downstairs filled with masculine rumbles of conversation and laughter, and I felt the safety I'd felt down in the kitchen triple.

In a fun change of fortune, Chester himself brought up supper to Phoebe and me, and I took great joy in watching him carry the tray to the bed and set it down just so.

"And my napkin?" I asked, settling myself against the pillows.

"*Mademoiselle.*" He bowed low, brandishing a square of gingham cloth.

"And for Phoebe?" I added, since she didn't appear to want to join in the game.

"But of course," Chester said, adopting a comical French accent as he fussed about us, picking up our glasses to take sips of water as if to ensure that Mrs. Bledsoe didn't intend to poison us in revenge for blackening her best washtub.

I continued to play the role of pouting princess and Phoebe kept her self-conscious silence until Chester left the room. Then, faced with the finest meal we'd seen since the steamboat's dining room, we tore into our suppers with a most unladylike abandon. Savory pork sausage links and potatoes that had been parboiled, then fried with onions and seasoned with salt and black pepper. A hunk of rich, dark bread spread with butter, and a small dish of blackberry preserves.

By the time I got to the end of the meal, I wondered if perhaps Chester hadn't been wise to check the water after all, because I was overcome with such fatigue I nearly fell asleep with a spoonful of preserves lodged in my cheek. Phoebe was tired too, and we grunted through a debate about whether to take our trays down to the kitchen, but settled on the side of laziness and placed them on the floor at the foot of the bed.

I have no idea who eventually took them away.

When I awoke later, I fully expected dawn to be around the corner, but one look out the window showed it to be the thick, still hours of the night. The open window made the room chilly, so I swung my feet over the side of the bed—wincing a bit at the pain in my back and shoulders—and walked over to close it. Lifting my arms proved an impossibility, however, and when I turned around, I saw that Phoebe had cocooned herself in the bed's only blanket. Mrs. Bledsoe had mentioned having extra bedding in a trunk in Mother and Daddy's room. My sense of entitlement had grown since arriving here, so I thought nothing of crossing the hall and fumbling around in the dark to find it.

I did extend the courtesy of being as quiet as possible, turning the knob of my parents' door slowly, carefully, silently. When the door was opened just a crack, I leaned forward to listen for my father's snoring, but heard nothing. Then again, I did hear something—their voices in conversation downstairs. I meant to just go inside, find a blanket, and creep back to my room, but the tone of their voices drew me. I'd lived my life listening to my parents. I'd heard them fight, my mother's shrill voice running circles against Daddy's short bursts of angry retorts. I'd heard them laugh at his comic renditions of their friends. I'd listened to low, passionate whispers—sometimes in broad daylight on the other side of the parlor door.

But what I was hearing now was different.

I remember once, standing out in our front yard with my father, the air perfectly still. No breeze whatsoever, like the entire world was clapped under a gray glass dome. "There's going to be a storm," Daddy had said. "God's just building up for it."

That was the essence of their conversation now. One steady volume interrupted by bouts of silence. An unnatural calm. I turned away from their room and made my way quietly down the hall, then silently down the stairs until I was on the third step. I couldn't see my parents, but I could tell the room was full of low lamplight, and I was able to hear every soft, monotonous word.

"You're quite sure. Everything?" Mother said.

"Ellen, I'm so sorry."

"And the house?"

"Selling was the only option. We would have lost it soon anyway."

"All of our things?"

"We couldn't have brought them with us."

There was a beat of silence during which everything I'd heard settled in my head. Gone. Everything gone. Not destroyed by any fire or storm. Simply…gone.

"I don't understand how this happened," Mother spoke, again in that eerily even tone.

"It's complicated, dear. Demand was up, but we couldn't—"

"I'm not a fool, Robert." The calmness in her voice remained, but it was rimmed with a sharp, steel edge. "I understand the workings of a business. I was with you, remember? I was there beside you through every bit and piece of it. What I don't understand is how you could have lied to me."

"That was wrong, I know."

"Or maybe I am a fool, and I just don't understand *how* I could be so foolish as to let all of this fall apart around me."

She sobbed a little then, and I could picture her, head bent low over the table, my father looking helplessly on—images I'd never been able to conjure before this afternoon in the stagecoach.

"And what," Mother said, sniffing a bit, "do you think Silas will do with the business? Does he have some sort of magic touch that will bring it all back?"

"I'm not sure—"

"You didn't ask?"

"He was willing to buy. It was a way out."

"Oh, what my sister must think of me."

"She didn't know. Silas and I agreed—"

"She knows now!" Mother raised her voice, and I heard the little thump of her fist slamming on the table. When she spoke again, it was softer. "She knows everything, and what a laugh she must be having—living in the spoils of our failure while I'm stuck with that insipid brat of hers."

I heard a sharp, small sound behind me and turned to see Phoebe sitting two steps above me. She was wrapped in the blanket from our bed. She came down to sit beside me, holding out the blanket to encompass both of us. I turned to Phoebe, my face full of an appeasing smile as if to apologize for my mother's thoughtless comments, but she simply stared forward, her stone-still face the merest shadow in the stolen light of the kitchen.

"I wanted to protect you," Daddy was saying. Mother's only reply was a derisive laugh. "I knew how much our life meant to you. Our society. I couldn't face losing all that. Seeing you lose everything you cared about."

"You are what I care about, Robert," Mother said, although her voice conveyed little passion behind the words. "You and the children. I am your wife. I'm to be your helpmeet."

"There's nothing you could have done."

"How do you know that? You didn't try. We might have been able to do something together. I could have prayed for you. Prayed *with* you."

"Don't you think I've prayed about this?" I heard the chair scrape on the floor and my father came into my view. He faced away from us, and Phoebe and I drew back further in the shadows lest he turn around. He looked smaller than I ever remembered seeing him, his shoulders stooped in unfamiliar defeat. "I don't remember the last decent night's sleep I've had. I'm up, middle of the night—sometimes all night—on my knees begging God for an answer. For direction."

"And this is the answer He gave you?"

"I thought so, yes."

"And you think it was His will for you to lie to your wife, to deceive your children?"

That seemed to deflate him completely. He turned around, but his eyes passed right over me; if he'd been looking, he would have seen me. He stepped out of my view again and went back to my mother. I leaned forward and ventured the tiniest peek around the corner of the stairwell and saw them—my mother seated regally in her chair, the lamplight filling the wall with her shadow, and my father on his knees before her, grasping her hand, his head nestled in her lap. If I didn't know it was such a sin, I could have hated her at that moment.

"I didn't know what to do." Daddy's voice was muffled by my mother's skirts. "I thought that if you saw this as an adventure rather than a defeat…if you could just think of it as an opportunity for a new beginning…"

His voice dissolved, and I hoped Mother was offering some measure of comfort, stroking his hair, perhaps. Bending deep to shush him with kisses. After a moment she asked, very quietly, "Just what do we have left?"

"Just what we're traveling with. The cash in my wallet."

"And it isn't much, is it?"

"No, but think of it this way, Ellen." Daddy's voice sported renewed strength. "We have more than most people ever dream of having. Back home it wouldn't buy us a month of living how we used to, but in Oregon, it'll buy us a farm. It'll be enough to start a smaller business, if you want to do that. There are people who haven't got five dollars to their name crossing this country the same as we are."

"Well, not quite the same," Mother said, and I was relieved to hear a hint of humor in her voice. Something had broken.

"True," Daddy said, his tone cautiously light. "Darling, I wanted this to be as painless as possible for you. I sank every dime I could into the steamboat and the coach ride. I couldn't very well see you squatting next to a wagon cooking johnnycakes."

"No, I don't suppose so." Mother's voice was almost warm.

"So you'll forgive me, Ellen?"

"You are my husband, Robert. God has charged me to submit to you."

"And He has charged me to love you. And all of this is because I love you. Can you understand that?"

"I do," Mother said softly.

"But submission and understanding—they aren't the same as forgiveness, are they?"

"No, Robert. Not tonight."

9

The next morning our family gathered together for breakfast in the Bledsoes' kitchen. Mr. Bledsoe was outside helping the driver hitch up the teams, and Mrs. Bledsoe was busy overseeing the loading of our baggage onto the boot of the stagecoach.

"Don't you rush, don't you rush at all," she'd said as she backed out of her kitchen with a small case in each hand. "You just take your time and eat your fill. I'll see to it that no one disturbs you until you're ready."

She must have heard everything too.

Our plates were filled with bright yellow scrambled eggs and biscuits that steamed when they were sliced open to take on Mrs. Bledsoe's white, pepper-flaked gravy. The stagecoach horses obviously shared their barn with a cow, because Phoebe and I had glasses of warm, fresh milk, while Mother, Daddy, and Chester stirred some into their cups of coffee. What a shame to have such bounty languish on our plates. My body ached with the effort of lifting my fork; Mother made no attempt to even pick hers up. Daddy and Phoebe both ate with methodical deliberation, forcing small bites through thin lips and taking great pains not to clink their forks against the plates. Only Chester attacked this meal with the vigor it deserved, creating his trademark stew of eggs, biscuits, and gravy in the center of his plate and using his spoon to bring heaps of it up to his mouth. He took a swig of coffee after every third bite, helped himself to a drink of my milk after every fourth, and seemed completely oblivious to the silent turbulence around him.

Mother dislodged one of her hands from her lap, reached for her coffee, took a sip, and nestled the cup back in its saucer. "Robert," she said, once her hand was safely back in place, "don't you have something to tell the children?"

"Should I leave?" Phoebe asked, her eyes narrowed to mere slits, making no effort to hide her disdain. "Is this a family matter?"

"Don't be silly," Mother said. "You are family, after all."

Daddy took one last sip of his coffee, pulled the napkin from where he'd tucked it into his shirt collar, and unnecessarily dabbed at his beard. "Well, everybody," he spoke to his largely untouched breakfast, "there are some things you all should know…"

He stirred the story around the table, a soft monologue of unforeseen disaster, filling in all the details I'd missed the night before. Competition from larger factories. Impending war in the South. Bad investments. Miscalculations. A slow, bleeding loss that brought us to this point. Mother looked down and fiddled with her napkin, allowing us to believe we were the only ones to have been deceived, but as Daddy talked about the expense and luxury of the steamship, a slight smile tugged at the corner of her mouth, as if she were about to hum a dinnertime waltz.

"Which brings us to where we are today." Daddy propped his

elbows on the table and rested his chin on his clasped hands. "I thought I was protecting all of you and that our journey would be a lark. I thought with a new home and a new life, you wouldn't see what was…missing."

I followed his gaze across the table toward Mother, who lifted her head to meet his eyes. "I've asked God to forgive me," Daddy continued, "for being so shortsighted. For not trusting Him the same way I didn't trust you. And I've asked your mother to forgive me for lying to her. Now—" His voice disappeared for a moment. "Now I come to you, Belinda and Chester, asking you—"

"Of course we do," I said. It was a terrible thing, seeing my father's spirit and strength eviscerated before me, splayed out on the table in front of us. "If anything, *you* should forgive *us* for making you feel like you couldn't come to us with the truth."

"Belinda, that's enough," Mother said. "You've quite forgotten your place."

"Just don't forget your place, Mother. By your husband's side. Whatever he decides."

Nobody at the table could have been more shocked at my boldness than I was, but still I didn't shrink back. I held my aching shoulders straight and looked my mother square in the eye, daring her to contradict me.

"Apologize to your mother."

"I'm sorry," I said, for Daddy's sake rather than hers, "but it wouldn't be fair to—"

"What wouldn't be fair would be to blindly continue on as we

have been. Now, the cards are on the table." Daddy offered an indulgent smile to Chester, who had been following this exchange with
an air of calculated boredom. "And we're at a crossroads. The money
that I'm carrying is all we have. It's plenty to start up new in Oregon. Farming, maybe a little store. Or we could go back home. Buy
a smaller house. Invest in the foundry—"

"Never," Mother said, and we all jumped a little at the level
of disgust in her voice, except for Phoebe, who shrank back in her
chair.

"No, none of that," Daddy said. "If we go on, it has to be for
the right reason. Not just because we're afraid to go back."

"It's a gamble." Somehow Chester's plate had been emptied, and
he reached across to stab a forkful of eggs from mine.

"Oh, spare us," Mother said. "We certainly don't need to hear
your—"

"Let him speak," Daddy said. "He's a man now. Go ahead, Son."

Chester cleared his throat. "When you've got a hand of cards,
you'd be a fool to throw your money on the table because you're afraid
of what you've lost already." Mother gave an audible little snort, but
Chester ignored her and went on. "You put your money down
because you believe—you have to believe—that what you're holding
are the winning cards. You can't waste time thinking about the hands
you lost. You've got to do what's best with the ones you're holding."

Daddy looked at Chester with an expression akin to gratitude.
Mother seemed less convinced, though, and even Chester seemed a
little surprised at the apparent wisdom coming out of his mouth.

"That's what faith is," I chimed in, eager to bolster my father's case. "And we have to trust God to be with us—just like we always have."

"Well, we can't expect God to just ignore our mistakes." Mother looked at my father.

"Not ignore them, Mother," I said, "but He does forgive them. And then He tosses them away. As far as God is concerned, we've been given a fresh start. A whole new journey. We can't assume that He would abandon us simply because of Daddy's misjudgment."

Mother shifted her gaze to me. "I am not going to have this conversation with a child."

"She's not a child." Daddy reached across to cover my hand with his. "She's a young woman who seems to have more faith in God than any of the rest of us do. And the Bible says our sins are tossed as far as the east is from the west. Well, right now we're about as far from the west as we are from the east. We can go either way, but I say we press on—"

"How does that verse go?" I asked. "Forgetting those things which are behind and reaching forth—"

"Philippians," Mother said, sounding defeated, "chapter three. 'Brethren, I count not myself to have apprehended: but this one thing I do, forgetting those things which are behind, and reaching forth unto those things which are before, I press toward the mark for the prize of the high calling of God in Christ Jesus.'"

"Amen," Daddy said, making Mother's recitation a prayer for our family.

Our family embarked on the next leg of our journey with renewed vigor. Perhaps it was the knowledge of having essentially nothing to return to that made us embrace the unknown, but within a few days, even Mother's face would beam a little when we talked about the new life waiting to be claimed.

While the conditions of our travel did not improve, we seemed to encounter more of God's little blessings along the way. The stagecoach was as harrowing and uncomfortable as ever, but we laughed more as we careened into one another. Our lodgings continued to range from crude to uninhabitable, but at least we were afforded more frequent overnight stops. We came together in prayer every evening and met each morning with a new sense of purpose.

Some of the stations were actually forts built to house soldiers posted to protect emigrants from Indian attacks. I found this amusing, as it seemed there were always a few Indians living within the forts' walls or just outside—quiet, peaceful people wholly unlike the painted savages that made Mother hold her breath. We occasionally saw those savages too, or at least the evidence of them as we passed the charred buildings left in the wake of their raids. Daddy tried to reassure us that we were quite safe—Indians rarely attacked a stagecoach, as we had nothing of value to them and posed no threat. But still, sometimes in the night we would hear the sounds of battle cries and in the day see them proud upon their mounts on the horizon, and I would ask God to keep a wide path between us and them.

My favorite part of any stop came just after supper. Daddy would take out his map and, sometimes asking the expertise of our driver or whoever manned the station, gather us around to show just how far we'd traveled that day. Mother barely feigned enough interest to look over his shoulder before declaring that a bunch of little dots and lines didn't mean a thing to her, and Chester stood impatiently, shifting from foot to foot, before being dismissed to find what entertainment lurked in the surrounding sheds or barracks. But Phoebe and I gathered round, holding the lantern as close as we dared, listening as Daddy asked about the day's journey that lay ahead. Where we might be able to have another extended stop to bathe and change our clothes. The chance of Indian attack. The grade of the road and the surrounding terrain. Phoebe soaked it all in, asking question after question, until one soldier at a nearly deserted fort declared it a shame that she was a girl, as she'd make a fine scout.

It was amazing to gather around that long, folded paper and realize that we were in a different territory—Kansas, then Nebraska, a dip to the south into Colorado, and now Wyoming. I listened not so much for myself but for my father, who had recaptured every bit of the spirit he'd had back when we boarded the train in Belleville.

It was late in the summer, just days left in August and more than two months into our journey and hours before the dawn, when our stagecoach came to a stop amid a ramshackle group of long, low buildings. The air was still and cold; we'd spent the night huddled together in the stagecoach in what ways we could. The summer nights had never been balmy, this was the first to have taken such a frigid turn. When the traces finally silenced, we piled out of the coach, allowed our bodies long, wrenching stretches, then hugged ourselves against the cold.

The moon was round and full, but other than that, there was no speck of light to be found anywhere—no cookfires, no lanterns, no signal left to usher our arrival. Glancing around, I could make out the shapes of men sleeping on the ground near firepits long cold. Whip walked over to one of them and nudged him with his boot. "Git up." He made no attempt to allow the others to rest in sound slumber. "Help me unhitch this team."

Often when we approached stations in the dead of night, we were greeted by watchmen with rifles at the ready to defend the place against an Indian raid. As I watched this man scramble up to consciousness, I wasn't sure which made me more fearful—that he might be in charge of guarding my safety or that he might mistake us for a threat and begin to fire madly from the pistol he was working so hard to get an honest grip on.

"Aw, gimme that." While the man's hat was still dropped low over his eyes, Whip grabbed the pistol by its barrel and dropped it to the ground. "C'mon now and gimme a hand with this team."

While Whip began to unhitch the team, my father broke away from our huddled group and approached the newly unarmed guard.

"Excuse me, sir? Where are we to go?"

The man leaned closer to Daddy, trying to make out a face in the dim moonlight. "Go where?"

"That's what I'm asking you," Daddy said. "Where can we go to get some rest?"

The man let forth a slow, wheezing laugh and spread out his arms. "Rest where ya like, buddy. We're none too particl'r."

"Don't you pay any attention to him," said a voice from behind. "Some people wake up mean. Others wake up stupid. Marty just happens to be a master of the two."

Marty laughed out loud at this, as did our driver. I turned to see a man standing at the boot of the stagecoach, unlashing our bags.

"You better watch yourself, Del," Marty said, "or you're gonna be one of them people that wakes up shot dead."

"Well then, I figure he's pretty safe as long he's sleepin' here," Whip said. "That is, as long as he makes it a point not to shoot himself."

"Can I get one of you to give me a hand here?" the one called Del asked, and I volunteered, eager to get a look at the man who could turn our taciturn driver into such a wit. "Well, that's nice," he leaned closer to look at me, "but it might help more if I had someone who was a mite bigger than the bags."

Standing closer, I could see he wasn't much older than Chester. He had a soft smile and broad shoulders, both of which held my attention as he swung our largest trunk down from its perch and handed it to my brother, who took great pains not to grunt too loudly under its burden.

"I think this is more your size." He handed down my small satchel. "You're kind of a little bitty thing."

"Thank you." I grabbed the handle.

I was glad for the darkness so he couldn't see how I much I was blushing. As I walked back to the rest of my family, my mind raced with witty retorts: *A little bag can hold a lot of treasures.* Or *some of the best presents come in small packages.* But of course I hadn't said any of those things, and what a fool I'd look to rush back with them now.

After the luggage was unloaded, Del told us to follow him to where we would lodge for what was left of the night. "It's not but one room, folks. Sorry. But there's cots and blankets, and I lit you a little fire soon as I heard you comin'."

He hadn't taken more than two steps when I noticed the limp—a heavy falling on his left foot while the right dragged somewhat to come abreast—and I was relieved to have something to focus my attention on besides the width of his back and the strength of his hands. He walked in front of us, and I think we all shortened our strides so as not to overtake him as we made our way toward the promised lodging. Once there, Del opened the door and walked away without saying another word, even as my father called out, "Thank you, Son."

Mother was the first to venture inside, and she was back out before her skirts had a chance to fully cross the threshold.

"Well, this will never do." She tugged her gloves more tightly to her fingers. "Get that boy back here and tell him this is not acceptable."

"I'm sure it's fine, Ellen." Daddy pushed past her and emerged just as quickly. "We'll just have to keep the luggage outside."

One by one we wedged ourselves into the tiny cabin and saw by the light of a lantern hanging on a hook by the door that, yes, it did have the promised cots. Two of them, flush against two of the four walls, each piled high with folded quilts. The third wall was taken up by a small stove and fuel box, and the fourth was used almost entirely as the door. I set an immediate course for the stove, holding my numbed hands out and relishing the prickling as its warmth revived them.

"You and Mother should take the beds, Daddy." I turned around to let the stove work its magic elsewhere. "There seem to be extra blankets, so the rest of us will be fine on the floor, won't we?"

"Of course," Phoebe said through gritted teeth.

"You all enjoy." Chester grabbed one of the blankets off the end of a cot. "I'm taking my chances out in the barn."

"I suppose this means we can bring the bags in after all." Mother dispatched my father to fetch them. Mother and Daddy collapsed on the cots; Phoebe and I wrapped ourselves in quilts and settled on the floor.

Earlier that night, as we had lurched along the darkened road, I would have sworn that, given a level surface and a modicum of heat, I would be deep into slumber before my eyes were fully shut. But now, as the breathing of my parents and Phoebe took on a measured rhythm, my mind remained fresh and alert. Rumbles of deep, male laughter made occasional forays into the night air, and I couldn't help but wonder what the latest joke was. And the floor was much less comfortable than I had anticipated; my body felt awkward trying to find a comfortable position. Maybe I was too warm even though the fire in the stove had begun to wane.

Or maybe I was thinking of the hand that laid the fire.

We walk by faith and not by sight;
No gracious words we hear
From Him who spoke as never man,
But we believe Him near.

10

Every morning since we'd left home, I'd spent the first few seconds of consciousness trying to remember where I was.

At first it was easy, since we spent a few nights in the Rutledge Hotel in St. Louis and a few more on the *Felicity*. But after that, nights and days and nights had become a stream of trees and dust and sky. Never mind that the night before, Daddy would always gather us all around with his maps of the trails and stations. They were nothing more to me than dots on a page where mountains were pencil sketches rather than treacherous inclines and rivers were benign blue lines that showed nothing of the terror of an unstable ferry.

The excitement of progress had long since dulled. Daddy's joyous announcements of "We're in Kansas!" or "We've dipped south into Colorado territory" no longer brought the same sense of accomplishment they once had. We each had our own way of measuring distance—Daddy through his maps, Mother by how long it had been since she'd seen another white woman, and Chester by the various currencies he took in his pockets whenever he could find a card game. As for me, I looked up every now and then, looked around, and thought, *This is as far away from home as I've ever been.*

Phoebe, still enchanted by the exotic names of some of our stops—Namaqua, Willow Springs, Twin Groves—sometimes tried to engage me in drafting an exciting tale for each stop's namesake. But we had even grown tired of that game. There were only so many ways to find romance in death and despair, and I often grumbled that there might not be any meaning to any of the names. Just because a station bears the name of Pierson doesn't mean that Mr. Pierson was a tragic hero or a gallant horseman or that he gave his heart to an Indian princess. "Names are just names," I'd grumbled to her on more than one occasion before slumping down in my seat to take a nap.

I don't think Mother would have allowed us to spend even one night at our current station if she'd realized the name of it was Crook's Clearing.

But when I woke up the next morning and staggered, squinting, into the full sunlit new day, neither she nor anybody else in our little party seemed in any hurry to leave. A large cooking fire was built in the center of the encampment, and Marty, the sleeper from last night, hunkered next to it, gingerly testing the flapjacks laid out in a pan. In a more surprising sight, Mother sat on a little stool next to him, her hair long and loose falling over the quilt wrapped round her shoulders, and held a steaming cup of coffee to her lips. Thinking back, the sound of her laughter had roused me from my sleep.

"What are we doing here?" I asked, lumping all of my questions into one: we'd never lingered so late in the morning; Daddy, Chester, and Phoebe were nowhere to be seen; and Mother had never been one to let her hair down with the riffraff.

"Oh, we won't be leaving today," Mother said with a lingering giggle and a dismissive wave of her hand. "Something about horses and shoes…" Her voice trailed off in a happy little sigh.

"Where's Daddy?"

"He's close-by, overseeing the whole operation. If we're not careful, he's going to take the last of the money and buy himself bellows and an anvil and call himself a smithy."

The last time I'd seen her this way was back on the steamboat after a third glass of champagne. I walked over to her and leaned in close.

"Did he put something in your coffee?" I whispered, tossing a suspicious glance over to Marty.

"Certainly not." She gave the cup a quick sniff just to be sure. "I simply had a wonderful night's sleep. Perfectly comfortable, perfectly warm. *Tout à fait parfait!* And to think," she continued, "an entire day not riding in that wretched coach."

"Not to mention true gourmet vittles." Marty piled a plate high with flapjacks and drenched them in brown molasses from a small square bottle. "*Bon appétit,* ma'am."

Mother dug in with a relish I'd rarely seen, declaring it the finest breakfast she could have imagined. "You simply must have some, Belinda."

"Better double up her stack, Marty. Or else she's just gonna blow away."

The familiar voice made me smile despite my embarrassment at his attention. I wanted to turn around, if for no other reason than to see if the face I'd gone to sleep envisioning was as handsome in the day as it was in moonlight, but I was solidly rooted where I stood. I heard his step circling, and suddenly he was in front of me, crouched down looking up. His eyes—the color of soft green moss—squinted against the morning sunlight. His hair was wet and had been combed back, still bearing the tracks of his fingers.

In all the novels I'd read with Phoebe, in all the stories she and I concocted together, there was always that moment when the lovers' eyes met. Phoebe loved to go on and on in this breathless voice about hearts stopping, time stopping, the earth itself moving beneath somebody's feet. We would giggle and laugh and swoon at the very idea of being so swept away. But I didn't feel any of that now. My heart was beating so loudly I could swear its call would be answered by a group of Indians just over the horizon.

I saw him lifting down our trunk, handing me my bag, limping toward the fire he'd built to keep me warm last night. Now the earth was hard and cold as my bare toes curled around blades of frosted grass, and I shifted from one foot to the other in a fight against the prickling pain. This movement caught his attention, and he looked down at my feet, then up again, rising to his full height so that I saw nothing but his coarse blue woolen shirt.

"You'd better tell your girl to get inside and get some shoes and socks on," he said with a nod toward my mother. "And Marty'll get her something to eat."

Then his distinctive step took him away.

❀

Mother's joy at having an entire day stretched out to our own devices was contagious. With a belly full of Marty's pancakes, my hair brushed to a sheen and braided, dry socks and shoes, I was sent to fetch Phoebe to enlist her in doing a much-needed wash of our soiled clothes. She was lurking in the barn, having brought Chester a second cup of coffee.

"He's beautiful when he sleeps, you know," she said as we left. "When I went in to see him this morning, he was still asleep. And his face—he's just…beautiful."

Normally her prattling about the irresistible attributes of my brother annoyed me, but this morning I caught myself wondering what Del might look like when sleeping, and it was a moment or so before I slapped the back of her head and told her to shut up about it already.

As we made our way back, the camp was coming to life. Doors of the scattered cabins opened and men of all ages, shapes, and sizes stepped out. Some half dressed, most not shaven, and all quite taken aback at the sight of two young girls strolling about. Few of them took any pains to hide their appreciation of our appearance, and while I didn't understand everything they said to us, their tone was clear enough to make me want to crawl in a hole. But they didn't faze Phoebe. She jeered over her shoulder— "Ah, keep it to yourself! You're acting like you've never even seen a girl before"—and kept walking, never turning back to let them see her smug little smile.

We found Mother back at our cabin, where she'd commandeered a washboard and a cake of surprisingly pleasant soap. The three of us walked down a gently sloping hill and found a smooth-surfaced lake nestled within a wall of tall green brush. Closer to the water's edge, thick shrubs seemed to hold any advancing water at bay. The center of the lake was dotted with tiny grassy islands. We took turns enjoying a quick, cleansing bath while the other two held a blanket to guard against prying eyes. When we were all done and dressed in clean clothes, Mother left Phoebe and me with the pile of soiled laundry.

"It's good to see her happy," I said once my mother walked out of view.

"She can be happy. She's not the one doing the wash." Phoebe scrubbed Mother's dress across the washboard.

I didn't say anything until she was finished and handed the dress to me to rinse in the lake's frigid water, then wring out and spread over a low bush to dry.

"She didn't mean what she said that night, Phoebe."

"I don't know what you're talking about." She was scrubbing her own dress now.

"Mother can say some pretty horrible things when she's upset. And sometimes when she's not so upset—when she's just not thinking. Why, if I believed every terrible thing she's ever said to me, I wouldn't think she loved me at all."

"You don't have to think she loves you, Belinda. She's your

mother. You know she does. Frankly, it doesn't make any difference to me." Phoebe handed her soapy dress over to me. "I'm not going to build my life around whether my blessed Aunt Ellen loves me or not. I already have a mother."

"Do you miss her?" It may have been an obvious question, but Phoebe rarely mentioned her parents, and she hadn't said a single word about them since our fateful night in the Bledsoe house.

"I did at first, but I had Uncle Robert and your mother to fill the gap. And now…well, I guess I just got out of the habit."

"You still have my parents, Phoebe. They care about you very much."

"We'll see, won't we? When we all get to the end of this little fairy tale journey that we're on and it's time to start building up something new."

"You're family." I laid her dress out next to Mother's. "We'll need you."

"To do what? Do you think I came out here to be your wash-woman?"

I had just knelt next to her, and she thrust my newly washed dress at me with such force that the splash from it sent icy droplets to my face.

"I know why you came." I dried my face with the upper part of my sleeve. "Actually, I think it's pretty obvious to everyone. Including Chester."

Phoebe wrung out a stocking, casting a furtive glance over her shoulder.

"And it won't matter one bit." I wrung the last bit of water out of my skirt and headed for the drying bush. "There isn't a thing you could ever do to make him love you."

"I don't believe that."

"Just what do you think is going to happen? He's known you forever. Since you were a baby. Do you think one of these days the scales are going to fall off his eyes and some divine light is going to shine down on you?" I walked back to wait for the clean stockings. "That some angelic choir is going to sing down from heaven"—I summoned by best operatic falsetto—"*Chester, here is the love of your life!*"

"It could happen," she said with a mischievous glint in her eye.

"No it won't, Phoebe," I said, keeping my tone light. "My brother has a penchant for beautiful girls with loose morals, and you, my cousin, will never be beautiful."

It took a minute for my joke to register, and when it did, she took the handful of clean, wet stockings and threw them in my face.

"You're terrible!" she said, but I could tell by her voice that she wasn't angry in the least.

"No, I'm smart." I shook out each stocking from its wadded-up ball to rinse the soap out. "I'm not going to make my life decisions based on whether or not I love somebody."

"You don't know that," Phoebe said, once again solemn in her chore. "You won't know until it happens."

We left the clothes to dry—Phoebe's dress nestled between two of Chester's shirts—and took to exploring. Our reward for the morning's hard labor came in the form of a wild chokecherry bush, and Phoebe and I began to gorge ourselves on the dark, ripe fruit.

"We need to take some back," I said. "They're Daddy's favorite."

So Phoebe made a basket with the edge of her skirt, which I filled with clusters of our newfound treat. Every few steps I dropped a chokecherry into my mouth, then one into Phoebe's, and we giggled at the faces we made whenever we bit down on a sour one. Our faces and hands were sticky with juice, Phoebe's skirt irrevocably stained. We mused about how delicious the berries would be covered in cream, baked in a pie, or made into a jelly and slathered on a scone. But since we'd been living on a steady diet of salt pork, potatoes, biscuits, and beans, it was hard to imagine that any sort of tampering would make these berries any more delicious. I worried that we might not have any left for Daddy at all.

"They're good, aren't they?" Del had once again managed to appear silently behind me, this time catching me in the act of stopping a meandering stream of chokecherry juice with my tongue.

"Mm-hmm" was all I could say as I stumbled a bit in my effort to turn and address him.

"And I don't believe we've met." Del extended a hand toward Phoebe—a ceremonial gesture at best, as she was occupied holding the berries in her skirt. "Name's Del—Delano Saunders, but I just go by Del."

"That's my cousin Phoebe," I said, perturbed that he'd never introduced himself to me and wondering if he knew my name at all.

"Good to meet you—both of you." He fell into an easy step with us in spite of his limp. "I just got finished playing a few hands of cards with your brother."

"Is that right?" I said. "Well, you'd better be careful there. He's likely to take you for all you've got."

"Wouldn't be much to that," Del said with a hint of throaty laughter. "And you might want to tell him to do the same. Not all of the guys here are as nice as me. I walked away with him owin' me a few bucks."

When we came into the clearing, I could see that a certain bustle marked the onset of the late summer afternoon. Pockets of activity were everywhere: men chopping firewood, clearing brush, repairing a roof. In contrast to all this, Chester lounged in a hammock slung between two posts.

"So, what is this place?" Phoebe asked in that tone she had perfected—not accusing, not demanding, but impossible to evade. "I mean was this an army camp? Are you a soldier? Or," she inclined her head toward his wounded leg, "*were* you a soldier?"

"Phoebe!" I said, but Del just laughed.

"No harm in a question if all you're lookin' for is an answer. No, I wasn't never a soldier. Some of these fellows were—like Marty, he was a cook. Others wandered off and ended up making camp here, hidin' out from the war. But the rest of us come from all over. I was ridin' for the Pony Express, like some of these other guys. But with the telegraph takin' over, that's about dried up. Now it's more or less a mess of thieves and vagabonds."

"And which are you?" I asked.

"Neither. God's commandments taught me never to steal, and this foot keeps me from wanderin' too far. I am here, Miss Belinda, merely to serve as your humble guide and host."

Phoebe and I exchanged a quick, knowing smile, then walked on, our eyes stoically forward. I wondered when he had learned my name.

At the edge of the camp, a dozen horses roamed in an impressive corral under the scrutiny of three men perched on the surrounding fence. Under a large tree next to the barn, a shirtless man with a chest the breadth of a pickle barrel nailed a shoe to the back hoof of one of our coach horses. Just as Mother had said, Daddy stood close-by, as if inspecting each step. I remembered his stories of his early days at the forge, working amid the fires, pouring the molten metal into the molds. And since learning of the company's demise, I'd often wondered if we all wouldn't have been happier living out our lives in the cramped little apartment he once shared with my mother.

"Come on, Phoebe. Let's take these to Daddy." I set a course for the smithing tree.

"Nah, you'd better not." Del reached for my arm to stop me in my tracks. "There's sparks flyin' and everythin' else over there. You'd best take those to your ma."

Phoebe snickered as I wrenched my arm out of Del's grip.

"I think I'm quite capable of finding her, thank you. Come on, Phoebe."

I set a pace that I thought would leave Del behind, but he not only kept up with us, he spurred on ahead and took down a basket hanging on a nail just outside the cabin.

"Here." He offered the basket to Phoebe. "You might want to put your dress back down in front of all these fellows."

I was ready to die of embarrassment, but Phoebe took the remark in good humor and would have allowed Del himself to scoop the berries out of her skirt if I hadn't wedged myself between them.

This was the scene Mother came upon when she emerged from our little cabin, her arms full of our woolen coats and shawls.

"The nights have been so cool lately," she was saying. "I thought we might want to have these a little more handy. What on earth have you got there?"

"Chokecherries, ma'am," Del said. The basket was full by now, and he held it out to her with such deference it was almost a bow.

"How lovely." Mother shifted the coats to one arm and daintily picked up a few berries. "And yummy too."

"Well, if you like these," Del said, "there's a little grove of wild plums 'bout a quarter mile from here. Maybe close to this evening, when it's a little cooler, I could show these young ladies, and they could pick some for supper."

"That would be delightful, I'm sure," Mother said with the air of a matron whose spinster daughter had just been asked to a summer cotillion.

"No, thanks," Phoebe said, fairly winking with conspiracy. "The wash should be dry by then, and I'll need to bring it in for pressing."

"Maybe we could ask Chester to come with us," Del said, "in case we need to climb any trees."

I wondered if his suggestion was meant to appease Mother's sense of propriety or my discomfort. In any case, it only managed to accomplish the first.

"That would be perfect," Mother said. "It's always best when Chester has something to keep him occupied."

I spent the rest of the afternoon following my brother's example, drifting in and out of exquisite afternoon sleep. Some generous soul had procured two more cots for our cabin, and the opened door and windows ensured a pleasant, cooling breeze. There was an odd sense of safety in being surrounded by so many men—rogues or other-wise—and an indescribable and perhaps undeserved sense of peace settled around me.

Each time I opened my eyes, I had the distinct feeling that another hour had passed, although it may have been a mere fraction of that. When a raging thirst finally drove me to get up, I found that Mother and Phoebe had abandoned me, perhaps to go check on the wash. I made my way to the water barrel which, according to Marty, was filled fresh each morning from the camp's well. I took one long dipperful after another, but my thirst seemed like it would never be quenched, although the collar and sleeves of my dress were drenched.

"Are you ready to go plum pickin' with me?"

I jumped, snorted some water up my nose, and choked on my

last mouthful. "Tell me," I said once I'd regained most of my composure, "do you always sneak up on people?"

"I guess I just worry that if you saw me, you'd up and run away"—Del reached out and tugged one of my braids—"and I'd never catch up."

"How about keeping your hands off my sister."

Chester had never been protective, but then again, there had never been anything to protect me from. And even this was mere good-natured banter. He put up his fists as if to fight, then smiled and reached out to shake Del's hand.

"I assure you I'm the picture of a perfect gentleman." Del held a small, empty bucket and gestured with it toward a little path leading out of camp. "After you."

We made three long shadows as we left the clearing, Chester and Del strolling an easy pace in front of me. At first I coveted the opportunity to listen to a conversation between two young men but soon learned they didn't have much to say that was radically different from the countless kitchen conversations I'd been subjected to. Someone had snared a rabbit, and Marty was preparing a stew. The last of the potatoes were going soft, so he figured he'd best mash the lot of them to make them stretch a little further—all of it so boring that I'd tuned most of it out and concentrated instead on my surroundings. Like how the clouded sky made everything seem like you were seeing the world through a veil. And the determined sound of Del's dragging foot.

So I wasn't sure exactly when their conversation turned from the mundane to the point where Chester had Del pinned to a tree, this time brandishing a very real fist in his face.

"Stop it!" I said, pulling Chester away.

"Just what have you told him, Lindy? What have you been talking about?"

"Nothing! I haven't talked to him at all!"

"Then how does he know?" He turned back to Del. "How do you know all of this?"

"Been hearin' about you all for weeks now." Del's voice was calm, even, as if hoping to bring Chester to the same temperament. "I know you're thinkin' that you're out in the middle of nowhere, away from the world. But it ain't like that. All these stations—we're like one little town spread out over half the country. Drivers talk, switch off routes, stories spread. I knew two weeks ago there was some rich family ridin' the continental, headed straight through to Oregon."

"That's not all," Chester said. "Tell her the rest."

"I said your dad's a…a dang fool goin' around with that kind of money. It's just a matter of time before your coach gets robbed, and count it a blessin' you've come this far without your own driver turnin' on you."

"God has blessed us because we trust Him," I said. "He'll always protect those who are faithful to Him."

Del held his hands up in surrender. "I ain't goin' to argue with you there. I know more about God's protection than most anybody else I've met. I'm just tryin' to warn you."

"Then consider us warned," Chester said.

He took the lead down the path; Del and I kept an easy pace behind him. I'd spent my life negotiating peace between my parents and Chester, between my parents themselves. This, however, had all the earmarks of two bucks in the fall. I wasn't about to get in the middle.

When we came upon a thicket of small trees, Del handed the empty bucket to me. "This is it."

My job was to stick close to one or the other as they picked the ripe fruit from the low-hanging branches.

"See, this one here's perfect." Del held a plum out to me. "Dark orange color, just turnin' red. Means it'll still have a bit of a bite to it but not too sour. Go on. Try it."

"No, thanks." I took it from his hand and dropped it in the bucket. "I'll wait until supper."

"Too bad you're headin' out tomorrow. Marty makes a great plum butter."

"Could you quit chattering on like some old woman?" Chester, having pulled a branch down to make the fruit more accessible, let it fly and dumped a handful of plums in the bucket, saving one to eat himself. "Tell me, Saunders, you say you rode with the Pony Express?"

"Yep." Del strained to reach a high branch. "One of the first riders they had."

"For how long?"

" 'Bout a year."

Chester chewed thoughtfully. "So, how long do you figure it would take to ride from here to Oregon?"

"Oregon's a big idea there, Chester. Give me something more specific than that."

"We don't even have to get all the way to the promised land. Let's say to Fort Hall."

"Ridin' flat out? I figure two weeks. Less if you could change horses instead of just restin' 'em."

"And you know this route pretty well?"

"Pretty good." Del spoke slowly, cautiously, as if the next word might spring a trap.

"You have horses here that would be up to it?"

"Now just what are you gettin' at?"

"I'm suggesting that I rob my father."

"Oh, now, Chester." I took a few cautious steps away from them. "That really is low, even for you."

"Relax, Lindy. It's not what you think. Well, not *exactly* what you think."

"And just what would that be?" Del said.

"She's worried that I'm just going to abscond with it in the night. Grab the family fortune and ride off to parts unknown. Or to parts well known. To California, maybe. San Francisco. To find something a touch more exciting than a plot of dirt in the new Eden."

"Seems like she has a lot of ideas," Del said. "Any truth to 'em?"

"My soul may not be as lily white as yours, little sister," Chester said, "but give me some credit."

"You can't just take Daddy's money," I said. "You tried that once, remember?"

"No, I asked *you* to try it once. And if I recall, you weren't the least bit helpful."

"But Phoebe was."

"Ah, yes, Phoebe. But this is different." Chester picked another plum out of the bucket and sat down under one of the trees. "Our new friend Del here has been kind enough to warn us of impending doom. That thieving bandits are on the lookout for a continental stagecoach toting a wealthy family. But none of them would think twice about a couple of old pals making their way to the Pacific coast."

"Yeah," Del sat on a fallen log, "but I'm not your pal."

"Nor are you mine," Chester continued. "But I need you, see? I'm just some Illinois tenderfoot who doesn't know a canyon from a cliff."

"Let me ask you somethin'," Del said. "This family fortune. Is it in cash? Or notes?"

Chester cut his eyes toward me, as if seeking my approval to answer the question, but I gave him no response.

"Most of it's in Illinois script," he said finally. "The rest is in gold. I figure I'd leave Dad with the cash. You come with me, and as soon as we hit someplace where we can change the gold into federal money, I'll cut you a percentage and send you on your way."

I strode over to my brother and kicked him, hard, in the leg. "I can't believe you! This is our father—our family!"

"Yeah—if this is family," Del said, "forget it."

"You're missing the big picture." Chester scowled at me as he rubbed his shin. "I'm not *stealing* it. I'm not even going to *lose* it. Mr.

Pony and I will pick a place and wait for Dad and the rest of you to show. Then we pay off our little guide here and go on with the plan."

"Kinda makes sense," Del said. "Notes are safer than gold any day."

"You seem to know an awful lot about the preferences of thieves," I said, hoping my brother would join me in my suspicion. But Chester remained undaunted.

"I figured we could leave tonight, get at least half-a-day's lead," he said.

"And if we're on horseback, there's no reason to stick to the trail," Del added.

"So if anybody's following our family—"

"They might meet up with the stagecoach—"

"There's a town just north of South Pass. It's got an exchange bank. Be a nice place to hole up for a few days. See if it's safe to meet up with your pa."

"And if it's not," Chester said, "we head out to meet them at Fort Hall. Got that, Lindy?"

"You're forgetting one very important thing, Chester," I said. "Our father would never hand that money over to you."

"That's why we're not going to ask him."

"Now, wait a minute there…," Del said.

"Lindy knows where the cash is. She'll get it tonight, hand it over, and explain everything in the morning."

"I can't do that," I said. "It's stealing."

I should have known better than to try to reason with my

brother when his mind was already made up, and especially in a matter of money. He turned his head, spit the plum pit a good ten yards, and scrambled to his feet.

"It's not stealing, little sister. It's protecting everything that we have left."

"Then why didn't you ever think of it before? Why didn't Daddy?"

"Because Dad's a dreamer. That's why he lost the business. That's why we're in the middle of this mess. And I'm not going to watch it all just ride away in the hands of some thief."

"No," I said. "You're just going to throw it all on some card table. Losing it, dollar by dollar until—"

"Just shut up!" Chester grabbed my arms and yanked me clear off my feet. "I get so sick of your self-righteous, holier-than—"

"Put her down," Del said.

When my brother obeyed, I found my legs shaking beneath me so that I stumbled a bit and was steadied by Del's strong hand on my shoulder.

"Now," he continued, "whatever happens from here is a family matter, and I won't be a part of that. You work it out and let me know. I'm always up for a ride."

He stood behind me, his hand still gripping my shoulder, and before I knew to pull away, he leaned over me and planted a short, soft kiss on my cheek.

"In case I don't see you in the morning, it was nice meetin' you, Miss Belinda. And I look forward to seein' you again."

He was nearly out of sight before I took another breath.

"What do you say, Lindy?" Chester said.

"Do you think you can trust him?" I asked, still feeling his kiss.

"Do you trust me?"

I looked into his brown eyes—so much like my own—and searched for the familiar glint, the twinkle of mischief that always accompanied his most troublesome requests. But I saw just him, my brother, cut to his core. Truthfully, I didn't know if I trusted this man standing before me; I'd never seen him before.

"I don't see why we just don't leave all of this in God's hands," I finally said.

"What? Don't you think God has two hands? that He can protect you and me both?"

The glint was back, just a shadow of it, but enough to give me my answer.

ater that night, our family gathered around the big cookfire in the center of the camp, bloated and happy after a delicious meal of rabbit stew and Marty's sweet cornbread. Mother had come to her senses and pinned her hair up but more loosely than was her usual style. She looked soft and pretty in the firelight, and more than once I saw Daddy looking at her with an expression I'm sure he never intended me to see. Del sat on the other side of the fire, and I chanced a few glances at him between the dancing flames, wondering if he—or any other man—would ever look at me that way.

The night was alive with stories and laughter. Marty took out a harmonica, and its haunting notes hovered around us. Sometimes, if he knew the tune, Daddy would sing, and Mother leaned on his shoulder, her eyes closed in contentment. Phoebe begged Del to tell us more about his adventures as a Pony Express rider, but he looked up at her and said quietly, "It's nothin' but ridin' a horse."

"But what about—" Phoebe said.

"I'm not much on tellin' stories." He ended the discussion with a modest smile.

Chester sat with us too, but he dug at the ground around him with a sharp little stick and jumped at every spark that popped from the fire. Seeing him fidget so, I could understand why he seemed to lose more money than he ever won. He became still only when his shifting eyes locked onto mine, reaffirming my promise.

He gave a slight, almost imperceptible nod, and I closed my eyes.

Father God, I prayed silently, *forgive me.*

I stood up, gave an exaggerated stretch, and announced to our little gathering that I was exhausted.

"After such a restful day?" Mother nestled into my father's embrace. "I feel like I could stay up all night."

"You do that." I glanced at Chester. "We'll see who's grumpy in the morning."

"Good night, Miss Belinda," Del said. I realized then that he was standing too.

"Good-bye, Del."

"Aw, c'mon, Sis," Chester said. "You're going to see him in the morning, aren't you?"

"Of course." I hoped my voice didn't hold the same sense of deception that Chester's did. "Good night, all."

I declined the offer of a candle to take into our cabin, preferring to keep my sin in the dark. I knew where my father's trunk was, having rearranged its contents myself in the guise of looking for a missing pair of stockings. Daddy had wanted to load it and all of our belongings tonight, but Mother had prevailed, wanting one complete day free of the labors of travel. Feeling my way in the darkness, I released the latches, lifted the lid, and ran my fingers along the sides, searching for the soft, flat leather pouch I'd tucked in just hours before. Once I found it, I clutched it in a moment of indecision before lifting it out and gently closing the trunk's lid.

I picked my way through our crowded cabin and found my cot. I'd spent many a night on this journey wishing for a pillow but never as much as I did tonight. With no place to hide the money, I lay down right on top of it and closed my eyes.

At some point during the night, my feigned sleep must have become real, because I was startled from it by my father's cracking snore. There was a gap between the planks in the cabin's wall, and I peered through it, noting that the fire had burned down to glowing coals and the entire camp seemed to be engulfed in sleep. I remained still, listening to the depth of Daddy's slumber and Mother's quiet, rhythmic echo. But something was missing.

"Phoebe?" I whispered into the darkness.

No answer.

I sat up and reached out to pat the cot behind me. Then I stretched farther, searching for her soft form.

She was gone. Or had never come in.

I scrambled around for my shoes, glad to find that they had not been disturbed, as I didn't relish trying to find my brother on a night that was not only dark but cold. Plus, something told me that wherever I found Chester, I would find Phoebe as well, and I might need the boots to kick her all the way back.

The door opened silently on leather hinges, and I stepped out, pausing to get my bearings in the dark. It certainly wouldn't do for me to wander off and get lost, only to be found clutching a leather pouch filled with the bulk of our family's fortune.

Chester had instructed me to meet him just behind the barn, where he was bunking with some of the other men. He and Del would be waiting, horses saddled and ready. The thought of meeting Del there made me stop and wish I'd thought to run a brush through my hair. He'd have to be content with a final vision of me, pale in the wan moonlight, my dark hair loose and falling across my shoulders.

That is, of course, if he chose to remember me at all.

I found the barn easily enough and saw two saddled horses.

"Psst! Miss Belinda," Del summoned from the shadows.

I picked my way over to where he stood, reins in hand. One of the horses startled at my approach, causing Del to make soft, soothing sounds as he gently petted the animal's cheek.

"Now you hush up," he crooned. "Nothin' to be scared about. It's just a pretty girl come to give me her blessing."

"Oh, I'm not here to see you." I stumbled over my words, thankful for the darkness to hide my blushing. "Where's Chester?"

Del gestured toward the barn behind him. "Seems that cousin of yours wanted to give him a little blessing of her own."

"Oh no," I said as images of what Phoebe might do to wrangle Chester into her romantic fantasy filled my mind. "Why didn't you stop her?"

Del chuckled. "I haven't known the girl long, but I have a feeling once her mind's set…"

I clutched my father's wallet ever closer, pushed past him, grabbed the unlatched door, and opened it slowly.

It was warm inside and sweeter smelling than I would have imagined. From what I'd seen, few of the men owned horses and those who did tended to let them range free. I was prepared for it to be at least as dark inside as it was outside but was surprised by a faint glow coming from behind one of the low walls that divided the room into four stalls. One mingled shadow played across the ceiling in the far corner, moving in unison with soft, whimpering sounds. I was about to charge forward to rescue what was left of my cousin's virtue when I realized that what I heard was Phoebe's anguished weeping.

"Aw, Phoebe, it's all right," Chester was saying in that warm, cajoling way he had that could make you forget all the wrongs he'd ever done you.

Phoebe didn't respond. I eased my way closer, breathless, wanting to give fair warning but also compelled by a shameful curiosity. A final step brought me to where I could see inside the stall while remaining hidden from their view, and I somehow managed to stifle my sigh of relief.

Chester sat on the ground, the low-burning lantern sitting to one side. Phoebe sat next to him, her face buried in his shoulder, as her body shuddered with the shedding of her tears. Chester held her close, one hand softly stroking her blond hair that seemed much thinner and paler in the lamplight. His eyes were closed, and he bent down to kiss the top of her head.

"I just don't understand." Phoebe's voice was muffled against his shirt. She pulled away then to look at him, and I saw her face, red and wet with tears, strands of hair plastered to her cheek. "Am I that ugly?"

"You're not ugly at all." Chester smoothed the hair away from her face and wiped her tears with his hands.

"Of course I am. I've seen those other girls—"

"But you haven't seen yourself. If you could see yourself right now—it's the most beautiful you've ever been."

"Then why don't you love me?"

"Aw, Phoebe. I *do* love you—"

"Not the way I love you, Chester. Not at all. You're the only reason I'm even here."

"Then I've done something right," he said, and I secretly smiled with him.

"And now you're leaving. And I might never see you again—"

"Now don't be silly. Of course you will. Ask Lindy; we have it all figured."

"But it won't make any difference, because I'll still be this hideous creature and you won't—you'll never—"

"Now Phoebe," he held her face in his hands, "do you know what's going to happen?"

"I think so," she said, her little eyes narrowed.

Chester smiled. "No, you don't. You don't know that the minute

I ride out of here, I'm going to fade away from that great big heart of yours."

"Never," Phoebe said, and I tended to agree.

"You just wait, girl. You're going into a whole new world out here. Men the kind and character that you've never seen before. You know what the problem was back home?"

She gave the tiniest shake of her head.

"You're too much of a woman for those Belleville boys. Me included."

"Do you think I'm fat too?" New tears welled in Phoebe's eyes.

Chester threw his head back, laughing, then put his hands on her shoulders and gave her a good-natured shake. "No, silly! I mean your spirit. I don't know any woman who has as much gumption as you do, Phoebe, and precious few men who do, for that matter. But out here, you're going to meet men who are just as wild at heart as you are. There's no way you're going to scare them off."

"Do I scare you?"

I saw the last of the resolve leave her. She slumped within his grip, and it was all I could do to keep from running to them, taking her in my arms, and reaffirming everything my brother said.

Chester held her very still and looked straight into her eyes, his deep brown ones holding her gaze even as he slowly shook his head. "No, Phoebe. You honor me. And if you knew the person I really am—"

"I do know," Phoebe said. "And it doesn't matter. I love you anyway."

At that moment, I loved him too. More than I ever had. I was about to make my presence known when I saw Chester take Phoebe's face in his hands once again.

"Phoebe," he said, "would it be all right if I kissed you good-bye?"

"Yes," she said, her voice little more than a breath.

He pulled her close, so slowly that I felt my heart would burst before he touched his lips to hers. The softest whimper escaped Phoebe's mouth before Chester pulled her closer and closer until she seemed lost in his embrace.

I brought my hand up to my mouth, ashamed to be witness to such an intimate moment, but treasuring the kindness of my brother's heart. Slowly, silently, I backed toward the door, and when I felt it brush against me, I opened it, knocking loudly.

"Chester? Are you in here?"

There was a scrambling of straw before Chester's head poked up over the stall. "Yeah, I'm in here. Is everything ready?"

I nodded.

He disappeared for just a moment, then came out carrying the lamp. Outside, the cool night air was refreshing to my burning cheeks, especially when the memory of what I'd just witnessed collided with the vision of Del, who had the slightest, slyest smile.

"You ready to go, Romeo?" he asked, handing over a set of reins and shuffling around to the other side of his horse.

Chester sent him a look of warning before turning back to me. "Did you bring it?"

I nodded again and handed him the leather pouch. Any thought I had of taking one more stand against this idea had long since melted. He grabbed me in a quick embrace and planted a loud, smacking kiss on top of my head.

"I love you, Lindy."

"I love you too, Chester," I said, my breath nearly crushed out of me.

"Take care of everybody."

"I'll try."

He released me and swung up onto his horse.

"Let's get out of here before the whole camp wakes up to see what all this huggin's about," Del said.

He was already on his horse, and it pranced, seeming just as anxious to leave as he was.

"Now don't you worry about anything." Chester leaned down as far as he could, and I strained on tiptoes to meet him. "I've got a good feeling about this."

"I trust you," I said.

Then Del gave the slightest nudge, and they were gone.

I'm not sure how long I stood there, waiting for Phoebe to come out and join me. But when it became obvious she had no intention to, I made my way back to the cabin, back to the safe sound of my father's snoring, curled up on my cot, buried my face in my arm, and wept.

Minutes later, I felt her behind me, stretched out and perfectly still. Neither of us slept. How could we, with a room so thick with secrets?

12

*T*he sun was just peeking up beyond the camp when Whip climbed up to his seat and took the reins. The four of us found our seats in the stagecoach—Mother and Daddy together, Phoebe and I facing them—and steeled our legs against that first lurch. Chester would normally stretch out his legs as far as he could at this point, lean back, and pull his hat low over his eyes, saying, "Wake me up when we're not moving." I never knew how he could sleep through such commotion, but evidently he did, because Phoebe and I would often pass the time saying vile things about him to see if he was really asleep. He never got riled, but every now and then he would betray himself with a slight smile.

Now, though, everybody was quiet. Anger, worry, betrayal, and disappointment mingled in the space between us and settled on our feet. Every now and then, Phoebe lifted the window shade to look out on the passing landscape.

"You're not going to see him," I told her, leaning close enough to whisper.

A deep rut bounced my father clear off the seat and onto the floor with his head nestled in Mother's lap. Normally such a sight would have garnered a barrage of giggles, but today Daddy simply climbed back onto his seat and stared forward. Not at me. Not at anything.

"It just doesn't make sense," he said after a time.

"He's a boy, Robert. Eighteen or not, he's still a boy. And who wouldn't pass up a chance to ride wild in this country? I feel blessed that he didn't ask you to join him."

"But why not ask me?"

"What would you have said?"

Daddy conceded that point with a nod. "Why not tell me, at least? Belinda?" He was looking straight at me now, and my body went still despite the bouncing of the stagecoach. "You were with him all afternoon. Did he say nothing to you?"

I felt lucky to have another rough jolt to think of how I would answer, and Daddy repeated the question when we were all once again settled.

"Yes, Daddy. He told me that he and Del were planning to ride ahead—"

"And you said nothing?" He rose to his feet and stood in the middle of the floor, holding one of the leather straps suspended from the roof to steady himself. He loomed over me, an unsteady vision as his face pitched closer, then away, his free hand swinging precariously closer to my face with each rocking turn of the wheels. "You sat through our supper, our prayer time, knowing what your brother planned to do, saying nothing?"

"Robert, please," Mother said, but he did not acknowledge her.

"I tried to stop him." I pushed my spine against the back of my seat.

"And just how, Belinda? How did you try to stop him?"

"I—I tried to talk him out of going."

"That's true, Uncle Robert. I heard her last night. Right before they left. She said that you'd be furious and that she wasn't going to lie about any of this to you. She said she'd never been her brother's keeper and she wasn't about to start now."

"So," Daddy said. "did he tell you why he left?"

"It was a bet," Phoebe said with such ease I almost believed it. "He and that Del character were arguing over who would reach South Pass first—a stagecoach changing teams, like us, or a single rider resting a single horse. They were trying to figure and talk it out, but then the easiest way to know for sure was to ride it."

"Oh, doesn't that sound just like Chester?" Mother said, and though my father blocked her from my view, I could see her shaking her head in that indulgent way she had in all things concerning my brother.

"Is this true, Belinda?" Daddy asked. He seemed much less threatening than before. Almost deflated.

"We'll meet up with him," I said, choosing my words carefully. "There's a settlement just north of South Pass. He'll be waiting for us there."

"Or," Daddy's eyes took on the twinkle he had passed on to his son, "*we'll* be waiting for *him,* by golly! What was the wager?"

"The what?" I said.

"Just bragging rights," Phoebe said. "That lasts a lot longer than money."

"Especially in Chester's hands," I muttered as Daddy took his seat again, smiling in unmerited admiration of his son.

It was stifling inside the stagecoach at full noon when the horses slowed to a walk, then stopped altogether with no station in sight. I poked my head out the window and could see the coach road clearly marked in the short grass that covered the flat land. There were mountains jutting up miles away in every direction, and I felt like the last of a handful of berries left to shrivel in the bottom of a very big dish.

"The next stop's not for at least another twenty miles," Whip shouted down. "Goin' to rest the horses here. May as well rest your-selves too."

We piled out one by one, and I raised my arms to let the sum-mer breeze blow all around me, cooling the sweat on my face.

"That fellow packed a marvelous dinner for us." Mother lifted down the wicker hamper I'd shared my seat with. "More of those delicious little plums, I believe. Biscuits and"—she rummaged around—"can you believe it? Cheese!" She lifted a little bundle cov-ered in white cloth to her nose and inhaled. "How wonderful!"

"Well, my love," Daddy planted a little kiss on her ear, "had I known it took only a lump of goat cheese to make you this happy,

I could have saved a bundle not buying that little bracelet you're wearing there."

Mother turned her head and returned a kiss to the tip of his nose. "I'm just happy I don't have to choose between the two of them."

We'd stopped on a gently rising hill. Just at the base of it, parallel to the coach road, a thick grove of trees promised a much cooler place for a picnic. But Mother had already spread out a blanket and arranged the food. More alluring than the shade, though, was the sound of a swift-running stream. My burning throat nagged for a drink.

"I'm going to get some water." I reached for the crockery jug. "Phoebe? Anybody want to come with me?"

"Wait just a minute and you can take the horses." Daddy disengaged from Mother and looked up at Whip, shielding his eyes with his hand. "You ready up there?"

"Ready? Oh, yeah." Whip seemed distracted, and he continued to stare off into the distance for quite a few seconds before slowly climbing down to unhitch the front team.

He took forever with the complicated mass of leather and buckles, and I turned toward the stream. "I'm dying here," I said. "Phoebe, you can bring the horses down to the water."

"Aw, I hate horses."

"Well then, isn't it a blessing that they probably hate you too?" I called out over my shoulder, stopping only when I heard my mother call my name. "Yes, Mother?"

"You really must try to be more kind."

"Sorry, Mother. Sorry, Phoebe," I called, mustering all the sincerity I could. Mother smiled broadly and waved me off.

When I reached the stream, I fell to my knees and scooped great, cold drinks in my hands. The water poured down my throat, down my face, soaking the neckline of my dress and my sleeves. I poured handfuls of it over my head and felt instantly cool—cold, even, as the breeze wafted over me and caused my teeth to chatter.

"Hurry up!" Phoebe's sullen voice came from behind, and when I turned, I saw that she held the reins of the two lead horses. "Aunt Ellen has the food all set out. And how nice of her to remind *you* to be kind to me."

"You are the most obstinate person I know." I poured out the jug's warm, stale water. "You decide to love someone, you love him. No matter what. You decide you hate someone? Same thing."

"I don't hate your mother." Phoebe stepped aside gingerly as the animals dipped their noses in to drink. "I simply stand amazed in the presence of her hypocrisy."

"Mother is just—"

I am still not sure what I planned to say at that moment. Whatever it was got lost as the horses reared, squealing, and knocked me backward into the stream. The cold water took my breath, and in the flash and flurry of hoofs, I thought I saw Phoebe laughing. I was wrong. Her hand had flown to her mouth to silence a scream, and as I floundered out of the water, proclaiming my understanding of why she hated horses, she reached out and clapped that same hand over my mouth.

"Hush!" She crouched down and brought me down beside her.

Then I heard it too. Gunfire. Shots ringing out just a few yards away on the other side of these trees, where my mother was spreading out a picnic dinner.

I lunged in that direction, but Phoebe held me back, whispering furiously, "Are you crazy? Get down!"

I used all my strength to twist my mouth free from her grip, and we crouched together, our breathing quick and shallow. My skirt was heavy with creek water, my stomach was weighed down with fear, and I would have been perfectly content to spend the rest of that day—the rest of my life—concealed in that thicket.

Until I heard my mother's scream.

From somewhere far away, Phoebe called me, telling me to stop, to come back to her, but hers wasn't the voice that compelled me. I was pulled by the sound of my mother. The eloquent, refined speech I'd listened to all my life was now disjointed and desperate. I heard high, screeching wails, not words.

Then I heard another shot.

Then nothing.

The branches I'd cleared away so carefully when I was seeking water now crashed against my face. When I came in sight of the stagecoach, my eyes immediately sought out the blanket where I'd last seen her preparing our lunch. But the ground was covered with all kinds of blankets scattered all about the clearing. Then I saw that these weren't blankets at all, but our clothing. There was my blue dress. Mother's brown poplin. Daddy's green shirt with the regrettable ink stain on the cuff. I'd packed all of this away myself. I'd helped lash it all to the back of the coach. The sight of it poured stones into my shoes.

Then the corner of the bright red riding blanket came into view, then more as I saw my mother lying upon it. She was pitched forward, her face dropped into the blanket's dusty wool. The only movement was the afternoon breeze toying with one corner of her upturned skirt.

"Belinda! Go back!"

I turned to see my father standing behind the coach's open door. Had it not been for the tuft of hair lifted straight off the top of his head, I might not have recognized him at all. Much of his face was obscured by his derringer leveled straight at me.

"Daddy?"

All the pieces scattered around me failed to make a complete picture. My father holding a gun; my mother slain. My eyes trailed away from my father, up the coach to the driver's box where Whip should have been, sipping from his flask, yelling at all of us to get ourselves back in the coach to hit the trail. But of course he wasn't there. He'd been unhitching the horses when I left. Only two of them remained now, prancing nervously in place, and when my attention was drawn to the uneasy movement of their hoofs, I saw Whip lying on the ground, face up, bright red staining his shirt.

Still, none of this explained why my father was pointing a gun at me. That is, until I felt a sharp blade press against my throat and my body press against someone who held me immobile in the crook of his elbow.

"Now, mister," he said, "I'm not even gonna ask you to drop the gun. You just look at me and your little girl here and tell me where the money's at."

Daddy kept the gun level. "I told you, I've given you everything."

"And I've told you I know there's more. What you got here ain't hardly worth my time. And it sure ain't worth that woman's life."

"Oh, Daddy, I'm so sorry."

I felt the slightest sting of the blade against my skin, and the man behind me hitched me hard against him. He stretched his other arm out, and suddenly I was looking down a pistol's barrel, aimed at my father.

"I'm only askin' you to make the job quicker for me," the man said. "I can rummage around all this as quick as you can, but I'm givin' you one more chance. Tell me where the money is."

"He doesn't know."

The man holding me seemed just as surprised at the intrusion as I was, for he loosened his grip just enough for me to turn my head and see Phoebe standing in the midst of our scattered belongings.

"He doesn't know because it isn't here," she continued. "His son, Chester, took it. All of it. And he rode off with it last night."

I felt the man behind me slump, just enough for me to wrest myself from his grip. At that second, a shot rang out, and I heard him fall behind me. I ran to my father, who dropped the smoking gun to the ground beside him and took me into his arms. Something broke inside me, and I clutched his shirt, feeling it wet against my cheek.

"I'm so sorry, Daddy—so sorry—I should have told you—"

"Hush, hush." He extended me comfort and forgiveness through his very embrace. "Are you all right? Are you hurt?"

"I'm fine. I just—Phoebe—" I turned to look for my cousin, but she wasn't where she'd been standing. Instead, she was running toward the man who'd held me and who was now struggling to his feet.

"Get in the stagecoach," the man said, wavering his gun between Phoebe and me. "Now."

Even as he kept his gun trained on us, his eyes wavered, looking between us and a figure riding toward us, whose thundering horse created a massive cloud of dust in its wake.

"Do what he says, girls," Daddy said, and his authority was the only encouragement I needed.

Phoebe and I scrambled in on the floor, barely closing the door before the sound of hoofs came to a stop. Then we heard the voice of the rider saying, "Well, well, little brother. Looks like you've been busy."

"Looks like," said the man who'd held me hostage. "It's a wash, though. Nothin' here."

"What's he talkin' about?" the rider said. "Where's the money?"

"I told him I don't know," Daddy said. "Apparently I've already been robbed. By my own son. Better luck next time." The bitterness in his voice spoke of a man on the brink of surrender.

"Be careful, mister," the first man said, and I thought I heard a hint of gentleness in his voice.

"I could say the same for you," the rider said. "This boy of yours. You didn't know he took your money?"

"No," Daddy said.

"He's lying," the one with the knife said. "The boy's headed south. To Denver."

"That true?" the rider asked.

There was a long hesitation before my father's shaking voice said, "Yes."

"Well then, mister, I don't figure you're much good to me."

I heard the unmistakable click of a gun being cocked, an explosion of noise, and laughter. Even as I looked up to see the smoke drifting just outside the stagecoach window, it was the sound of the laughter that haunted me. Phoebe and I clutched each other, and it was only because of the pressure of her hand on my mouth that I didn't scream.

"What do you say, Laurent?" the rider said. "Feel like headin' to Denver?"

"Nah. You know I ain't one for the big towns."

"Suit yourself, Brother." I heard the scrunching of leather as he mounted his horse, then the sound of hoofs as he rode away.

Phoebe and I still held each other on the floor of the stagecoach. My ears rang and my eyes and throat burned. There was nothing real about what was happening around me. Nothing had made any sense since my last sip of water. Even now, as the coach door flew open and this stranger grabbed my arm and hauled me out, lifting me over the slumped form of my father. He was shouting questions into my face, questions I couldn't answer because I couldn't hear. This scene around me was all vapor, a mirage mingled with the clearing smoke. I hung, limp in this stranger's grip, waiting for truth to rematerialize.

Then I heard Phoebe say, "You can't kill her."

He threw me roughly to the ground, and Phoebe came to me, took me in her arms, and ran her hand in comforting circles on my back. When she spoke, I felt like I was a little girl again, curled up in my mother's lap at the close of some big dinner party as she talked over my head with her friends about things I couldn't begin to understand.

"If you ever want to see that money," Phoebe said, "you need her. She's the only one who can lead you to her brother."

"Get up." He once again pointed his gun at us.

I obeyed out of numb resignation more than fear, helped up by Phoebe's strong arm. He put his free hand to his mouth and whistled, calling a saddled horse to his side.

"Now get her up there."

He gestured with his gun for Phoebe to help me into the saddle, and I didn't balk until my foot was in the first stirrup.

"No!" I backed away. "We can't just *leave*."

"It's going to be all right," Phoebe whispered close to my ear. "He's been shot, he's bleeding. He'll be dead before sundown. Just do what he says, Lindy."

"But what about—"

"There's nothing you can do for them now, Belinda. They would want you to be safe. They loved you."

"This is all my fault." I fell against the horse, taking strange comfort in the warmth of its flank. "All my fault."

"You couldn't have known—"

All of a sudden, Phoebe was yanked away from me by the man who stood behind us, holding the reins of one of the horses from the team.

"You get up on this," he said.

"There's no saddle," Phoebe said.

"And there's no reason to keep you alive. I'm just feelin' generous. Grab a blanket or something and climb on up there and let's get goin' before somebody comes ridin' along to join us."

"You'll have to help me," Phoebe said with such a matter-of-fact tone one would think the two had been arguing with each other for years.

She turned to the scattered items strewn about, and the man turned to me. I tried to hold his gaze, but I looked continuously over to Phoebe, who was sifting through piles of garments. When she made her way back, I thought I saw the familiar cuff of my winter coat peeking out from beneath the blanket she carried.

She didn't think we were coming back.

Minutes later, she was throwing a blanket over the horse. She and the man squatted down to catch her foot. He emitted such a cry of agony as he lifted her that I thought for sure he'd spook the horses anew. Once he'd finished, he put his hands on his knees and bent low, spitting pinkish foam into the dust at his feet and breathing heavily for a full minute before turning his attention to me.

That was the first time I missed an opportunity to get away.

13

The land that once flew by in a blur of color seen through an open window now took on texture and dimension as the horses picked their way over the rough terrain ascending the foothills of the mountains that, just hours before, seemed miles away. We'd left the main trail immediately, heading straight north. I learned this from Phoebe when we were allowed a few minutes' privacy at a stop to rest the horses.

"How do you know?" I whispered, standing guard between her and our abductor.

"The map," she said. "I looked at it every night with your father."

Then the pang of loss hit me. I'd kept my grief wrapped tightly around me, like so many linen cloths wound around my chest, wrapped around my head. I'd ridden for miles in stone silence, the weight of my parents' killer heavy on my back, listening to his labored breath rasping down my neck. The cool breeze on my face complemented the growing ice within me, and after the first initial burst of speed, the horses had been slowed to a plodding pace, hypnotic in its rhythm. Each time the thought of my father or the vision of my mother entered my mind, I held my grief a little tighter, knowing there would be a better time to cut it loose and let it fall away.

And this was it.

A rushing noise filled my ears, and I fell to my knees. I gathered my skirt in my hands and brought the wadded material to my face and pressed it hard against my eyes. I poured my unvoiced screams into this depth, keeping them safe within the folds. I sobbed until I shook, exhaling deep, jagged breaths until I was desperate for another, and when it came, it mingled with salt and dust. So I choked and gagged and dropped my skirt away from my face and turned to spit out the bile that had been fighting for release along with the rest of my pain.

"Oh, God!"

None of the prayers I'd learned in Sunday school fit the vastness of this moment. This didn't seem like the time to thank Him for His blessings or to offer myself as His humble servant. It was all fine and good to ask for His guidance when such came with a map and a father. But here I was with a murderous stranger and a self-serving cousin. How would He reveal Himself to me through them?

Just over my shoulder, Phoebe was once again telling me that everything was going to be all right, that she had a pretty good idea of our bearings, that he was getting weaker by the minute, and if he didn't bleed to death and fall off the horse, we could easily finish him off ourselves and make our way back to the main road. But her words whisked away in the mountain breeze, and the utter silence of promise settled in their wake.

Be still.

I closed my eyes against the glory around me and held up my hand to lay my fingers against Phoebe's ever-moving lips. When she was silenced, I took it away and held both hands open in front of me, feeling the wind dance across my palms.

"Father God," I said, but the words were blown back to me, and I knew I could never voice this prayer to Him. None of the rote phrases from the hymnals and prayer books could begin to touch my need. With every syllable stopped at the back of my throat, I railed against Him for taking my parents, leaving me—*forsaking* me—here in this wasteland, delivering me into the hands of an enemy. I told Him He was cruel, ignoring our prayers for safe passage. Fooling us with faith. Making us believe that, as His children, we were immune from the underhanded evil of this life.

Be still.

Tears flowed unchecked, drying in streaks on my face. Not even the warmth of the sun settling across my back could budge the cold within me. The air carried the smell of sage—but its sweetness stopped before I could take it in. Further up the mountain, strong green pines stood against the wind, filtering it through their sharp needles, though I longed for its full onslaught, something strong enough to carry me away. I rocked back on my heels and opened my eyes to a vast, unblemished blue sky. Never before had I felt so small.

Then Phoebe's hands clasped my outstretched ones and she was helping me to stand. "We need to go," she said. "Now."

I allowed Phoebe to lift me to my feet, and we fell into each other's arms. For the first time I was merely thankful, not covetous, of her strength.

There didn't seem to be any hint of a destination. Now leaving the gentle foothills behind, we ascended the increasingly steep terrain. Though it was still light, the sun itself had long since disappeared, and despite the breath of our captor, I could feel the night's chill creeping across my neck. When we came to a spot that was fairly level, behind an outcropping of rock to block the wind, Phoebe declared we were stopping for the night.

"I'll tell you when we stop." Our abductor leaned heavily on me as he leveled his pistol at Phoebe.

Phoebe didn't flinch. "Then I guess those'll be your last words on this earth, because if you don't get some rest soon, you're going to keel over right off that horse and down this mountain."

"I'm just fine," he said, and I felt him gather his strength. "You think this is the worst I ever been hurt?"

"That just proves you're strong, not smart. But you're the man with the gun. What do you want to do?"

"Get down," he said at last.

"By the way," Phoebe dropped down from her horse, "what's your name?"

"Why do you want to know?"

"In case you die tonight. We might want to leave you with a note pinned to your shirt."

"Laurent." He inhaled sharply as he dismounted, leaving me to find my own way down.

It seemed to grow darker by the second. Phoebe and I were moving mostly on instinct as we laid out a circle of stones for the campfire. Once she had arranged the kindling, she asked for a match, but Laurent was already squatting at the ring's edge, striking flint against steel, eventually bringing forth a brave little blaze.

"I don't suppose you have anything to cook over that fire," Phoebe said.

"Here." He tossed Phoebe a small canvas sack. "I got some dried beef in there. Canteen's got some water in it. An' there's a bottle of whiskey. Fetch it down and get me a drink."

"We don't have to obey you." Phoebe turned to me. "We don't have to do a thing he says."

"Suit yourself." With great effort he stood and pulled the saddle off his horse and set it on the ground. He stretched out on the ground next to the fire, propping himself up with the saddle. "Eat. Don't eat. Drink. Don't drink. It's all the same to me."

I squatted down and held my hands out toward the flame, wishing there were some way to scoop the warmth into me. I wished for numbness, but instead my body ached from the long day's ride and seemed to sting from the inside out with cold. Something dropped onto my shoulder, and though startled, I was too weary to jump.

"Here's your coat." Phoebe slumped down beside me, holding Laurent's bag.

I ran my fingers over the fabric as if it were a foreign object. I lifted it to my face to inhale what I'd hoped would be the familiar scent of home, only to smell horse. "I could have used this earlier."

Phoebe picked up a long stick and stirred the fire, scattering sparks. "I've been saving it for a special treat."

I looked over and saw her face, pale in the fire's light, void of any perceptible emotion. No fear, no humor, just a placid acceptance of circumstance. After shrugging on her own coat, she opened the bag and began to rummage, pulling items out and laying them on the ground between us. A small pan, a large knife. A rolled pair of socks and a comb. Three handkerchiefs.

"Now, bring that on over here," Laurent said once Phoebe pulled out the bottle.

She set the bottle down, choosing instead to pull the knife out of its leather sheath and let the firelight dance on its blade.

Laurent laughed, something that seemed to cause quite a bit of pain. "For all I know, you might need to bring that on over too."

For the first time, I got a good look at him. He was tall and lean, his hair dark and curly—much like Chester's. His eyes were so dark they were almost black and rimmed with long lashes. He might have been handsome with the stark planes of his face but for a scar that stretched from the corner of his mouth nearly to his ear, looking like a maniacal grin. He had taken off his long leather duster, and I could see that the blood stain on his shirt had spread from his right shoulder nearly to the tail.

"You don't talk much, do you." He looked at me as he dropped back against the saddle.

"She doesn't have anything to say to you," Phoebe said.

"She ought to." He looked at me. "She's got a right to say plenty."

But I could never begin to voice the revulsion I felt for this man. Vile, unspeakable curses teemed in my heart and pushed themselves up until they lodged somewhere in my throat. I would speak them later, sometime when my head wasn't brittle, when it seemed I'd be able to open my mouth and not simply scream.

Part of me thought I should fear him—we were at his mercy, after all. But I didn't. Still holding the gun in one hand, he struggled to unbutton his shirt with the other. He seemed almost frail, and in that moment, I didn't see him as the man who had murdered my parents but the man my father had wounded. He wasn't frightening; he was pathetic. I walked over and knelt beside him—not sure if I meant to aid him in his task or revel in his wound.

I don't know what I expected to see once I pulled the shirt away from Laurent's body. Any stage of undress was completely unacceptable in my mother's home, so my exposure to the naked male chest was severely limited. But even the little I'd seen couldn't have prepared me for this sight. Behind the shirt was a hastily wadded-up fabric he had thrust against the wound. It was soaked with blood, and I gingerly took it between my thumb and finger and pulled it away, exposing a small, round hole just below the man's collarbone.

"Does it hurt?" I whispered, feeling disloyal in my question.

He closed his eyes and nodded.

"And just what are we supposed to do about it?" Phoebe demanded.

"Need you to get that bullet out." Laurent opened one eye, nearly black in the dim firelight.

Phoebe laughed. "And just what makes you think we'll do that?"

He opened his other eye and fixed his gaze on me. " 'Cause you ain't no killers. Now, gimme a drink o' that whiskey."

She handed him the bottle, and he took a long swig, heedless of the traces of liquid running into the stubble around his mouth.

"Now," he held the bottle back up to Phoebe, "I need you to bring that knife on over, tap it right inside the wound, and see how deep that slug is."

"No." Phoebe settled herself on the other side of the fire. "And you get yourself away from him, Belinda."

There had always been something in Phoebe's voice that commanded obedience, and this was no exception. Just as I was gathering myself to stand, though, there was a soft *thud* on the ground next to me where Laurent had allowed the gun to fall from his grip. He grabbed both of my hands—just above the wrist—and pulled me close to him. Close enough that I could smell the whiskey. Close enough to see isolated, defiant whiskers growing in the path of his scar. I tried to pull away, but he transferred his grip, holding both of my wrists in one hand, and put his other hand behind my head, pulling me even closer.

"I didn't mean to kill your ma." His voice was so soft I knew Phoebe couldn't have heard him. "She startled me is all."

"I don't believe you," I whispered back.

"Believe what you want. But I ain't gonna die tonight, not from this. I bled all I'm bound to. Gettin' the bullet out's just for some measure of comfort."

He released me, but I didn't move. I kept my face close to his, my eyes inches away, making him my hostage and thrilling at the power I felt. I could kill him now, kill him with the very knife he'd held to my throat. Shoot him with the very gun he'd used to kill my mother. Finish the job my father left gaping wide open.

"Were you the one who shot my father?"

"I'm sorry that happened. He seemed a good man."

"He was."

"He could've killed me, you know. I gave him his chance. Fair, square, and wide."

"But he didn't."

"No, miss. And this here bullet might hurt like the devil himself, but it ain't gonna kill me."

I sat back on my heels and looked at him. Despite the evening chill, his hair lay damp against his forehead, his face a sheen of sweat. Every breath seemed to be dragged from a pool of shallow pain. I don't know if it was a gesture intended to draw me closer, but Laurent lifted his hand, listlessly, his fingers suspended haphazardly, and I was reminded of a picture I'd seen in my *Illustrated Stories of the Bible*. In it, a man lay on a straw mat, surrounded by the disciples. His blind gaze stared straight ahead, but his hand reached out for Jesus. I'd spent hours gazing at that picture, thinking how clever the artist was to paint the man's eyes with such unseeing flatness. When I looked at Laurent now, I saw that man. Eyes flat, hand reaching. I knew in the story that Jesus healed that blind man, and while I didn't have any power to heal, I certainly didn't have the power to kill.

Without another word, I made my way to the other side of the campfire where we'd laid out the items from Laurent's sack. I found the knife and brought it back to where the man lay, his head tilted back against the saddle, his hand dropped once again to the ground.

"What do I need to do?" I knelt down.

"Finish him off," Phoebe said from across the fire.

But the only voice I heeded was Laurent's, and I set out to follow his whispered instructions. I spread the wound open as wide as I could, willing my hands to be steady, and inserted the tip of the blade. I heard and felt the faint tap as the blade met the bullet and, marking the depth with my finger, showed it to Laurent, leaving it to him to determine if it was in too deep. It wasn't.

I got up and wedged the knife's handle between two of the rocks within the fire ring and allowed the blade to bathe in the flames.

"Bring me the whiskey," I said to Phoebe, "and take off your petticoat. I'll need some bandages."

"Why not use one of your petticoats?"

I smiled. "Yours are bigger."

She rolled her eyes, stood, and thrust the bottle into my hand. Then, as if a stranger weren't lying mere inches from her, she lifted her skirt and untied her petticoat at the waist.

"Tear it into strips." I dreaded the task before me.

Once again at Laurent's side, I lifted his head off the saddle and held the bottle of whiskey to his lips, allowing him swallow after swallow until he closed his mouth against the amber flow. I asked Phoebe for a strip torn from her petticoat, which I wrapped around my hand to protect it from the heat of the knife's handle.

"Are you ready?" I asked, holding the knife above Laurent's chest.

He nodded. "Sit on top of me. You're little, but you'll need to hold me down."

I sat on Laurent's chest, straddling him, his arms flat against his sides and pinned by my knees. Five years ago, he might have been my brother, breathlessly crying, "Uncle!" until Mother charged down the stairs to tell us we were both too old and too refined for such horseplay.

Now, I pressed the blade of the knife against the flesh surrounding the wound. Laurent contorted his body and let forth a scream wrapped around a gut-felt profanity, nearly knocking me off my perch.

"Hold still." I set the knife in my lap, feeling its heat even through the layers of my skirt and petticoats.

I closed my eyes against the sight of the new trickle of blood and gingerly touched the bullet's wound before taking a deep breath. Soon, two of my fingers were surrounded by warm, soft flesh as they sought the slug. I could feel the tension in Laurent's body as he willed himself to be still against the pain, and soon I felt it, a little round ball. I curled my finger around it and urged it to the surface, then scooped it into my palm and, inexplicably, slipped it into my skirt pocket.

"It's out."

Immediately, and without my summoning, Phoebe was at my

side with a length of bandage. I took it and ripped a smaller piece, which I wadded up as tightly as possible before drenching it with whiskey. I once again held my breath as I plunged the bandage into Laurent's wound, packing it in as deeply as it would go. Over this I placed another bandage, folded into a thick square. Laurent sat up and lifted his arms as Phoebe and I wound and cinched her former petticoat around him. Once he was settled back again, I offered him one more drink. This time, when he opened his eyes, I could have sworn I saw a look of gratitude.

"You reckon it's safe for me to sleep a bit tonight?" he asked, hinting at a smile.

"As safe as any other." I joined Phoebe on the other side of the fire.

"Here." She handed me a strip of dried beef.

I hadn't taken time to think about being hungry, but perhaps that had something to do with the shaking of my hands and the overwhelming weariness that made me feel like a pile of sand dissolving under the weight of water. I took the meat and tore off the end. It was dry and tough; if it had any flavor, it was beyond my ability to taste. I'd never chewed anything for so long in my life. By the time I finally got it worked to a swallowing consistency, Laurent was asleep and Phoebe was tapping my elbow with the whiskey bottle.

"Drink some," she said. "It'll help."

"No. Mother would never—"

"Oh, come on, Belinda. You're shaking. And cold. If we were back home, your mother would be fixing you a brandy and water."

"This isn't brandy."

She sighed, reached for the canteen, and poured a little into the bottle. After swirling it a bit and taking a taste, she handed it back to me. "Now drink."

I put the bottle to my lips, closed my eyes, and tipped it. Even diluted it burned but wasn't entirely unpleasant. I felt a flush come to my face and chest—my entire body being warmed from within. I took one more long drink.

"We can't go anywhere tonight." Phoebe took the bottle back. "Tomorrow morning though, first light, we'll go. He's not in any shape to stop us."

"No, we need to stay with him. He'll take us straight to Chester and Del."

"*I* can get us to Chester and Del," Phoebe said. "Maybe we can go back to where—we can go back and get the map."

"I can't go back there." The mere thought of revisiting that scene brought it all into focus with such clarity, the last drink threatened to rise up and choke me.

"I just need to get us to the trail. From there we'll follow it— any direction until we get help."

"God sees us where we are, Phoebe. He'll help us get—He'll help us."

"Well, I know that. But we can't just sit around. We can leave in the morning."

"There's a verse in Psalms where King David asks God to see him in his hiding place. This is my hiding place, wherever this

Laurent takes us. You can leave if you want to, but I'm staying here."

Phoebe shook her head and corked the bottle. She took off her coat and lay down, curling up on her side and covering herself with it, pulling it up to her chin. "If you change your mind, let me know."

14

A thick mountain mist turned the world pastel, and while I thought it might be wiser to wait until it lifted, Laurent was up and making preparations to leave the minute the light shifted from black to gray. Phoebe's desire to escape loomed in my mind, and I sent her my blessing to leave each time our eyes met as we broke camp. None of us spoke much to each other. My mouth was dry and my head ached, presumably from unaccustomed imbibing. Laurent moved slowly and carefully, directing us to do anything that required lifting—including saddling his horse—with short words that came out as puffs of pain. Phoebe's mouth was set in the thin little line that spoke more of her disapproval than any shouting ever could.

Laurent directed me to ride with Phoebe on the horse he'd commandeered from the stagecoach while he rode alone on his.

"We're going up some tricky trails," he said once settled in his saddle. "Stay close."

"How do you know we'll follow you?" Phoebe asked, having yet to mount our horse.

"You're not followin' me; I'm followin' you. Stay close so you can hear me, else we might just tumble right down this mountain. Any other questions?"

"No sir."

Phoebe grabbed a handful of the horse's mane and pulled herself onto its back. I did the same, though not nearly as adroitly as she, relying on much hoisting and tugging on her part to get me settled in front of her.

"Head out," Laurent said.

In answer to Phoebe's question of which way, he gestured in a direction I could only recognize as up.

It must have been nearly noon before the mist completely burned off. I felt like I was fighting to steal each breath from the thin air, and the pounding head that greeted me upon awakening only intensified.

The cautious, precise pace must have been maddening for our horse, as it had been accustomed to flying across well-traveled roads at breakneck speed. Of course, the opportunity for breaking one's neck was just as ample on this journey, especially on the occasional bit of rocky terrain where a glimpse to the side revealed a steep drop-off. As a result, our horse moved in a state of nervous agitation coupled with moments of sheer ineptitude. The only thing that fidgeted more was Phoebe, who kept up a litany of gasps and sighs and complaints.

"Are we going to a cave?" she said over her shoulder at one point. "There's a story in the Bible about a man who lived in a cave. He was infested with demons, and Jesus had to drive them out into a herd of pigs. You infested with demons, Laurent?"

I hissed at Phoebe to stop, but she would not be deterred.

"So, what do you think it'll be, Belinda? Where do you think we're going to end up? California?" I felt her turning back again. "Is that it, Laurent? Are we going to get to the other side of this mountain and see the ocean? Is that your plan?"

"Just hush." The pounding in my head was nearly unbearable, and the dryness and discomfort I'd felt in my mouth and throat had now contracted to a single sharp pain any time I swallowed or spoke. "You aren't making this any more pleasant."

"That's because there's nothing *pleasant* about this. In case you haven't noticed, cousin, we're captives. Hostages. Prisoners." I could feel her twisting with each word, tossing it defiantly back to Laurent. "We'd be better off with Indians. Or maybe that's what he is. A savage in disguise. Is that it, Laurent?" she shouted. "You going to tie us to a stake somewhere and burn us alive?"

"I hadn't planned on it until now," he said. I hated that I heard the humor in his voice. "We ain't got much more to go, so in the meantime you'd best listen to your little cousin there and hold your tongue before I get any ideas."

"Well, you don't scare me," Phoebe said. "You're not going to kill us. We're your key to the money."

"Most doors only need one key," he said. "You just keep quiet till we get where we're goin', and I won't have to decide which one."

I felt her tensing up to speak again, but a sharp nudge from my elbow poked her into silence. For the rest of our ride there was only the sound of the dense forest around us.

We had already stopped twice to rest the horses, so when Laurent called us to halt for the third time, I climbed down, resigned to a long day's journey, when he surprised me by unloading his horse.

"On foot from here." He winced with the effort of taking off the saddle. "I can get most of it. Think you girls are up to carryin' this?"

"We're your prisoners, not your mules," Phoebe said.

She stood, passive and mute, refusing to carry even a single blanket. By now I felt on fire, burning from the inside out, and found the idea of holding the smallest canvas bag so overwhelming as to make me want to curl up with the saddle and wait to die.

"Well then," Laurent said, "come on. It's not far."

Staggering a bit under the burden of his saddlebag, he set off with such confidence he must have been privy to some invisible landmark. Phoebe followed him, and I followed her, using the dark green and lavender calico print of her skirt to guide me. By now it seemed the path between my mouth and stomach was stuffed with straw. Sweat coated my face and brow, soaking under my arms and my back. I thought of nothing—not my parents, not my brother. I had no fear that Laurent might well be leading us to some place of execution. In truth, there was a part of me that found the idea a relief.

At some point the skirt stopped, and I stumbled right into its wearer, nearly knocking both of us down.

"Go on inside," Laurent was saying. "Rest up. I'll be back with another load."

I looked up, thinking I must be hallucinating. The thick woods we'd been trudging through opened to a small clearing, at the center of which was a small log cabin. Phoebe stood staring, her mouth agape for a few seconds before turning to me.

"Belinda! Are you all right?"

My eyes welled with tears, and my gathering sobs burst through my burning throat. Shaking my head served only to slosh the pain from one side to the other, so I let myself fall into Phoebe's arms for the final few steps of our journey.

The features of the cabin evolved as my eyes adjusted to the dimness. A little cookstove stood in one corner with a coffee pot perched on top and various pans hung above a long wooden box that ran nearly the length of one wall. On the other side of the stove was a water barrel half as tall as me, and a little washstand with a blue speckled bowl. In the middle of the room were two straight-backed chairs and a table with dishes stacked neatly on it. Two narrow cots completed the room's furnishings, and a more welcome sight I had never seen.

"Here." Phoebe helped me shrug out of my coat. "You need to lie down."

Under any other circumstances, the thin mattress covering the stretched canvas would have been unacceptably primitive and uncomfortable, but I couldn't tell the difference between it and the finest goose down.

Phoebe touched my face and furrowed her brow. "You're burning up."

My teeth were now chattering, and I curled my body to find some measure of warmth. She unlaced my boots and pulled them off before covering me with a blanket that smelled of pine needles and tobacco.

"I need some water," I said.

"I know. There's none left in the canteen, so we'll have to wait until Laurent gets back."

I nodded. I could wait. And until then, I could sleep.

I woke up to tea.

"With honey." Phoebe moved a spoon around in a tin cup as I sat up.

"Where are we?" I managed to croak after the first warm, sweet swallow.

"I'm not sure." She leaned forward, whispering. "He's right outside, chopping firewood or something. I think he'll let us go once you're well."

"Go where?"

"What does that matter? Anywhere away from here. He's dangerous, Belinda. A killer, remember?"

"Of course I remember."

"I'm sorry. But you should see him now, out there chopping those logs. Single-handed, you know, what with the wound and all. I just hope he doesn't decide to take that ax to us and—"

"Phoebe! You're being ridiculous."

"Even so, your falling ill might be the best thing that could have happened." She leaned even closer. "I don't think taking prisoners factored into his plan. Mark my words. We'll rest here for a few days until you get better, and then he'll throw that door wide open for us."

I glanced over at the door which was, at that time, wide open. Dusk was falling, and I heard the rhythmic sound of an ax splitting logs just outside.

"I don't think we're prisoners anymore." I took another sip. "I think we're guests."

Just then Laurent walked into the cabin, his arms full of kindling, which he took to the wood box by the stove.

"She awake?" he asked without turning around.

"Yes." Phoebe had been sitting in one of the straight-backed chairs, having pulled it alongside the bed. Now she stood, seeming a presence equal to his in this small room. "Not that you care. What she needs is some food."

He tugged his gloves off and dropped them on the table before crossing over to the cot and sitting in Phoebe's newly vacated chair. When he reached his hand toward me, I felt no compulsion to shrink away. Placing the back of his hand gently on my forehead, then cheek, he said, "She's burning up."

"My, my," Phoebe said. "Thief, murderer, and doctor. How fortunate for us to be in such capable hands."

A shadow fell across Laurent's face. He looked away from me, stood, and headed back to the door.

"I got a cookfire goin' outside. Got some beans warmin' up out there. Should be ready in a while." Then he left, shutting the door behind him.

"You should be more careful, Phoebe. It can't do us any good to make him angry."

"Oh no, my darling cousin." Phoebe resumed her place beside me. "That look on his face? That wasn't anger. That was shame."

For the next hour or so I lay on the cot, drifting in and out of awareness, watching Phoebe inspect every nook and cranny of the room. My throat continued to burn, and I felt as if my entire body were covered with a thin layer of fire. At some point I convinced Phoebe that my virtue would remain intact if I took off my dress, as the sweat-dampened material and constricting seams made the garment nearly unbearable.

"You suppose old Laurent has a nightgown hidden around here?" Phoebe asked, poking through a long, flat trunk she'd discovered under one of the cots. "Like maybe this was grandma's house, and he's the big, bad wolf?"

I smiled weakly.

"Or maybe," she continued, pawing through the garments in the trunk, "this was the cabin he built for his lover. He built it here, high up on the mountain, so he could hide away with her."

"Because her parents didn't approve," I added, ignoring the pain of speech.

"Yes, of course."

She had evidently found something to her liking and dropped the garment in her lap. She snapped the latch on the trunk and pushed it under the cot again before helping me to my feet and holding me steady as I stepped out of my skirt and petticoats. I shrugged out of my blouse, but decided decorum insisted that I wear my chemise.

The garment she'd pulled from the trunk was a shirt, made of the softest pine green flannel. It felt wonderfully comfortable the minute she dropped it over my head, and I hugged myself once my arms found their way into the cavernous sleeves. The hem of it dropped just to my knees, and I was grateful for my long stockings to fill in the gap.

I climbed back into the cot and closed my eyes.

"He wasn't a killer back then," Phoebe continued. "In fact, he had a promising career as a…"

"Painter?"

"Do you see any art in this place? No, not a painter. A carpenter."

"But her father was a banker."

"Exactly. And the only way they could be together was to get her far away from her father. So he left one spring, came here, and built this home with his bare hands."

I heard her take a few steps. Opening one eye, I saw that she was draping my soiled dress over the back of the other chair.

"But when he went back to get her…," I prompted, once she was sitting down again.

"When Laurent went back to get her, she had just been married to the son of her father's partner. That started a murderous rampage. First his lover's husband, then anybody who got in his way of building—well, stealing—the fortune that might gain him the respect he never had."

"Nice story."

My eyes flew open at the sound of Laurent's voice. He stood in the doorway, holding a black cast-iron pot with a towel wrapped around its handle, looking the least murderous as I'd ever seen.

"How much did you hear?" Phoebe asked.

"I came in when I was murdering my lover's husband."

He set the pot on the table and stirred the contents with a long wooden spoon. Steam was rising up from it, and soon the cabin was filled with a deep, delicious aroma.

"Sorry, girls, but the real story ain't half so excitin'. I share this place with my brother. Our pa was a trapper. Nothin' romantic about it."

I'd never seen Phoebe so flustered. Flushed, embarrassed, she twiddled her fingers in her lap for a few minutes before gaining her composure.

"So, you gonna eat first or feed your friend?" Laurent said.

"Go ahead," I told her.

Laurent set the bowl at the empty place at the table, motioning for Phoebe to bring her chair back to its place.

"Well now," Phoebe said. "Won't this be cozy? Just the three of us trapped here."

"Nope." Laurent filled another bowl. "I plan to get you girls out of here first chance I get."

15

I'd grown up on stories of enchanted cottages tucked away in deep, dark forests where innocent girls were lured to their doom. When I was ill as a child, Mother would sit by my bedside and read them to me for hours on end, holding my Brothers Grimm book at an angle so I could see the illustrations of wide-eyed children huddled behind woodpiles as they outwitted ogres. In the days that I languished in and out of fevered sleep, Phoebe did much the same for me. The only difference was that, in her stories, the heroes weren't anonymous princes or woodcutters, but Del and Chester, riding to great adventures in the Wyoming wilderness. She told tales of their imagined exploits, making them ford raging rivers or pull children out of raging fires. They battled Indians, foiled bank robbers, or found rocks of gold littering the beds of mountain streams.

The climax of each yarn was the dramatic rescue of us. If Laurent happened to be listening, Phoebe took great delight in narrating a violent confrontation wherein Del held Laurent at gunpoint while Chester swooped me up in his arms and carried me out of the cabin and down the mountain where a stagecoach was waiting to take us back to Belleville.

"Chester doesn't carry *you*?" I asked once, managing a faint smile.

"You're smaller. And sick." Then she leaned closer. "Besides, he can swoop me all he wants later."

This made me laugh, just a little, but enough to send me into a coughing spasm that threatened to split my head open. Even Laurent, sitting at the table drinking coffee, smiled and shook his head before getting up and walking outside.

He left us alone quite a bit—sometimes for hours—once coming back with a rabbit he'd trapped. For the rest of the afternoon he sat outside on a log next to an open fire while it roasted on a spit. I still hadn't recovered much of an appetite, so I had just one small piece of the meat shredded into a steaming bowl of bean broth, but I watched as Phoebe and Laurent sat at the table, tearing into it with gusto.

For just a moment, Phoebe forgot her antipathy toward Laurent and complimented his cooking. He smiled and said the secret was in the slow turning of the spit. And I, in that moment, escaped the circumstances that brought us all together and took three breaths of perfect peace.

On the fourth night I woke up drowning. Freezing cold, surrounded by total blackness. Soaking wet.

Phoebe had told me earlier that day about the mountain lake just over a ridge behind the cabin. It was a steep climb down to it, she'd said, but at the bottom was a giant pooling of melted snow, the clearest and cleanest water she'd ever seen. So this, finally, was how Laurent was going to dispose of us. After a prisoner's final meal of roast rabbit, we were simply tumbled over the ledge, left to sink, suffocating, to the bottom. I flailed my arms, searching for Phoebe— surely he would have tossed us in together—and opened my mouth in an illogical gasp for breath.

To my surprise, breath came. Then another. In a matter of seconds, the whole room was illuminated, and Laurent's shadow fell across the wall as he touched a match to the kerosene lantern on the table.

"You're not drownin'," he said.

"What are you doing in here?" Every night since we'd arrived, Laurent had slept outside next to the campfire.

"I heard somebody screamin' about drownin'."

There was a hint of irritation in his voice, but something indulgent too. He brought the lantern over to me, knelt down, touched my face, and smiled.

"Your fever's broke."

"I guess so," I said.

"Well, that's a good thing anyway. Want some water?"

I nodded. How could I ever have thought I was underwater, given the dryness of my mouth?

Laurent took the lamp back to the table, turned the wick down, and poured a cupful of water from a glass jar on the table. He brought this over to me and waited until I was sitting upright before handing me the cup. The first sip was so cold it almost burned, but then my throat felt immediate, cooling relief, and I took long, even drinks until it was gone.

"Thank you." I handed back the cup and lay back down.

"Get those covers up around you," he said. "Don't want you takin' another chill."

I heard a clatter as he opened the stove, and I watched him lay wood and kindling within it. He dipped a long stick down the chimney of the lantern and transferred the flame to the stove, blowing gently to fan it before closing the little door. That done, he pulled out one of the chairs and settled himself at the table, resting his head in his hands.

"Aren't you going to go back to sleep?" I whispered.

"In a minute," he said. "Let me get the fire burned down. Don't want no sparks."

"Would it be all right if I went over and sat by the fire for just a while?" I asked. The clamminess of the bed was nearly unbearable.

He got up and moved to the chair farther away from the stove. I swung my feet over the side of the bed and stood, my legs shaky with disuse. I hadn't taken more than five steps without leaning on Phoebe's arm since walking through this door. It took a while for the heat of the stove to penetrate the chill of my soggy shirt, and as I drew my knees up to my chest, curling up on the chair, I got a whiff of my own sour smell and wished I had something clean to change into.

"Feelin' better."

"Yes," I said, taking his words for a question.

"Think you're fit to travel?"

"Maybe in a few days. Right now I'm wondering if I'll be able to make it back to the bed."

Laurent simply nodded and continued sitting very still, looking down at the table.

"I guess it's a good thing you brought us here." Only Phoebe's faint snoring—a familiar and comforting sound to me now—punctuated the silence. "Why did you?"

"I don't know."

It was my turn to sit quietly, full of questions but in no hurry to get the answers.

"I never meant to kill nobody," he said after a time.

"You told me that before."

"I told you I didn't mean to kill your ma. I'm tellin' you now that I never set out to kill nobody."

"Well, you've had a few days to come to that realization."

My head was clear for the first time since arriving, and I'd spent much of the time in that fog trying to reconcile the image of the man who seemed to be taking such great pains to care for me with the monster who had gunned down my family.

"I'm not sayin' I ain't done my share of robbin' people. But the killin', that was always Hiram's doin'."

"Is that your brother?"

"Yep."

"Why did you tell him my brother went to Denver?"

"To send him away from you. Don't ever want him to find you."

"He's got to come back here sometime, so why bring us—"

"I don't know."

"Stop saying that. You *have* to know."

"That's just it. I *don't.*"

Phoebe let out a long, raspy snore and stirred a bit on her cot, and Laurent paused and lowered his voice again.

"I followed that stagecoach for a good two miles thinkin' Hiram's comin' up from the other direction. Cuttin' it off. I come up on it, and that driver starts shootin'..."

He rubbed his eyes with the heels of his hands, as if trying to rub the vision out of his memory. But I wanted to hear it, and I steeled myself for every detail.

"I never killed anybody before," he said, still hiding his eyes.

"I don't believe you."

He took his hands away and looked at me. Even across the table, in the dim light of the single, low flame, I could see straight into his eyes. They were steady. They were still. And something in my heart told me I was about to hear truth.

"It was always Hiram did that. So when that driver shot at me, I panicked. Started shootin' scared." He laughed, a dark, rueful laugh, and rubbed his beard. "Rotten coward like Hiram always said. Then the shootin' stopped. All that smoke cleared. And you came walkin' out of the trees."

"And you held a knife to my throat."

"I wanted him to shoot me."

"He did."

"But he didn't kill me."

"He's not a killer."

"Neither am I."

"So, it wasn't you who shot my father."

"No."

"Why did you hide Phoebe and me?"

He looked down again, studying his hands. "I can't explain it. The minute I saw you comin' out of those woods, I hear this voice. And it's tellin' me not to hurt you."

"So you held a knife to my throat?"

"Then when I dragged you out of that coach, I hear it again. Some voice tellin' me not to hurt you."

I couldn't help but smile. "I think that was Phoebe."

"No, it wasn't."

He looked up at me and stretched out a hand. Had mine been resting on the table, I think he would have touched it. Instead, his rested in the space between us, reaching for me.

"It was a voice. Inside my head but talkin' just as plain as you and me are now. And it's sayin', *'Not a hair on her head.'*"

Just then, I felt that same hair tingle at the root.

"So you brought me here," I said.

He nodded. "Didn't know what else to do. Figured here I could keep you safe. Get up some supplies to take you to—"

"Meet up with my brother?"

"Maybe. I hadn't thought it all out."

Right then a sense of power, the same power I'd felt when I held Laurent's knife to his chest, came over me. He was every bit as frightened and confused as Phoebe and I were. Maybe more.

"Will you help us get to him?"

He nodded again. "Just tell me where you're goin'."

I placed my hand on the table, just inches from his. "Get us down from this mountain first. Then we'll tell you everything you need to know."

The heat from the stove had warmed me through, and though I wasn't really tired, I had an overwhelming desire to go back to bed. As I walked past Laurent on my way to the cot, he reached out and grabbed my sleeve.

"I'm goin' to take care of you," he said. "Make up for what I done."

"Do you really think that's possible?"

He released my sleeve after I gave the slightest tug, and seconds later I was nestled down under my blanket. Laurent continued to sit at the table, his back to me. The cabin was completely silent. Too silent. I looked over to the cot where Phoebe slept and saw that she was looking straight at me.

"Good night again, Phoebe," I said before turning my face to the wall.

My strength tripled the next morning the minute I slipped on my dress—newly laundered by Phoebe—and stepped outside. The dark confines of the cabin were swept away with the first gust of mountain-cold wind, and though I felt strong, I also felt compelled to grab Phoebe's arm for fear of blowing away.

Holding me steady, she showed me a small lean-to behind the cabin. Inside were sacks of cornmeal, beans, tea, and coffee setting on a shelf supported by two barrels.

"I think one of them is full of whiskey," Phoebe whispered, even though we were alone. "I don't know about the other one. And see those cans? There's milk, oysters, maybe even peaches."

"Well, if he was planning to kill us, it wouldn't be from starvation." I ran my finger along a neatly formed pyramid of shiny tin.

"He is quite the little squirrel, isn't he?"

Laurent had left us to our own devices that morning, as he did most mornings, and the echoes of our midnight conversation were still ringing in my head.

"How much did you hear last night?" I asked Phoebe.

"Almost everything."

"Do you think he was telling us the truth?"

We were walking farther from the cabin, going down a clearly marked path on our way to fetch water—something, I came to understand, that had become Phoebe's daily chore. I don't know that she'd ever had a chore back home.

"Watch your step." She pulled me up short beside her before gesturing with her empty bucket. "Look. Isn't it beautiful?"

We were standing on the rim of what looked like a bowl scooped straight out of the mountain. Not a bowl, exactly, because the walls did not slope gently down from where we stood on a ledge just a few feet away from plummeting into a lake at the base of this unexpected valley. I'd never before seen water so still. The wind that threatened to blow me right over the edge seemed unable to reach the lake's surface, and it shone in the sunlight like mirrored glass. Indeed, the trees and rocks that lined its other shore were perfectly reflected, and I imagine if God Himself had a face, this is where He would come to study it.

"That's not where we need to go to get the water, is it?"

"Don't be silly," Phoebe said. "The water there is formed from melted snow. Nearly solid ice in the dead of winter, but in the spring it melts and runs off into little springs."

"How do you know all this?"

"He told me. Come here."

She took my arm and led me away from the edge, back toward the cabin—I could actually see it out of the corner of my eye—then past it, going deeper into the woods, following the faint sound of water until it became a full, lush, gurgling stream. Phoebe knelt at the water's edge and filled the bucket.

"It's still quite a walk back to the house," she stood tall and squared her shoulders, "but worth it. This is the best water, after all. Isn't it?"

Phoebe walked right past me, heading back to the cabin. I stood there, a bit puzzled by the uncharacteristic cheerfulness of her labor, before struggling to keep her pace.

"You still haven't answered my question," I said.

"What question?"

"About Laurent. About whether or not he was telling me the truth last night."

"Oh, that. I want to believe him. It would make everything… easier."

"It wouldn't bring my parents back. Wouldn't get us away from here."

"No, but if he's telling the truth, then we're not in any danger. And to be honest, I don't feel afraid of him anymore." Her voice was soft, almost shy, and a glance over revealed her cheeks to be pink, a slight smile tweaking the corners of her mouth. "I think he'll take care of us."

"Here?"

"Yes. Or maybe he'll even help us find Chester and Del."

"We can't forget what he did, Phoebe. No matter what the circumstances were, he's still a murderer."

"I know." She slowed her steps to a listless stroll, placing one foot in front of the other, eyes down studying each step. "But after these past few days, that part doesn't seem…real."

She couldn't have shocked me more if she'd thrown the bucket of water full into my face.

"Well, it seems real to *me*." I stopped in my tracks. "That was my mother! My daddy—"

"I know, but—" She stopped too. "You've been sick…and sleeping these past days. You haven't had a chance to get to know him. If you did, well, you just wouldn't believe that he could be capable of—"

"So, bringing us back to the question at hand. You believe him?"

She nodded, but swallowed her words.

"He'll still have to answer for what he's done. At the very least, to God. But if he feels as bad as he says, he should turn himself in."

"That's not up to us to decide." The defense in Phoebe's voice confirmed my suspicions.

"You like him, don't you?" I started walking again, and she joined me.

"No. You know my heart belongs to your brother."

"And you don't think you'd be able to push your feelings for that gambler aside to make room for a thief and murderer? My, Phoebe, what discriminating taste you have."

"Oh, shut up." She nudged me with her shoulder. "Now, you tell me. Do you think you'll ever be able to forgive him?"

"Who, Chester? Or Laurent?"

She giggled. "Both, I guess. But Laurent. Do you think, knowing all of this, that you could forgive him?"

I sighed. Even if I could believe what he said, forgiveness was a completely different question. One I couldn't answer.

16

The next day was ushered in with a thunderous rainstorm— the last we'd see before the onset of snow, according to Laurent—making the footpath treacherously slick with mud. After allowing two days for the conditions to improve, Laurent came into the cabin early in the morning, swearing—then apologizing—and throwing his hat on the floor.

"Horses are gone." He held a hand up to refuse the cup of coffee Phoebe offered.

"What do you mean, *gone?*" Phoebe asked, her eyes narrowed in suspicion.

"Gone from where I left 'em."

"From where you left them a week ago?" Phoebe fairly slammed the cup on the table. "Didn't you tie them up?"

"No, I didn't *tie them up*. You can't tether a horse for days on end."

"So, what did you do? Politely ask them to wait for you? I had no idea you were so gifted in languages, Laurent. Of course, it shouldn't surprise me that you speak horse, seeing that half the time you behave like a complete—"

"Phoebe!" I said. It was bad enough she sounded like a bitter fishwife, she needn't be a vulgar one as well.

"I winter in this cabin every year and leave my horse at the foot-path. Usually I can whistle him up until the heavy snows come. Right now, he ain't around."

"He comes back every year?" I asked.

"This one has, past five," Laurent said. "Hiram, he usually ends up stealin' himself a new one. Figures it balances out 'cause someone out there got his."

"So what do we do?" Phoebe asked, managing, as always, to sound accusatory.

"Too close to winter to head anywhere on foot." Laurent finally picked up his coffee.

"But it can't even be—" I searched my brain for a date, trying to calculate how long it had been since the days were warm with summer.

"It'll snow before we know it," Laurent said. "But I'll head back down there today. Keep tryin'. Plan on leavin' first light tomorrow."

As the day wore on, though, I knew we would not be leaving at first light.

Left to ourselves that morning, with my health and the surrounding terrain fully restored, I was eager to spend some time exploring the surrounding woods, enjoying the bracing gusts of mountain air filling my lungs after so much time cramped up in a dark, crowded room.

"Let's walk to the crevasse," I told Phoebe. "I want to throw a stone down and see what the lake looks like with ripples."

"How fortunate you are to be so easily amused." She was sitting at the table, her head draped on her arm. "Maybe I can find you a little ball of string and you can just bat it around here for a while."

"Well, we can't stay cooped up in here all day. Let's go down to the creek and get water for the canteens."

"We don't even know when we're leaving."

"But we know we *are*. We need to fill the barrel anyway."

"So, go. You know the way."

"It's more enjoyable if we go together."

"Look, Belinda. I was your water girl for days on end. Would it kill you to do it yourself just one time?"

Although I'd often observed Phoebe's verbal eviscerations on unsuspecting family members, I'd rarely been a target myself, and I physically recoiled at the sting. Rather than retaliate, however, I took a closer look at her and noticed an unfamiliar glint in her eyes. It was more like a glaze, really.

"Do you feel all right?" I said.

Her cheek, bearing its usual patchy ruddiness, was hot to the touch, and the minute I felt it, her eyes filled with tears; she turned her head away from me, burying it in her arms.

"Phoebe! How long have you been sick?"

"Shut up." Her voice was wet and muffled against her sleeve.

"Why didn't you say something?"

"Because it's time to *go*."

I put my head down on the table and peered through the dark tunnel of her folded arms, hoping to catch her eye. "Phoebe, we can wait until—"

"I'll be fine!" She reared her head, then balled her fists and slammed them on the table. "I'll rest up today and be good to go tomorrow."

"There's no hurry."

"You heard him! Winter's closing in—"

"A few more days won't matter. He'll understand."

"No." Phoebe wiped her nose with the back of her sleeve. "Don't tell Laurent I'm sick."

I laughed. "Phoebe, dear, I think he's going to figure it out. One look at you—"

"He never looks at me, Belinda. Nobody ever looks at me."

"This is not the time to indulge in self-pity." I dipped a rag in the water barrel, wrung it out, and gently wiped Phoebe's face. "You can bet he'll be looking at you once you collapse halfway down the trail and he has to carry you back here."

"I'll be fine," she said again, only this time there was the slightest hint that not even she believed it anymore. "I'm stronger than you think."

"That's just it." I took her arm and led her—amazingly without protest—to her cot. "You don't have to be this strong. Not today, anyway. Just lie down, close your eyes, and sleep. You'll have plenty of time to be strong later."

It was comfortable inside the cabin—just the slightest chill—so I saw no need to make her get under her blankets. I took off her shoes and suggested she might be more comfortable if she took off her corset.

"I'll stand watch for Laurent to be sure he doesn't walk in while you're changing. We can keep it hidden under the pillow if you like."

"Don't bother," she said, and I was glad to see a glimpse of her familiar, wicked smile. "I haven't worn it since we got here."

"You're joking," I said, dropping my voice to a whisper and looking over my shoulder as if a conspirator to this quiet act of rebellion. "Where is it?"

"I threw it over the ledge. Down by the lake."

"What if someone sees it?"

"Like who?"

Again, I gave a meaningful glance over my shoulder.

"Oh, please. It's at least a hundred feet down. You can't even tell what it is."

"Well then, I guess you're comfortable enough."

"Oh yeah." She settled in and closed her eyes. "Besides, there has to be some benefit to being a hostage."

When Laurent came back later that afternoon, I could tell by the scowl on his face that the elusive horses had failed to appear, but his expression changed immediately to one of concern when he saw Phoebe.

"I'm afraid she's caught my cold."

"Just as well," he said, quickly adopting a gruff demeanor. "Can't go nowhere without the blamed horses anyway."

He shouldered right past me to the table and scooped out the remains of a pan of cornbread baked over the outside fire last night.

"Mind if I take the rest of this?" He wrapped the bread in the cloth that had been covering the pan.

"Take it where?" I wished I'd been quick enough to snatch off a corner for myself.

"Goin' out to look for them horses." He filled a canteen with water and took the whiskey bottle off the shelf, stuffing all of this along with the cornbread into a small canvas sack. "Goin' to take one of these blankets too. Just in case."

"You're leaving us alone all night?"

"Won't be no different from when I'm here. I'll still be sleepin' on the ground, 'cept I'll be sleepin' better not listenin' to you two yammer all night."

"There won't be much of that." I looked over at Phoebe, who was sleeping soundly, her mouth hanging open.

"Keep watch over her." He took a blue wool blanket from the foot of the cot and rolled it tight. "And put on a pot of beans if you want any for supper tonight. Know how?"

I nodded, though I wasn't sure at all.

"I ain't goin' far. Two, three miles, then circlin' back. If I can't find 'em...well, we'll just see."

Laurent stuffed the blanket, food sack, and a rope into a worn leather pack and slung it across his back. He walked over to the cot where Phoebe slept and stood there for the briefest moment, watching her. She fidgeted just once under his gaze, snored, and turned over on her side. When a thin lock of hair fell forward to rest on her nose, she brought one hand up as if to bat it away, but it was a useless, listless gesture. Laurent knelt down and gingerly, like a man afraid to rouse a dormant bear, reached out to smooth the hair off Phoebe's face.

"Be careful," I said.

Startled, he stood and repositioned his pack. "Sorry. I didn't mean—"

"I meant be careful while you're gone. We'll be waiting for you."

"Yep." He adjusted the straps on his pack and headed for the door.

"And your brother?" I said, following right behind.

Laurent turned around in the doorway. "What about him?"

"You don't think there's a chance he'll come here while you're gone?"

He turned his hat over and over in his hands, studying it before answering. "I don't know. If he does, sit tight. Won't be more'n a day."

After he left, I went into the little pantry behind the house to scout out what I could find for supper. There were three sacks of dried beans, so I took one scoop out of an open one and set them to soak for the rest of the afternoon. Laurent had done all the cooking since we arrived, with Phoebe, I noticed, taking some part in assisting him, but I'd paid little attention. I looked at a sack of cornmeal, knowing that it, with a little water and molasses, would make a batch of johnnycakes, but the exact portions and technique remained a mystery. A bit of rooting around brought forth a jar of pickled vegetables—carrots and radishes—and a tin of crackers. That would do for me, and I could only hope that Phoebe would experience the same lack of appetite I had. If nothing else, there was plenty of tea, and I might be able to add a little milk, if she had the presence of mind to show me how to open the can.

I brought my fare into the cabin and checked on my patient, who was just beginning to rouse herself from sleep.

"How are you feeling?"

She spewed forth a cough in response.

"Would you like me to fix you some tea?"

She shook her head. "Water."

I got her a drink, then helped her out of her dress and dropped the same shirt over her fevered shoulders that I'd worn the entire time I was sick. It wasn't nearly as long on her as it was on me—coming just to her knees—and this time when she laid back down, I made sure she was under the covers with an extra blanket folded on her feet.

"Comfortable, isn't it?"

"Men are so lucky." She snuggled in. "Where's Laurent?"

"He went to look for the horses. He promised to be back by tomorrow evening."

She leaned up on her elbows. "He left us?"

"Just for tonight." I wiped her brow with a cool cloth once she'd lain down again. "Now, get some rest."

The rest of the afternoon was lonely. I puttered around, while Phoebe flitting between bouts of coughing and sleep. I ventured to the stream twice to bring back water to fill the water barrel after using what was left to wash up the cornbread pan and coffee cups from this morning. Laurent had strung a clothesline between one side of the cabin and a post set in the ground, and I hung Phoebe's dress there to air. It occurred to me from time to time that I ought to be afraid, stranded in this mountain cabin, but that thought was chased away by something far stronger. I remembered how my father reassured Mother when she expressed her doubts about this journey, saying that God had not given us a spirit of fear but that His strength was our strength. I stood in that little cabin, stirring the first pot of beans I'd ever cooked—the first of *anything* I'd ever cooked—and found myself utterly at home. I knew every inch of this room. For this night, every bit of it was at my disposal. I was the caretaker; I was the authority. For this night, at least, this was my home, and the satisfaction of that thought thrilled me to my toes.

Unfortunately, the first culinary product of my independence was not as thrilling. Apparently Laurent had a secret source of seasoning I was not privy to, so the beans ended up bland and crunchy. Phoebe smiled, though, and bravely worked her way through a bite or two before declaring that she simply wasn't up to eating anything.

It wasn't until the evening's business was done—everything washed up and put into place, the final trip out to the tree line taken—that the thought of a long, dark night alone brought with it a sense of fear. I tucked Phoebe in, then settled myself into my own bed. The fire in the stove had all but burned down, so we had the slightest flame to keep the cabin from being plunged into total blackness.

"Phoebe," I whispered across the room, "can I come over and say my prayers with you?"

She made a sound that I assumed to be affirmative, so I hopped out of my bed and trotted across to hers. Kneeling, I took her hands in mine and bowed my head over them.

"Dear Lord, thank you for another blessed day. Thank you for the food and the fresh water and this warm place to sleep. Please help Phoebe to feel well again, and guide me as I take care of her. And please keep Laurent safe as he looks for the horses. Amen."

I squeezed Phoebe's hand and scuttled back to my cot, feeling a little better already. I had settled in and could feel the first tendrils of sleep when Phoebe let forth a string of rich, wet coughing, followed by a small whimper.

"Are you all right?" I asked.

"It hurts to cough."

"I know."

"Belinda?"

"Yes."

"Why didn't you pray for him to *find* the horses?"

aurent wasn't back the next morning. Or the next afternoon. As the evening shadows fell, I sat on the fallen stump in the clearing in front of the cabin, straining to catch a glimpse of him in the darkness of the surrounding trees. Until Phoebe called me inside.

"I'm sure he's fine," she said, her voice noticeably weaker than it was yesterday.

"Of course he is." I forced a chipper note into my voice as I added another piece of wood to the stove. "Tonight, we keep the fire going as long as we want. It's freezing out there."

Indeed, the night was bitter cold, and I couldn't imagine how any man could survive out in it.

"Maybe you should keep the fire burning outside too," Phoebe said, "to help him find us."

"He'd risk the cold before he'd take the chance of hiking up in the dark."

"How can you be sure?"

"I can't," I said. "It's just a feeling."

I'd fared better with tonight's supper, having followed Phoebe's instructions to make a decent batch of fried mush drizzled with molasses. The beans benefited from a day's reheating, and Phoebe declared me the third best cook in the house.

"Third?" I said. "I don't recall you doing much cooking."

"But when I do," she said, "I know I'll be better than you."

We had steaming cups of tea, to which I added the final drops from the last open can of milk and just a tiny bit of the white sugar I'd found in a small wooden box. Her fever had subsided, though her skin had taken on a clamminess that worried me. But her spirits were up, and our conversation helped allay my fears.

"So." I motioned her to move closer to the wall to make room for me to sit on the edge of the cot with her. "Where do we think Laurent is? Maybe he—"

"He's made camp not a hundred yards from here. When the sun comes up, he's going to look over his shoulder, see this place, and feel like a complete idiot."

"And so will we for worrying."

We shared a few minutes of comfortable silence sipping our tea, listening to the wind whistle around the corners of the cabin.

"Then what about this?" I said. "How do you think Del got his limp?"

"Frostbite," Phoebe said.

"Come now; it's not that cold in here. The stove—"

"No. I mean it was frostbite. Half of his foot is gone."

I stared at her with gape-mouthed surprised as she calmly took another sip of her tea.

"How do you know this?"

"I asked."

"You asked Del?"

"No, silly. I asked that cook, Marty, while you and Romeo were off picking plums."

"Tell me!"

Hearing something new and truthful about Del seemed almost as exciting as seeing him again, but Phoebe made me wait until she drained the last of her tea and had given me the cup to take back to the table before saying another word.

"It's not very exciting," she began once I'd settled in beside her again. "He was taking a load of mail out…somewhere. California I guess. He got caught in a snowstorm, rode as far as he could, but then had to stop out in the middle of nowhere and wait for it to stop."

"You're right," I said. "That's not very exciting."

"Apparently he didn't have any shelter, and he had to hunker down and use his horse as a wind block for three solid days."

"Is this part true? Or are you embellishing?"

She held up her hand as if taking an oath. "This is everything Marty told me. Now, do you know the biggest danger for a horse in a snowstorm?"

"Freezing to death?"

"Suffocating. Their snot freezes over their nostrils, and they can't breath. Well, it seems Del took off his boot and strapped it onto the horse's muzzle."

"For the entire three days?"

"For as long as it took. When the storm stopped, he gauged that he was only about two miles from his last stop, but instead of going back there, he went on another twenty to the next one. By the time he got there, it was too late."

Phoebe finished the story with considerable effort, and while I was eager to talk more, I could tell she was exhausted. I stood up and fluffed her covers, enjoying her smile as the blanket settled around her, then moved to the foot of the bed to be sure her feet were covered.

"Why did you tell me this now?"

She shrugged. "I wanted to tell you before he did."

"Do you have any other secrets to tell me?"

She closed her eyes, and I knew she was remembering what it felt like to be held in Chester's arms. I was about to tell her that *I* had a secret of my own, that I had seen everything that night, but before I could she said, "No."

"Liar."

"I'm not lying, Belinda. There's a difference between a secret and a treasure."

It was dark as pitch and bordering on unbearably cold when Phoebe's voice roused me out of a warm, pleasant sleep.

"Do you see this? Belinda! Do you see this?"

"Just a minute."

I took a deep, bracing breath before hopping out of bed. My teeth started to chatter the minute my feet hit the floor, and the chill spread throughout my body, causing my hands to shake; I didn't think I'd ever get the lamp lit. Once I did, I opened the stove where the fire had been reduced to just a few embers. There was little left in the wood box, but enough for me to build up a small blaze.

"Belinda, do you see?"

I brought the lamp with me to Phoebe's bedside, hoping to better see what had excited her so, but it was her own appearance that shocked me. Her skin looked to be covered in a thin layer of pale wax as her eyes darted around the room in near madness. Leaning forward, I heard a faint, irregular wheezing, and each breath of hers seemed to be a miniature battle fought and won.

"Phoebe! How long have you felt like this?"

"I can't see them with the light so near."

"Maybe if you sat up a little, it might help you breathe easier."

I set the lamp on the floor and helped raise Phoebe up. We had no pillows, so I took one of the blankets off my cot and wadded it up behind her.

"Turn down the light, Belinda. I want you to see them."

"You're not making any sense, Phoebe." I touched her head. "And no wonder, you're burning up again. Let me get a cloth."

I fetched a cloth from the shelf and dampened it. I expected Phoebe to recoil when I held the cold cloth against her face, but she didn't flinch. All the while as I dabbed her forehead, her cheeks, even her neck and shoulders, she remained perfectly still while her eyes continued their relentless roving.

"Turn down the light."

"In a minute."

"I want you to see."

"I will, Phoebe, I will."

"They're angels, Belinda. Turn down the light."

"Oh, Phoebe, you're imagining things. It's the fever."

"They're outside. All around us. Millions of them."

"Of course there are angels." I adopted my most soothing, authoritative voice. "God sends His angels to protect us. But we can't see them, Phoebe."

"I do. Flying, all around." Each sentence was punctuated with a tortured breath. "Turn out the light."

"All right," I said, "but first I need to build up the fire."

Cut wood was stacked outside the door, which I opened just enough to lean out and grab the top few logs. The sting of the night air hit me full in the face the minute I peeked out. The wind had died down, but in its stead was a new bite. Crisper. And wet. I looked up and saw that the dark blanket that usually draped over our little clearing had transformed to an eyelet lace as soft white flakes—millions of them—danced and fell to the ground.

True to my word, I stoked the fire and blew out the lamp. I made my way to Phoebe's cot and once again settled myself beside her.

"Do you see them now?"

"Yes." The single square window above my cot was a mass of swirling white. "But they're not angels, Phoebe dear. It's snowing."

"You don't know, Belinda," she said, and I couldn't very well argue.

Although the space was narrow, there was enough room for me

to stretch fully out and lay beside her. The heat emanating from her fevered body warmed me, and I felt a little guilty for taking advantage of its source. No other element of her illness brought the slightest comfort. Her breaths were wet and shallow, and the occasional fit of coughing still came upon her. But they too, had grown to something fierce, bringing with them a thick mucus, which she spat into a rag.

"Does it hurt to breathe?" I asked over my shoulder.

"It hurts worse to talk."

"Then don't." I smiled into the darkness. "You talk too much, anyway."

I closed my eyes but did not go to sleep. Phoebe might see the protection of angels in the snow, but to me, each white flake drifted with a new fear. *Please, God,* I prayed, but my requests seemed as numerous as the crystals in the sky, and my heart was too heavy to list them. *Father God, take care of us.*

He must have come and gone with the stealth of a mouse, because I opened my eyes to the smell of brewing coffee and the sight of an empty cabin. But his sack was on the table, and wet footprints tracked the floor.

Behind me, Phoebe's breathing had been reduced to shallow panting. I sat up and turned to look at her in the morning light. What I saw nearly stopped my heart. There was the faintest blue tinge to her skin, which remained feverish and clammy to the touch.

She appeared to be sleeping, though her eyes fluttered at times, and her mouth gaped open slightly, with traces of white gathered in the corners of her thin, chapped lips.

"Oh, Phoebe."

I grabbed her hand, and she returned the faintest squeeze.

"He's back," she said.

"I know he is, but you're too sick to go anywhere right now."

"I never want to leave this place."

"We can stay here as long as you like." I gripped her tighter. I wanted to infuse her with promises, with life and breath and blood.

"It's beautiful here. Did you see the snow?"

"Not this morning."

"Go look."

I slipped my feet into my boots and stepped outside. The world had been transformed to something pure, a whiteness that clung to tree branches and covered the ground completely, save for a narrow, broken path leading up to the door and around the corner.

"Laurent?"

The cold muffled my words, seeming to carry them no farther than the little puff of steam they produced. Even so, he appeared, the collar on his jacket turned up, the brim of his hat pulled down, and his arms laden with foodstuffs from the lean-to. His only greeting was to look into my eyes, and I stepped out of the doorway to let him in. He dropped the food on the table and hung his hat and coat on the peg by the door.

I'd stepped back inside and was pouring Laurent a cup of coffee when I sensed him standing close behind me.

"How long has she been like this?" He was bent low, whispering into my ear.

"Since right after you left," I whispered back, not turning around. "But probably before that. She didn't want us to know."

"It's bad."

"I know. Did you find the horses?"

"Nope." He took his coffee and walked outside.

I dragged one of the chairs to Phoebe's bedside and settled down. I couldn't entice her to eat anything, but she did drink some water and promised to try something a little later now that a decent cook had returned.

Laurent came inside just long enough to add wood to the fire, start a pot of beans, and look at Phoebe before heading back out. Hours later, when Phoebe was sleeping once again, I laced up my boots, put my coat on, and went outside. Much of the snow had melted in the afternoon sun, but there were a few small drifts in the shade of the cabin. Laurent had worn paths with his pacing, turning the clearing into a mess of mud and snow. I followed one set of footprints and found him looking off toward the lake.

"It's cold out here," I said.

"Not yet. It'll get colder."

I pulled my coat tighter around me. "What can we do for her?"

His hands were plunged deep in his coat pockets, and he seemed to be punching the fabric within. "Nothin' I know of. Never took care of a sick person before."

"Neither have I. We always had doctors and—"

"Well, I ain't never had nobody." He raised his voice for the first time since that day at the stagecoach. "Nobody ever took care of me, and I ain't never looked out for nobody but myself."

"I'm sorry to be such a bother to you. Perhaps if you had allowed my parents to continue on their journey to Oregon, we wouldn't be such nuisances to you now."

I turned around, ready to stomp back into the cabin, but he caught my sleeve.

"You ain't a bother," he said.

"Let go of my arm." When he did, I walked back inside.

Phoebe managed to take a few sips of broth later that afternoon, and she seemed to have a clearer presence of mind when she sat up and asked where Laurent was.

"Outside," I said.

"In the snow?"

"I don't think he likes being cooped up with us."

I helped her get out of bed long enough to fluff and smooth the covers.

"I want to see the snow," she said, and sick as she was, she could still furrow that brow to let me know there was no use arguing.

"Most of it's melted," I said.

"I don't care."

"You'll freeze to death."

"Just for a minute. I don't even have to go outside. Just take me to the door."

I wrapped a blanket around her shoulders and helped her walk across the room. Keeping one hand around her waist, I opened the door, and the vision beyond it took away what little breath she had and brought on a short but powerful fit of coughing. I held her steady until it subsided, then stood beside her, taking in the view.

"You should have seen it earlier," I said, once she was still. "It was perfect."

"I miss out on everything."

"Maybe it'll snow again tonight. I'll be sure to get you up early to see it."

"That would be nice," she said.

I felt her strength wane, so I took her back to the bed and helped her settle in, then sat on the edge of the cot.

"Do you want me to tell you a story? The latest adventures of Chester and Del?"

She shook her head. "Not right now."

It was just as well, because there was a look of peace on her face that frightened me so, any words were wadded in my stomach.

"Maybe later?" I managed to say.

"Maybe later."

She closed her eyes and seemed to drift off, but I couldn't bring myself to leave her. I sat on the bed and watched her sleep, feeling my own breath shorten to match hers. Then I fell to my knees and buried my face in the crook of her sleeve.

When my grandfather lay dying in his bed, Mother gathered us all into a room and told us that we must all pray very hard for him to be at peace. I remember sitting in my starched dress on a damask-covered chair in the parlor, my hands folded in my lap and my head bowed. I swung my feet, listened to the clock tick, and took a few surreptitious glances around the room only to find all of my cousins completely compliant with their eyes screwed shut.

Except for Phoebe. At the exact same moment I looked at her, she looked up at me, and I quickly bowed my head again. Later, when Mother came in to tell us that our grandfather had passed, Phoebe looked up at her and said, in the sweetest voice I'd ever heard, "Oh, I'm so sorry, Aunt Ellen. If only we'd prayed a little harder."

Then she'd turned and looked directly at me with those narrow little eyes, and I'd wanted to run across the room and kick her.

But I didn't want to kick her now. I wanted to pray for her like I'd never prayed in my life. There was no ticking clock to draw my thoughts away, no room full of cousins to tempt me to mischief. I poured my soul into her sleeve, speaking out to God, begging Him to heal her. Now. To make me strong enough for both of us. To show me why He'd brought us here.

My mind wandered to memories of my parents as the pain of listening to Phoebe fight for breath made their death once again raw and new. But they were gone, with the Lord. She was here, and God could heal. Why would He make her suffer so much? Why would He make *me* suffer so much? What had I ever done except love Him? Follow His teachings?

It was so, so quiet in the room. Just the sound of Phoebe's labored gasps and my whispered petitions. Occasionally the door would open, and I'd hear bootsteps on the floor, the stove open, logs added. Sometimes the steps grew near and even stopped just behind me. Once there was a hand on my shoulder—just for a moment—then taken away.

I opened my eyes once, and the room had grown dim. Later, again, and the room was dark. At some point, exhausted, I must have slept, because when I opened my eyes this time, I was in my own bed, and the room was light. And silent, as if muffled by the snow. I looked up and saw Phoebe, pale and still and cold.

The door opened, and I turned around to see Laurent standing against a backdrop of solid white.

The angels were back, and they'd taken her away.

We may not touch His hands and side,
Nor follow where He trod;
But in His promise we rejoice,
And cry, "My Lord and God!"

e buried Phoebe on the edge of the ridge that over-looked the mountain lake. Laurent and I each had responsibilities; he was gone for much of the day digging Phoebe's grave while I stayed behind to dress her. I couldn't share these final, intimate moments with anyone—let alone a man who remained a stranger. So I struggled with Phoebe and her chemise, her pantalets, her petticoats, skirt, and blouse. I talked to her the whole time, thanking her for not making me cinch a corset, envying the stitched detail on her flounce. I brushed her thin hair and gathered it to one side, securing it behind one ear with a ribbon and draping the rest over her shoulder. It wasn't a style she'd ever worn, which was regrettable, because it was quite becoming.

Laurent came back in that quiet way of his and stood behind me. "She looks pretty."

"Yes," I said, and she did.

The face that always seemed to be in battle with its blotches was now a uniform shade of translucent white—no furrowed brow, no scowl. In contrast to the paleness of her skin, her hair took on a richer, deeper tone.

With something akin to reverence, Laurent slipped one arm beneath Phoebe's shoulders and another under her legs to lift her up while I stripped the bed of all but one blanket, which I spread flat upon the cot. He laid Phoebe back down and crossed her arms across her breast.

"You have anythin' else to say to her?" he asked.

I shook my head, though I knew I'd be talking to her for the rest of my life.

He took one side of the blanket at its corners and brought it over to cover Phoebe. Gently working down the length of her body, he lifted her, tucking the excess fabric underneath. He did the same with the other side, until she was cocooned in bright blue wool. From somewhere he'd produced a thick needle and thin twine, which he used to sew the fabric together. Finally, just above her head and below her feet, he cinched the blanket tight and tied it off with rope.

"That's it, then."

"Wait a minute!" I panicked and grabbed his sleeve. "Her coat!"

"Keep it. You'll need it more than she does."

He picked the bundle up again, as if it weighed nothing. If for no other reason than this moment, I was glad to have removed the bullet from Laurent's shoulder. The only other time she knew a man's embrace was the tender moments with Chester in the barn at Crook's Clearing. I sent up a prayer of thanks to God that she had that precious memory to keep with her in her final days.

I pulled on my coat and followed Laurent outside. The snow was coming down in thick flakes that obscured everything around me.

"Stick close," Laurent said.

I walked head-down behind him, seeing nothing but his boots and the tracks they left, until we came to the grave.

Everything was white. The sky, the ground, save for one brown, gaping hole and the earth piled beside it. I took a few more steps to look down at the lake, which was a shade of gray as snowflakes landed, speckling its placid surface. The air had a sweet smell to it, like newly starched clothes. I breathed it in deep. And held it.

When I turned around again, Laurent had already lowered Phoebe into the ground, and this time I took a few steps to look down into her grave. He'd dug deep, and the little blue bundle seemed small, certainly too small to contain Phoebe with all of her sass.

"Want to say somethin'?"

I had been thinking about what I would say at this moment. It seemed only fitting that Phoebe should have a proper funeral, but I'd been to so few in my life, I wasn't sure of the words to use.

"I wish I had my Bible."

Laurent gave a weak smile. "Can't help you there."

My mind raced through invisible pages, the words zipping by, but nothing seemed to fit what I felt right now.

"The Bible says…" I started, hoping something would come to me. "The Bible says that…"

I felt the snow weighing down my eyelashes. I held out my hands and watched the crystals land on my coat sleeves. Phoebe would have loved this. She would have been scooping the snow into hard-packed balls and lobbing them at me from behind any barrier she could find.

"In the Bible…"

Laurent stood beside me, shifting his weight from one foot to the other, taking his hat off, putting it back on, taking it off again. I reached my hand out and, surprisingly, he took it.

"The Bible tells us that those who wait on the Lord will renew their strength. That they will mount up on wings like eagles. That they will run, but not be weary." Laurent became very still beside me. "Phoebe was always strong. And I know how much she hated these past few days. But now," I lifted my eyes to the snow-filled sky, "she is with You, Lord. Stronger than she could ever be on earth. And filled with more joy than she ever imagined she could have."

It was a confusing moment, trying to reconcile my grief at the loss of my cousin with the envy I felt that she was somewhere eternally safe. Icy rivulets of melted snow ran down behind my collar, and she was perfectly warm. My only source of protection and companionship was the man who killed my mother, with whom she now stood in a circle of glory at the feet of our Lord. It didn't seem fair, at that moment, to be the one who had tried so hard to do everything right.

I sensed Laurent trying to take his hand away, so I gripped it a little harder.

"Now, *we* must wait on the Lord. That strength is for us." Then, trying my hardest to sound like an official reverend, I said, "Join me in prayer. 'Our Father, which art in heaven—"

I paused, waiting for him to join me in this recitation; when he didn't, I went on alone, my voice sounding thinner and smaller with each word.

"Our Father, which art in heaven, Hallowed be Thy name. Thy kingdom come, Thy will be done in earth, as it is in heaven. Give us this day our daily bread. And forgive us our debts, as we forgive our debtors. And lead us not into temptation, but deliver us from evil: For Thine is the kingdom, and the power, and the glory, forever. Amen."

"Amen," Laurent echoed before taking his hand away and slamming his hat on his head. "Get back inside. Warm up some coffee."

"I want to stay here."

"You don't need to see this."

He picked up the shovel next to the pile of upturned earth and plunged it in. I could tell he was determined not to make another move while I remained, so I headed to the cabin.

It was nearly dark by the time Laurent came back. The snow fell continuously, and I'd begun to wonder if he'd had to use the shovel to dig a path back to the door. I poured him a cup of coffee and sat across the table from him, drinking my own. There was nothing prepared to eat, but I don't think we were hungry. Neither of us spoke as the cabin grew cold and the coffee colder, and when the room was more shadows than light, he touched a match to the wick of the lantern.

He stared down into his cup. "Got to ask you somethin'."

I looked at him and waited.

"With the snow and all. Can I sleep in here?"

"It's your house."

"It's yours too, now."

"I don't want to go to bed right now."

"Me either. I'm just sayin'. When it's time."

Still another long stretch of silence. He and I, staring at the walls. Snow piling outside, the ghost of Phoebe thick within. I heard the tick-ticking of a clock, then remembered there was no clock, and the sound was my boot heel knocking against the table leg. I wondered if the sound annoyed him and realized he'd never tell me if it did. Then, moving with a stealth that never failed to surprise me, Laurent stood up and walked over to Phoebe's bed.

"I want to sleep in that one," I said, heedless of the harshness in my voice.

"I figured," he said over his shoulder.

He pulled out the trunk from underneath the cot and rummaged through it, producing a bright red shirt, which he laid without comment on the foot of the bed, and something else before snapping the lid shut and returning to the table.

When I saw what he'd brought back, I felt myself on the verge of a smile. A deck of cards. He tapped the deck on the table, shuffled, tapped, and shuffled again.

"You play anythin'?" he asked.

"My brother does. I wasn't ever allowed."

"Ever want to learn?" He set the cards in front of me, and I cut the deck. "Name your game."

"I don't know any games."

"Poker it is." He dealt the cards.

19

*I*t didn't take long for us to develop a routine, giving structure to our days. I woke up every morning to the luxury of a fire burning in the stove and coffee ready to drink. Laurent would be sitting at the table, motionless, but the minute I stirred from my bed, no matter what the weather, he'd put on his coat, hat, and gloves and head outside.

I'd stay under the covers as long as my body would allow before getting up to relieve myself in a surprisingly ornate chamber pot that Laurent discreetly emptied throughout the day. I dressed each day, having slept in the long red wool shirt he'd provided the night of Phoebe's funeral. When he came back in, we'd share a small breakfast; then I'd wash up the plates and cups while he chopped firewood or brought in food supplies.

After that, it was time to play cards.

Initially we played from hand to hand—wagering nothing—until I learned the game. Then one day he came in, put the cards on the table, and handed me a little leather pouch.

"What's in here?" I asked.

"Open it."

I dumped the contents out on the table. Beans, dried and uncooked.

"Hundred for you." He dumped his own pouch onto the table. "Hundred for me. We play till one of us is broke."

I soon came to understand how my brother could be so seduced by this game. Nothing gave the same thrill as scooping a handful of Laurent's beans across the table after producing a mere pair of sevens, and never could I imagine that three queens could be defeated. We'd play until one of us had nothing left to bet, then the beans would be divvied up again for the next day's game. On mornings where luck seemed to alternate from hand to hand, we'd continue until there wasn't enough light coming in through the window to tell a heart from a spade.

Our other meal was served up whenever the card game was over. If I were particularly hungry, I might bet recklessly—twenty beans on a pair of tens—hoping to bring a swift end to the game, but I soon learned that the longer I waited, the less likely I'd be hungry again at bedtime. My favorite days were the days Laurent cooked a big batch of beans, because that meant the fire would burn all day as they simmered, and I could play without having to wear my coat.

At suppertime we'd light the lamp, and I insisted we pray before eating.

"Not much for prayin'," he said the first time.

"That doesn't matter," I said. "Anyone can pray—everyone should, actually—and this one is simple."

Then I reached across the table for his hand, bowed my head

and began, just as I had at Phoebe's graveside, "Our Father, which art in heaven…"

After the first few days, he started to chime in on a phrase here and there. At first his words were even more obscure than usual, barely escaping his clenched jaw, but then I slowed my speech, and he had to slow his. We paused and spoke in perfect tandem. Sometimes I let him say, "Amen," by himself. Then we'd eat in the same companionable silence in which we'd played cards, rationing the day's distractions as carefully as we doled out food and fuel. The luxury of talking was reserved for our final waking hours.

To say that we ended our evenings with lively conversation would be misleading. The tradition started just days after Phoebe died, when I found myself rambling on about one of our girlhood exploits—a time when we convinced our parents to let us sleep in the barn, only to wake up in the morning to find great big chunks of our hair missing.

"Phoebe ran screaming out of that barn, 'The mice chewed my hair!' And I just sat there crying because it looked so awful. It turned out that it wasn't mice at all. My brother Chester and his friends snuck in on us and chopped it off as a joke."

"That's awful," Laurent said, but I could tell by his slight grin that he was more amused than outraged.

"Our mothers had to cut our hair clear up to our ears." I demonstrated the length as if acting out a death sentence. "It took a year to grow back."

"What happened to Chester?"

"Nothing, as usual. He could always charm his way out of punishment."

Laurent went outside when it was time for me to go to bed—I guess to give me some privacy—and the night I told that story, I fell into contented sleep.

That's how evenings became story time. Once our dishes were cleared away, I would tell Laurent some tale or another, either reliving childhood memories or recounting great heroic tales I remembered from school. He listened with such attention that I felt sorry for his having grown up so deprived.

The routine held true every day, with the exception of the Sabbath. Early on I forced myself to recite each day's date. Otherwise, it seemed the short days and long nights of our isolation turned time into one big melting mass.

On Sundays, I insisted that we not gamble or play cards at all.

"The Sabbath is a holy, somber day," I told Laurent. "We must devote this day to worshiping God."

"Ain't never been to church," he said.

"Then I'll bring church to you."

After the breakfast things were cleared away, I took special pains to comb and freshly braid my hair, tying it with a ribbon I fashioned from the ruffle on my skirt. Laurent surprised me by shaving for the first time since I recovered from my illness, exposing that deep, ragged scar.

Rather than sit at the table, for that is what we did every day, I made Laurent move the table to the space between the two cots, and we sat with our chairs facing each other—not quite knee-to-knee. The day's lesson would focus on whatever Bible verse I could clearly recall.

"John, chapter three, verse sixteen." I began with the text most familiar to me. " 'For God so loved the world, that He gave His only begotten Son, that whosoever believeth in Him should not perish, but have everlasting life.' "

I made Laurent repeat the verse back to me until he could say it by heart. Once he did, I declared Sunday school over and moved into the church service. For this, I stood behind my chair while I delivered the sermon I'd practiced in my head the night before.

I opened my first sermon with the question, "Who is God?" and I paced back and forth behind my chair, expounding everything I knew of Him as Creator, Protector, Savior.

I did a three-week series on the Ten Commandments, paying special emphasis to "Thou shalt not kill" and "Thou shalt not steal" while bypassing the one about coveting a neighbor's wife.

I concluded a sermon on Psalm 23 by telling him that I had been in the valley of the shadow of death. "You were right there with me, Laurent. And even though I was afraid at first, the Lord did comfort me a little. Right now I'm on a mountain, but I still feel like I'm in that valley sometimes. And still, the Lord comforts me."

"So, you ain't afraid?" he asked.

"Not as much."

After the sermon came time for Sabbath meditation. Back home that meant sitting quietly in our room or on the sofa in the parlor for hours on end. It meant the same in this home too. I would stretch out on my bed; Laurent would restore the table to its place in the middle of the room and sit there. The best escape from the chill was to take a nap—which I often did—only to wake and find that he hadn't moved an inch.

After our Sunday suppers, the evening story was always some heroic, biblical tale: Moses and the pharaoh; Noah and the ark; Joshua and the walls of Jericho. All this time, Laurent was like that lake in the basin behind the cabin. It held every flake dropped down to it, keeping them all behind that cool, placid surface. And every day it seemed I could see the power of God's Word reflected in his face. The glint that usually gave his eyes such a hard edge disappeared, as did the rigid set to his mouth. His beard was growing back, not only obscuring the scar, but softening the sharp planes of his face. His hair was growing longer and curling, reminding me of Chester's, and I could fully understand Phoebe's budding infatuation.

One Sunday I realized we were in the month of December, the season of Advent. During the week, I recounted stories of my Christmases growing up, describing in detail the favorite doll I got when I was five and the little music box that was left among the ruins of our stagecoach. I ate my modest bowl of beans thinking of the feasts that would adorn our table. I shivered in the ice-cold room, longing for the warmth of the yule log blazing in the fireplace in our parlor.

But with each Sunday of the season, as I told the story of the nativity, with the angels and shepherds, and saw this story for the first time through Laurent's eyes, I thought I shouldn't be anywhere else but here.

Last Christmas, after Irene Dunsfield came down with a timely case of mumps, I was given the role of the Virgin Mary in our Christmas Eve program. On that night, I stood in our church, illuminated by a hundred candles, and spoke the words of Mary's song to a hushed audience.

Now, isolated in this tiny mountain cabin, with an audience of one, I reprised my role as our after-supper story. I opted to stand on my chair, instructing Laurent to turn the lamp down as low as the flame would allow, then close his eyes until I was ready. Once I'd taken a blanket and fashioned a costume for myself, I ascended my stage and told Laurent to open his eyes. I've no idea how he reacted to my appearance, because in true dramatic fashion, I kept my eyes fixed above and delivered my song.

> My soul doth magnify the Lord,
> And my spirit hath rejoiced in God my Saviour.
> For he hath regarded the low estate of his handmaiden:
> for, behold, from henceforth all generations shall call
> me blessed.

For He that is mighty hath done to me great things;
and holy is His name.
And His mercy is on them that fear Him from genera-
tion to generation.

I don't know if I was expecting enthusiastic applause or a solemn amen, but I was not prepared for Laurent to stand, bringing himself nearly eye level with me, and smile. Not the tight-lipped, one-sided grin he allowed whenever amusement took him by surprise, but a full-on beam, framed by his beard, illuminated in the lamplight, and evidenced clear into his eyes that shone with a mist I'd never seen before. He took my hands in his and brought them to his lips; his beard dusted the backs of my fingers. Then he stepped back and helped me down from the chair.

"Merry Christmas, Laurent."

"Merry Christmas, Belinda."

It was the first time he'd ever spoken my name.

He went outside, as he did every evening, even though a steady snowfall had packed a small drift in front of the door. I took off my costume and crawled into bed to say my prayers. For the first time in a long time, I cried myself to sleep.

The next morning I woke up to the familiar warmth of the room and the familiar smell of the coffee. And something else. Missing was the familiar sight of Laurent sitting at the table.

But as my waking eyes adjusted to the room, I understood why. Cuttings of evergreen lined the shelf on the wall, filling the room with a fresh, sweet scent. Still more graced the center of the table, artfully arranged around three unlit tallow candles. Also on the table, at my place, was a canvas-wrapped bundle tied with a length of rope.

Laurent himself was sprawled out on his bed, snow dripping off the boots that hung over the edge, sleeping.

I climbed out from under my covers—heedless of my red nightshirt—and toured the room, looking at all of his efforts close up, breathing in the scent of pine. The taboo of touching a Christmas gift loomed large in my mind, so I allowed just the barest tracing of my finger along the coarse fabric of the bundle, unable to imagine what might be hidden inside. The coffee cups dangled from their hooks on the wall, so I took two down and poured a cup for myself.

Before I could take my first sip, Laurent was up and beside me. I thought there might have been some shyness between us after last night's display. Instead, we exchanged a warm "Good morning" before he excused himself to go outside while I dressed for the day.

The gift and garland weren't the only hallmarks that this was a holiday. When Laurent came back inside, his arms were full of treasures from the pantry, things long denied, as he carefully rationed our supplies to ensure we'd make it through the winter. Today he had cornmeal, brown sugar, and molasses, and two tins—one of milk and the other, peaches. I sat at the table while he made a breakfast of fluffy, sweet corncakes and even enjoyed a bit of milk swirled in my coffee.

"Open it," he said as soon as we were settled with our food.

"Nope. Not until after the breakfast dishes are done. Family tradition."

"Fair enough."

We ate in our usual companionable silence, and I forced myself to eat slowly, savoring my treat. Perhaps later we could bring in fresh snow and make molasses candy.

When the dishes were all wiped clean and dry, I sat in front of my gift again, rubbing my hands together in anticipation. "I'm sorry I don't have anything for you."

"I ain't never had a present. So I wouldn't know what I'm missin'."

I picked up the package, unable to guess what might be hidden inside. The rope was fashioned into a simple bow, which I untied—savoring this experience as much as I had the breakfast—and leisurely pulled away the canvas.

"Oh, my goodness…"

They looked like boots but were creamy soft and brown and unlike anything I ever could have imagined for myself.

"It's rabbit." He reached across to touch the fur that lined the top inside and out. "Inside's lined with wool. Took that from an old pair of my brother's socks. But I washed them."

The stitching along the top and back was a series of perfect, tiny loops, and a pretty, swirling design was stamped into the top of the foot.

"You made these?"

"They're moccasins. What Indians wear. Figure they'd be warmer than what you have now."

I took off my old boots and slid these on, thrilled at the feel of thick wool and rabbit fur that hugged my feet.

"They're wonderful, Laurent. Thank you so much."

He looked so pleased, I knew it didn't matter to him that I didn't have a gift in return. But it mattered to me, and in that moment I knew what I would give him.

"Laurent, I want you to know something."

"What's that?" He cocked his head to look under the table and admire his handiwork.

I took a deep breath. "I forgive you."

His smile disappeared, and he became the same hidden, guarded person I'd known until yesterday.

"For everything," I continued. "For what happened to my parents. For bringing me here. I want you to know that I don't blame you anymore. I—I just forgive you."

He dropped his head and nodded. When he looked at me again, he wore an expression akin to pain.

"Do you think—" his words caught in his throat, which he cleared before starting again. "Do you think that God can forgive me too? Not just for what happened with—to your family. But all them other things."

"He already has."

"What do you mean?"

"When Jesus died on the cross. All the way back then, He offered you forgiveness. Do you believe that?"

He nodded.

"Then you're forgiven."

"You don't know what all I done."

"It doesn't matter. God knows. He knows everything. And the Bible says there's no sin too great for Him to forgive. It's a gift." I stretched my legs out, admiring my boots. "It's a gift like any other. All you have to do is accept it."

"And then?"

"Well, imagine for a minute. What do you think your life would've been like if you had been my brother?"

"You mean growin' up how you did?"

"Yes. What if you'd had the opportunity to live in my home? What if my parents were your parents?"

He let out a rueful laugh. "When you tell them stories, it's like you was livin' in another world. This little house is the only home I've ever known. Just my brother and my pa, both of 'em drunk as rats most the time." He brought his hand up to his face and ran a finger along the scar. "Got this the time I broke my pa's whiskey jar. He forgot he had that glass in his hand when he smacked me. I don't figure I ever had no chance to be nothin' but what I am."

"But that's what forgiveness is." My heart quickened at the thought of it. "God tells us that when we accept His forgiveness, when we truly believe in the sacrifice of His Son, it's like we get a whole new life. Like we're born all over again to get a fresh start to be something better than what we were before."

"What kind of a new life would *you* need?" he asked with sadness in his voice. "Can't see you ever done anything to forgive."

"Of course I have. But that doesn't matter. God doesn't see any difference between your sins and mine. And once you really take Him into your heart—the way I have—we'll really be the same. You'll be my brother."

"I'd like that." The words were thick in his throat.

"Don't just tell me." I laid my hand on his. "Tell Him."

"All right." He stood up. "But I think I'd like to go outside."

20

Winter strengthened its hold after Christmas. Whereas before we had the occasional day when the sun would shine and Laurent would accompany me on a short walk out in the fresh, blinding air, now the wind kept the snow in a constant state of flurry, and the temperature dipped to a range that brought pain with every breath. Everything blurred. The view outside the cabin was a smear of gray. Inside, we rationed the light, refusing to light the lamp until delaying one minute more would make it impossible to find the matches.

Everything within me—my mind and body—grew dull too. Hunger became very real for the first time as each day our portions got smaller. This wasn't the sharp, insistent pain that I remembered when I couldn't wait until the end of the school day to get back to my house to a stack of fresh sugar cookies. Rather, it was a subdued, constant presence in no way confined to my stomach but permeating throughout, consuming me with my own emptiness.

One evening as we said our prayers together, I heard Laurent say, "Give us this day our daily beans." After we'd said, "Amen," I gave him a quizzical look.

"Won't be no more bread," he said before digging in.

Some days I woke up to have breakfast alone. "Didn't think

you was ever gettin' up," Laurent would say on those mornings. "I already ate."

"It's a sin to tell a lie."

"Then it's a good thing I'm forgiven."

I began to wonder if we'd have to surrender our poker beans to the boiling pot, but even that activity had lost its charm. If it wasn't too dark to see the cards, it was too cold to hold them in my numb fingers. My head was so full of cold and dark and hunger, that kings and queens melted together, losing all their former charm.

Laurent insisted that we needed to stay still to conserve our energy. That meant sometimes entire days spent huddled under the covers on our cots, fading in and out of troubled sleep. I no longer slept in the red flannel shirt. Every day—all day—I wore my dress and my coat, with Phoebe's coat over it. My rabbit-fur-lined boots never left my feet.

We still told stories, though now we often spoke them out into the darkness. And Laurent now recounted a few fun, happy memories from his childhood as well as reliving the torture of his violent father.

"You need to forgive him," I'd say, even after hearing about a brutal beating.

"I have," he finally said, his voice gentle in the dark.

Then came the night I could not get warm. Usually if I just lay still enough, breathed deep enough, I could reach a level of comfort to allow me to sleep. But this night, hunger gnawed at my bones, and my skin stretched over them to the point of splitting open. All this, with the last of the fire burning in the stove. When the cold took over the final ember, I imagined I'd be turned to ice.

"Belinda?"

It was solid blackness inside the cabin—so much so that I couldn't tell when my eyes were open—but I could tell from the proximity of his voice that he was kneeling right next to my cot, his head level with mine.

"Yes?"

"It's cold."

I almost laughed. All winter long, any time I said, "It's cold," he'd replied with "Not yet." To hear him admit it now seemed like a victory.

"I'm only sayin' this 'cause I'm worried. It'd be—you'd be warmer if—" He stopped, and I could picture him looking down, scowling at the floor. "You should lay down beside me."

My blood ran a little colder as every word of warning Mother ever spoke to me wormed its way through my muddled head.

"It ain't what— You're my sister. I'm sayin' before God that I'm here to keep you safe. Keepin' you safe is keepin' you warm."

He was silent then, waiting for me to send him away, but I didn't. I felt one more blanket, then another piled on top of me, then lifted away as Laurent took my arm.

"Let me lay down first. Against the wall."

I silently obeyed and stood on the icy floor. I felt shifting and movement behind me, then his hand was on my arm again, and I was being pulled down. My feet found their way under the covers, then the blankets were pulled up under my chin. It was almost like any other night I'd spent on this cot until I felt a strong arm drape itself over me and draw me close to another, warmer body.

"It's a good thing when it's this cold," he whispered over my shoulder. "Means the thaw is just around the corner."

"Goin' down the mountain just a bit today," Laurent said. He'd spent the previous evening cleaning his rifle, which he slung over his shoulder after putting on his hat and coat. "See what there is to hunt."

We'd gone five days without a new snowfall, and what was piled up around the cabin was becoming soft and wet. The sun shone almost warm and inviting in the afternoons, but I could do little more than walk outside, turn my face toward it, and wish there was some way to feel full with light. I didn't know how he had the strength for adventure; I hadn't seen him take more than a few sips of coffee in days. His dark eyes were set deep in hollow sockets, and there was a tremor in his hands as he put his knife in the sheath he wore on his belt. He paused in the doorway and gripped the sides of the threshold before stepping outside.

"Be careful," I said.

"Go on back to sleep."

I closed the door behind him, crossed the room to my bed, and burrowed under the covers. The next thing I knew, I was dreaming that Laurent came back, bursting into the cabin with none of his usual silence and stealth, shouting, "Fear not, kid! Big brother's here to save you!"

I opened my eyes to the muted darkness under the covers and remained still, listening to heavy footsteps move around the room. There was a *thud* of something heavy being thrown onto the table and the *thunk* of wood being tossed into the stove. A fire in the afternoon must mean a reason for celebration. I pulled the top of the covers down just far enough to peek.

Even with his back turned to me, I knew this wasn't Laurent. This man took up so much more space, made so much more noise. A long, black coat stretched over broad, thick shoulders, and his bare head was covered in straight, closely shorn hair. The simple act of putting on coffee was a matter of rattles and bangs laced with intermittent curses.

I knew this voice.

I covered my head again and tried to stop breathing.

A chair scraped across the floor and creaked when he apparently sat on it. More rustling and rattling, then a match was struck and the room soon smelled of sweet tobacco. The chair scraped again, and footsteps fell heavy on the floor. Even through the covers I could feel the blast of cold air as the door opened. The footsteps walked back in and over to the shelf, then stood there, still. Then they were here, so close to me I flattened myself against the cot and prayed for God to make me small enough to disappear.

Somewhere, outside, my name was winding its way up the mountain, coming out of the trees.

"Belindaaaaaa!"

The covers above me were gathered up and pulled away, and then there was deep, rumbling laughter. I saw Laurent grasping the doorway, bent over, fighting for breath. He lifted his head and found my eyes. "Are you all right?"

I nodded, even as the covers were thrown to the floor.

Laurent looked at the man standing over me. "Didn't expect to see you till spring, Hiram."

"Well, little brother, maybe spring came early. Besides," he crouched down, eye level with me, "looks like you've had enough here to keep you warm."

"Get away from her." Laurent wedged himself between Hiram and me. "I mean it. You're not to lay a hand on her."

"Relax," Hiram said, almost on the verge of laughter. "Where'd she come from?"

Don't tell him, I screamed inside my head.

"That stagecoach," Laurent said. "Them people we killed was her folks."

"Ah."

Hiram stood up and went to the table, where he rummaged through his bags and found a bottle of whiskey. He poured a generous amount into one of our cups and held it out to Laurent, who shook his head.

"And that, Brother, turned out to be a complete waste of time." Hiram took a long drink and narrowed his eyes, holding out the cup to point to Laurent. "But I get a feeling you knew it would be."

Laurent bent low, bringing his face close to mine, and whispered, "It's goin' to be fine. I promise you. You're safe."

"Didn't anybody ever tell you it's rude to be whispering in a corner? Ah, look who I'm talking to—the man that can't stand the thought of any human company. Apparently at least not till now—"

"I'm warnin' you, Brother." Laurent stood to face him.

Hiram threw his hands up in a gesture of surrender. "Whoa, there. Don't get me wrong. I'd never deny you your right to a little company. Matter of fact, did you know that not ten miles from here, up at Silver Peak, there's the sweetest little whorehouse run by a—"

In one swift motion, Laurent unsheathed his hunting knife and, after knocking the whiskey cup out of Hiram's hand, laid Hiram out on the table, pinning him there with his forearm, holding the knife to his throat.

"Not another word, understand?" Laurent said, panting with the effort. "I'll kill you here."

"Stop it!" I was out of my bed and at Laurent's side, my hand on his arm. "You're not a killer."

"Well, that's true enough," Hiram said. "He's about as worthless at that as he is everything else."

The blade—the same one that had once been held against my throat—trembled in Laurent's hand.

"Saw your horse down there," Laurent said, not relaxing a bit. "You go on away from here now, or tomorrow mornin' we're takin' it—just the girl and me."

"That all you want, little brother? All this for a horse?"

If his light reply was intended to make Laurent relax, it didn't work. If anything, Laurent bore down harder and held the knife steadier.

"Fine," Hiram said at last. "Take it."

Laurent slowly stood straight and resheathed his knife. Hiram stood too, rubbing the spot between his ribs where Laurent's elbow had pinned him to the table. All this time, Hiram's thin cigar had lain smoldering on the cabin floor. He bent over, picked it up, tapped off the excess ash, and put it back in his mouth.

I don't know if it was the proximity of my father's killer, the previous excitement, or my temporarily forgotten hunger, but suddenly the floor seemed very unstable, and my feet and legs turned to liquid. Laurent's arms caught me just on the verge of collapse and held me standing against him.

"Hold on there." Hiram's voice maintained that irritating thread of near laughter. "Doesn't look like she's going to be fit to travel anytime soon."

"I'm fine." I gathered my strength. "Your cigar's making me sick is all."

Hiram laughed, expelling more smoke. "Well, I'm truly sorry if this is going to ruin your appetite, because I think you both could use a little beefing up. You look like you died a week ago and forgot to fall over."

"Been a long winter," Laurent said, his voice controlled. "Now it's over."

"So it is," Hiram said. "Now, I don't know about the two of you, but I'm starving. You are, of course, welcome to join me. I only brought enough for two, but she looks little—a bit too little, Brother, if you ask me. But I'm not one to judge—"

"Just shut up right there, Hiram. You don't say nothin' disrespectful to her. Or about her."

"I'm sorry," Hiram said with exaggerated courtliness.

By now the fire Hiram had built up in the stove had warmed the room, and he made a grand production of taking off his coat and hanging it on the peg before going to the table, rubbing his hands together, and tearing into the packages.

"To start, I've got a nice venison sausage." Hiram held up several links. "Then a nice round of sourdough bread, some coffee, some whiskey," he winked, "and some beans. Though it looks to me like you all might have had your fill of these already."

Neither of us spoke. Just the sight of the meat caused my mouth to water. But then I looked at the man who held it, the malicious glint in his eye, the cruel smile stretched beneath his mustache, and even the imagined savory taste of the venison turned rancid.

"No, thank you," I said before turning and going back to sit on my cot.

Behind me I heard Hiram say he was going to go outside and enjoy a little nature while Laurent and I came to an understanding. Then Laurent was sitting on the cot with me, his hand on my shoulder, leaning close to whisper.

"You got to eat somethin', Belinda."

"I'm fine."

"Just to build up your strength. I know I got to. Can't ride like we need to like this."

"I said I'm fine. I won't touch anything that comes from him."

"I can understand that, but food's food. It ain't got no sense of evil to it."

"But he does."

A winter's worth of isolation had numbed much of my pain, and there were times I was ashamed of how long I'd gone without dwelling on the memories of all I'd lost. But seeing this man again brought me back to that moment, huddled in Phoebe's arms, hearing that shot. And I hated him.

"Think on it, Belinda," Laurent said. "When it all comes down, he ain't no worse than me."

"There's nothing the same between you two. He's not sorry! He doesn't even care."

"Maybe he just ain't had a chance to yet. Now, you want to stay here and starve to death? Or you want to get down off this mountain and leave Hiram up to God?"

I looked down at the floor, refusing to answer.

"Remember, he's got bread. We can say that prayer right again. I figure we dole that out, take a few days to get our strength back, and—"

"No!" I spun around to face him. "No *few days*. You told him we would leave tomorrow!"

"But it might be best to wait just one day to—"

"No! It's always *one day.* Then another day and another. Tomorrow!" I felt the tears gathering in my eyes, and my voice was growing hoarse with the effort not to scream.

He smiled. "Will you eat, then?"

"Yes."

The joy and relief I felt at the thought of leaving this place lasted only as long as it took for me to realize that I might never see this man again. A tiny pocket of fear opened up, and even though I was sitting just a breath away, looking into his soft brown eyes, I began to miss him.

"Where are we going to go?" I said.

"Someplace to get you started home."

"What about you?"

"Same thing."

21

*T*here's something wonderful about going to sleep on a full stomach. That last night in the cabin, I slept like a little candlewick that had just been snuffed out. Laurent cooked the sausage with beans and added the last bit of our flour to make a thick, rich stew. I sat at the table all the time it bubbled on the stove, growing further and further away from my initial misgivings as the warmth of the stove and the aroma of the meal worked to soothe my troubled spirit. Behind me, on the other cot, Hiram slept, having complained about riding through the night to reach his brother.

"You just sleep then," Laurent had said, and he seemed relieved to be rid of Hiram's presence for awhile.

In the meantime, we sat, our spirits and bodies buoyed with fresh coffee and bread, and resumed our long-abandoned card game, whispering our bets and raises, not wanting to stir the evil on the cot. At the final hand, I was up twenty-seven beans, and declared myself the winter winner.

Hiram roused himself just as our supper was ready to eat. He and Laurent waited until I had eaten my fill—which I thought might mean the entire pot but in the end turned out to be less than one full bowl—before they would sit down together. After taking a final bite of meat and soaking the last of my bread in the rich broth, I made my way to the bed, so full and warm and excited about the next day's journey, I wasn't sure I'd make it across the floor. Of course I did, but my eyes were closed before I'd even brought my feet up, and I fell asleep without pulling up the covers.

Neither man was inside the cabin when I woke up, even though the light coming through the window said it wasn't quite dawn. I bounded out of bed and over to the washbasin, which had been unused for weeks. Now it was full, the water not quite ice cold, with a clean towel folded next to it.

I felt for the first time in months like a normal girl ready to face a normal day, and I rolled up my sleeves and splashed water on my face. I didn't want to think about my hair, even as I felt my scalp crawling with dirt and oil, but I took Laurent's comb and raked it across the top of my head. I plaited my hair in two long braids and tied them with fabric strips torn from the red flannel shirt I used to sleep in. Finally, I slipped my feet out of the rabbit-skin moccasins and sat down to pull on my boots, feeling my feet rebel against the confines of the leather.

When I walked to the stove, the sound of my heels against the wooden floor was so surprising, I looked over my shoulder to be sure I was alone. Once there, I poured myself a cup of coffee and tore off a hunk of the bread to dunk in it. Short of our last Christmas supper, nothing had ever tasted so delicious.

The second surprise of the morning came when I opened the door to step outside. I almost turned right around to escape the blinding glare of the sun, but the pure, genuine warmth on my face was too enticing. The snow on the ground was soft and wet and made a *slushing* sound as I walked through it. We hadn't had a fresh snowfall in days, and what surrounded the cabin was mixed with mud. Everything sounded different. Perhaps it was the absence of the ever-blowing wind, because today the air was thin and still. In the dead of winter, the world felt thick and muffled, but this morning I sensed I was being set free from an oppressive grip. I took in a deep breath of it, then another.

I walked around the cabin looking for Laurent, but he was nowhere to be seen. Most likely he was with Hiram checking on the horse, and the thought of it brought a bubbling of joy.

Getting off this mountain. Leaving Hiram to God.

I went back inside just long enough to grab my coat—smiling at the fact that I would only need one—and left again, closing the door behind me.

It was hard to believe that even yesterday this walk would have been impossible, and I pushed down any sense of fatigue, telling my legs and my feet that they were just fine. The walk would be worth the sacrifice.

I wasn't sure if I would be able to find the grave; the winter snows would have certainly erased all traces of it. But Laurent had erected a sturdy wooden cross at its head, and as I came up over the final small hill, it beckoned to me, straight and tall, if a little weathered. He had also marked the grave itself with large stones, and I could see the shape of them mounded beneath their winter covering.

Phoebe.

I had no grave to visit in honor of my parents, but the grandness of this one sufficed for all three. It had as a backdrop the majesty of a mountain; as its covering, untainted white snow. There were no strangers bordering this final resting place, no sea of names carved in stone. Just one wooden cross, standing in the midst of so much purity.

The softness of the snow hid the sound of his footsteps. It wasn't until I heard his voice that I knew this sanctuary had been invaded.

"What did you do to my brother?"

I didn't want to turn around. I kept my eyes trained on the mountain rising across the valley and tried to force myself to be calm. At least until Laurent got here. Instead, I was thrown into a panic as Hiram grabbed my arm and spun me around, holding me so tightly I felt my arm would be crushed to powder.

"Let go of me," I said.

Perhaps being so near Phoebe gave me a bit of her courage. When he complied, I was proud of myself. But the next moment, my face exploded in pain from the shattering blow of his fist, and I landed on the ground, right on top of Phoebe's grave. I looked up. He blocked the sun.

"What did you do to him?" I asked, knowing Laurent would never let Hiram be alone with me like this.

"Nothin' I ain't done a hundred times before," he said. "Brothers fight, you know. But this time—" Hiram bent over and grabbed the front of my coat and hauled me to my feet, bringing his face within inches of mine. "He's got some crazy idea that he's going to go to the law and turn himself in. Did you know that?"

I didn't. We'd never talked about what Laurent's future held, but it didn't surprise me either. He'd reconciled himself to God; it only made sense that he would want to reconcile himself to the law as well. Actually, I was proud, and I guess some of it must have registered on my face, because Hiram hit me again, knocking me back to the ground. This time he threw his weight on top of me and grasped my throat in one hand. I couldn't scream.

"And if he goes to the law, how long do you think it will be before they come for me? Huh? He'd probably lead them right to me."

Bits of spittle frothed at the corners of his mouth and flew in my face. He emphasized his words by jerking my throat, slamming my head into the snow.

Where is he? Where is he? Where is he? My breath was crushed within me under Hiram's weight. My head and heart cried out to God, and I must have somehow voiced my plea because the sound of my prayer brought Hiram to a new state of fury.

"Don't you pull that on me," he said.

To my relief he let go of my throat and rolled off me to sit in the snow while I remained on the ground, gasping for breath.

"That's the other thing, him spouting on about God and for-giveness and such. You worked some kind of spell on him, little girl.

You took my brother away, and it's going to be the end of me." He gave a low, bitter laugh and gazed out across the canyon. "Guess it's natural, though. Being stuck out here and all. It's bound to make a man crazy, make him think crazy things. Maybe even do some crazy things."

His voice changed then, became slow and soft as he turned his head to look at me again. "Maybe you just have a way with you, little girl. Though you're not so little, are you?"

He was above me again, his knees sinking into the snow on either side of my legs. Even though his hands were nowhere near my throat and his body wasn't touching mine, I felt myself once again unable to breathe. Unable to scream. Above me he blocked out the sun and the sky, becoming one looming shadow speaking dark things. About me. About my body.

Then I felt my skirt being lifted away. His hand between my legs, wedging them apart.

Oh, God! No!

And then he was down upon me again, my body shot through with pain. Hiram buried his face in my neck, and I opened my eyes, staring straight into the sun, thinking if I could see it, God could see me. I begged. Begged Hiram to stop. Begged God to save me.

"Belinda!"

Hiram was spewing such ugliness into my ear I could hardly believe what I'd heard. But then I heard it again, my name called out with such anguish I didn't recognize the voice.

"Belinda!"

Within seconds, though, I was flooded in light as Hiram's body was torn away from mine. I looked up and saw Laurent, his face obscured by a trickle of blood that had been left unchecked.

"You get away from her!"

Hiram had been thrown to a pile beside me in the snow, and he sat there, panting like a dog before slowly rising to his feet.

"Sorry, Brother," he said. "Guess our pa never did a good job teaching us to share."

That's when I noticed the gun in Laurent's hand, aimed straight at Hiram's chest.

"You're not going to kill me," Hiram said. "You're not a killer. Not even before you became this holy man."

Laurent held the gun steady, but took his eyes off his brother long enough to look at me. "You all right?"

I nodded. I was alive, anyway. I pulled my skirts back down around my legs and sat up, knees tight to my chest, wrapping my own arms around me.

"Then get on back to the house."

I didn't want to leave him, but I stood up slowly, fighting against the protest of my body, and began to back away.

"Give me the gun, little brother." Hiram took a step closer to Laurent.

"Belinda! You get on back to the house." Laurent never took his eyes off Hiram.

I backed away a few more steps, afraid to turn my back.

"Unless you're willing to shoot me now, in cold blood, give me that gun," Hiram said.

He took the final step that brought him within an arm's length of Laurent, the barrel of the gun just inches from his chest. In a gesture so quiet, so peaceful, there was a crossing of sleeves, and Laurent's hand was hanging empty at his side.

"Now then," Hiram said, "this feels a lot more natural, doesn't it."

Laurent turned to me, his eyes filled with a pain I knew had nothing to do with the blood on his face.

"I'm sorry." His voice broke into a sob, and he stood there, so much smaller than his brother, his shoulders slumped and heaving as he cried. "I wasn't there. I couldn't get—"

For the first time, I looked at Laurent with a heart full of love, and I ran to him and threw myself into his arms.

"It's all right," I said, my own tears hot against my skin. I pressed my swollen face into his shirt and felt his arms hold me tightly to him. "I love you."

"See? Now this is nice," Hiram said, and I felt his filthy hand touch the top of my head. "I don't see any reason the three of us can't just play nice—"

I was on the ground again, this time thrown there by Laurent, who pushed me out of the way before lunging at his brother. The two of them struggled for footing. They became one body, a thrashing of arms and legs, heads butted together, then thrown back. They might have stayed that way forever, neither willing to disengage.

Until the gun fired.

The sound was muffled but unmistakable. Both men stepped away from each other, each with a look of shock and surprise. Then Laurent looked down and put his hand to his gut. When he brought it back again, it was covered in blood. He studied it, then he looked at me.

"I'm sorry," he said again.

Hiram dropped the gun in the snow and looked at his own hand. "I didn't mean to do that, Brother." He grabbed the lapels of Laurent's coat. "Do you believe me?"

"I believe you." Laurent's voice was little more than air. "I believe you." He took a step back, tears showing in his eyes.

Hiram was crying too, and he clutched at Laurent's coat as if clinging to the life waning within. Step after step they took in tandem, Laurent backing farther and farther away from me. I caught my breath when I realized they were steps away from the crevasse.

"Look out!" I screamed.

Hiram's face was buried in his brother's coat. He was begging now, begging Laurent to forgive him. Laurent stopped and lifted his brother's face to look him square in the eye.

"I forgive you, Brother," he said, before looking straight at me and smiling. He brought his hands up, clutched Hiram's coat, and took the final step back.

Then they were gone.

I heard nothing except my own screams. I fell to my knees and crawled to the point where their tracks ended, but I couldn't bring myself to look over the edge. My first instinct was to fall down there with them. Faced with being left here, utterly alone, it seemed the most comforting thing to do. But then there, on my knees, I realized I wasn't alone.

Father God, take me away from here. I don't have the strength, and I don't know where to go. But You do, Father. Somewhere deep in my soul I remembered the prayer of the virgin. *Look at me! Regard me in this low place. Raise me up, O God, and take me wherever You will. For You are mighty, O Lord.*

I don't know how long I stayed there on my knees in the snow. But at some point I got up and started to walk. Giving no thought to my direction—no thought to anything, really, except the continued pace of one step after another—I walked right past our little cabin and headed down the mountain.

I walked and it was daylight. I walked and it was dark. The idea of stopping brought with it the fear of never getting up again, so I continued on. Past the point where I could feel my feet. Past the point where I was moving under my own power.

I walked and it was daylight again. I walked and it was dark again.

There was nothing but silence both in and all around me, and soon I realized even the sound of my boots crunching in the snow had ceased. As if snapped like a thread, I fell, and the thought of immobility brought me great peace. I closed my eyes, perfecting the darkness, and felt the cold envelop me like a finely stitched quilt.

Each beat of my heart sounded like the step of a loved one walking away, and my body went limp with relief.

Off in the distance I could hear a voice calling, and I smiled. I knew then, without a doubt, that when I opened my eyes again, I would be Home.

That, when our life of faith is done,
In realms of clearer light
We may behold Thee as Thou art,
With full and endless sight.

22

Softness billowed all around me, and my body felt a sensation so foreign I could hardly give it a name. *Warmth.* I kept my eyes closed long after I knew myself to be awake, certain I had died and that the constant rustle around me was the friction of angels' wings. It seemed the heavenly host spoke in the guise of the whispering women constantly at my side, sometimes alone, sometimes gathered together. But then, as much as I delighted in this welcome rest, I became aware of a sharp, stinging pain in my hands and feet, and I realized I was still in a world full of suffering. I waited until the surrounding silence assured me that I was alone before opening my eyes.

The room was dark, with heavy curtains drawn against the sunlight. My head was nestled so deep into a soft feather pillow that I had to raise it to look around the room. Against the far wall stood a tall bureau with three dresses hanging on hooks beside it. A pitcher and bowl sat on a washstand, and a pair of glass-domed sconces with snuffed-out candle stubs flanked the mirror above it. The door was open slightly, and I could see a dim hallway. Somewhere—it sounded as if coming from below—I heard the voices that had haunted the last of my dreams. Conversation. Laughter.

One voice seemed to break away from the others, followed by

the sound of feet climbing a set of stairs. As the steps came closer and closer, part of me wanted to close my eyes and hide away just a little longer. I let my head fall back on the pillow and waited.

She was, without a doubt, the fattest woman I had ever seen.

"Well, just look who decided to come to the party."

If it weren't for the red-stained lips mouthing the words and the bosom threatening to spill over the top of her dress, I might have thought that old Whip had come back to life in the body of this enormous woman. Her voice had the same ragged depth as his.

"Hey, Sadie!" she called over her shoulder. "Get on up here and tend to this little squirrel you dragged in!"

Within seconds I heard another set of footsteps on the stairs, and I faced what was possibly the tallest woman I'd ever seen. She whispered something in a language I didn't understand and crossed to the bed, settling beside me and stroking my hair.

"Thank God you are all right, my little one," she said.

Her clipped syllables pierced something deep within me. Not memories exactly, but the undeniable sense that this woman had carried me. Had lain down beside me. Had taken the wet clothes from my body. Before, she'd whispered to me in a different language—German, I guessed, having heard our butcher back home speak it to his family. Even though I couldn't understand any of her words, I sensed from her that we shared something deeper than any conversation could touch.

This is Sadie. And she knows.

Yet another set of footsteps, and a third woman was in the room.

She had a sweet round face surrounded by unruly tufts of brown curls, and a smile that looked like a pretty pink bow. As soon as she walked in, she let forth a delighted little squeal.

"You're awake! You're awake!" she said, accompanied by the softest clapping of her little hands. "Are you hungry? Are you thirsty? Can I get you some tea? Or porridge?"

My tiny knot of a stomach tightened, jumping to life at the mention of food. I attempted to open my mouth and tell this woman, "Yes, please, food," but my lips were dry and sealed, threatening to split and bleed at the slightest parting. Behind them, my tongue and throat felt swollen. I tried to raise my hand to signal my need in spite of the stinging pain—rivaled only by that in my feet—but no effort would bring it more than an inch off the mattress. So I searched the face of the cheerful woman and was immediately rewarded when she clapped again and hustled out of the room.

From that moment I learned that my reluctance to speak would have no impact on whether my needs would be met. Every time I opened my eyes, one of the three was at my bedside with a tray. Most often it was the sweet, plump woman named Mae who spooned broth and porridge into my mouth. The day I parted my teeth to take a nibble of toast, she praised me to the rafters. I almost smiled. And when she brought me a bowl of steaming beans, cooked in a thick broth seasoned with onion and black pepper, I actually did.

For nearly a week I remained confined to the bed, dozing throughout the day and night, silently reveling in the warmth of the room. The pain in my hands and feet was excruciating, especially as the skin blistered and cracked, but the one called Sadie checked them every day, holding them gently aloft, bringing them close to her face as if to smell some sign of danger.

I learned by listening that the large woman was named Jewell, and she was the uncontested leader in the household. She was not a mother, nor were Sadie and Mae sisters, and the nature of their relationship and how they came to live here together remained a mystery for a time. All that mattered to me was that they seemed willing to take me in, unquestioningly.

Compared to the other women, Jewell seemed the least concerned with tracking my progress. She visited often enough—several times a day, in fact. She would sit on a chair by the window, and when she asked questions, she seemed more than happy to be refused an answer.

"Girl," she'd say, "what in devil's name happened to you?" Then, without even the pretense of wanting a reply, "Aw. It don't matter. There's not too many of us out here that haven't been through it. So don't you go lettin' yourself feel no shame. I can see you're a good girl. I can always tell a real good girl."

Her voice sounded like the way my throat felt when I had a sip of Laurent's whiskey. She spoke low, as if afraid that Sadie or Mae might intrude on our one-sided conversations. I figured she must have thought I was a true mute, somebody safe with her secrets, because when one of the other women did come into the room, Jewell was immediately loud and brusque, peppering her speech with mild profanity and bawdy jokes in contrast to the soft, dreamy tone she had when we were alone.

"I used to have me a little house," she told me, "and a boy who was just about your age when I left." Only when she mentioned her son did Jewell give any hint of her pain. Judging by her reaction when Sadie and Mae entered the room, I'd be surprised if either of these women knew he existed.

Once my feet and hands had healed, I was allowed to take a bath. Sadie hauled a small tub up to my room, and she and Mae took turns bringing water to fill it. They *tsked* at the sight of my body, and I crossed my arms in front of me.

Jewell came in to add a few drops of scented oil to the water, making it feel like silk as I slipped in. Then Mae poured a bucket of warm water over my head and lathered my hair with a soap that smelled of mint and honey. I didn't think I'd ever want to get out, but soon enough the water began to turn cold, and Sadie held out a new, clean gown. Mae had tailored it, sewing a new hem so I could walk without tripping, and fashioned the excess fabric into a ruffled nightcap to keep my head warm during these final weeks of frigid nights.

My bath complete, Sadie and Jewell each took a handle of the tub and struggled to carry it, sloshing, out of the room while Mae brushed my hair. The feel of the bristles against my scalp frightened me at first. I remembered combing my fingers through Phoebe's pale strands, such a silent, futile task in comparison to the rhythmic stroking I heard now, occasionally interrupted by the sound of bristles in battle with snarls that had been left, untouched, since before Christmas.

"Oh, I'm sorry, little one. Did I hurt you?" Mae said, mistaking the pain behind my tears. I shook my head.

She plaited my hair into two braids that she draped over my shoulders, and placed the new cap on top.

"Would you like to see, honey?" Without waiting for an answer, Mae sprang over to the bureau, picked up a mirror, and brought it back to the bed. "See how pretty you are?"

I didn't lift a hand to hold the mirror myself, so there was a sense of disembodiment as my reflection floated in front of me. Much as that night when I'd stared into a shard of glass as I descended our cellar steps, I felt myself searching for my soul. I remember wondering if what all my cousins had experienced was real, and now for just a moment I wondered if the girl in this mirror had really lived through everything she thought she had.

"You've just plumped up so much." Mae pinched my cheek with her free hand. "Why, when you first got here you were nothing but skin and bones. People say that all the time, but in your case it's the gospel truth."

I worked up a weak smile, because doing so always pleased Mae.

"Oh, look at you." She gave my cheek one more pinch before taking the mirror back to the bureau. "I think you're well enough for a cookie. Does that sound good? I have just enough sugar left for one batch."

I smiled a little broader and nodded. A cookie. Just like I would have had at home on any Saturday night.

As soon as she left the room, I wept.

My first foray out of the room took me into a hall where the rough wood grated against my sensitive feet. I walked with one hand gliding along the wall, terrified to trust my legs after such long disuse. When I came to the threshold of the stairs, I stopped and turned around, saving that journey for another day.

In the end it was Sadie who coaxed me down the steps one morning—holding my arm as I descended—and into the first floor parlor. I don't know why I was so surprised at the luxurious furnishings; somehow I thought I'd never see brocade sofas or paintings or carpets again. But there they were—nothing like our home back in Belleville, but more plush than anything I expected.

"Now," Sadie said, "you can come downstairs any time you like. Sometimes, in the evening, there might be some men down here, but do not let them frighten you. They are actually quite kind, but you do not need to stay near them if you are uncomfortable."

She continued to lead me through the house, allowing me to poke my head into the kitchen, where Mae stood at the stove frying cornmeal cakes that she would later serve drizzled with syrup. Chester would have loved those. Sadie helped me back up the stairs, pointing to each door, telling me whose room was whose, and when

I started to enter the room where I'd been staying, she gently took my elbow and led me down one more door.

"Of course you may stay in my room as long as you like, but we have been working on this room for you."

Like the other upstairs rooms, the walls were whitewashed, but this room had a light airiness that Sadie's lacked. White muslin curtains hung at the window where the sun appeared as a mere slit slicing through the corner of the room. The bed in here was smaller than the one I'd grown accustomed to—as though it had been crafted just for me—and was covered with a quilt sporting a sage green ruffle. A little scrap-braid rug shared the colors of the quilt and would give me a soft place to stand when I used the pretty white pitcher and bowl to wash up in the mornings. There was no dresser, but there was a little trunk at the foot of the bed, and my dress, newly washed and mended, was hanging on a hook next to the washstand. A candle stood upright in a delicate saucer on a three-legged table covered with a white lace doily. A chair by the window would allow me a lovely view.

"Do you think it is pretty?" Sadie asked.

I nodded.

"I had a room very much like it when I was just about your age."

When she told me this, her face took on an expression like Jewell's had when she spoke of her son, making me wonder how many ghosts haunted this place and if there was room for a few more.

"Well then," she said, "you should wash your face, put on your dress, and join the rest of us downstairs for breakfast. How does that sound?"

I nodded again, then wrapped my arms around Sadie's waist and laid my head against her spare bosom. She went rigid, and though she was right within my arms, I felt she was miles—and years— away. I held her tighter, waiting for her to soften against me, but she didn't. After a while she gave me an awkward little pat on the top of my head and disengaged herself, telling me that breakfast would be on the table any minute.

The women had grown to accept my silence, and somehow my lack of speech added to the sense of peace I felt in this new home. Perhaps this is why the Bible urges us to be slow to speak. Before, I was constantly engaged in some verbal sparring—with my parents, my brother, with Phoebe, even Laurent when I had the strength. But here, there was no cause to argue. They anticipated my needs, and I accepted what they gave me. I smiled when they laughed and listened when they spoke. For all they knew I'd never uttered a word in my life, and if any of them ever heard the cries and mutterings that I sometimes woke myself with in the middle of the night, they never mentioned it. I felt blessed to have found shelter with souls as wounded as mine. I didn't have to spell out my pain; they knew it all too well. And I could talk to God without opening my mouth.

But that morning, sitting with all of them in the warm little kitchen, I longed to join in the conversation. These women were telling stories—grand adventures in exotic places full of colorful characters. I longed to tell my own stories, to breathe some life back into my parents by telling of their love for each other or to ask if my brother and Del had journeyed through this place. I couldn't, however, simply launch into speech after so many weeks of silence. I wanted some invitation, some indication that I was accepted here, not as a mere foundling but as a friend.

"Girl? Girl?" Jewell's voice interrupted my thoughts. "Now I can't just keep on callin' you 'girl.' It's time you had a proper name."

A hush fell at the table; Sadie gave Jewell a most hateful glare.

"You're a tiny little thing," Jewell continued, unfazed by Sadie's look. "I'm gonna call you Biddy."

"No, Jewell," Sadie said, surprising me with the anger in her voice. "This one is not yours to name."

I snapped my head around to glare at Sadie. This was my home now, my refuge. There was no place for Belinda here—not for the little girl who knew God only as a character in Bible stories, who sat mutely through Sunday school classes ignorant of His power. I was alive because of Him. This new life deserved a new identity.

"It's all right," I said, as surprised as they were to hear my voice. "I like that name."

23

And so I became a part of the household. I learned that this was a place called Silver Peak, a little camp tucked away near a fledgling silver mine. It seemed almost cruel to think that through all those months trapped with Laurent I had been this close to warmth and women. In some way it reinforced the danger of the mountains, knowing that just a few peaks and valleys could keep this haven so well hidden.

Even though I settled in comfortably, it was a while before the true nature of Jewell's home dawned. At first I thought they were just women like me—older, yes, but abandoned by their families and brought here to make a life together under Jewell's loving care. Indeed, for weeks nothing untoward or improper happened at all. All the while I had convalesced in Sadie's room, and during my early forays downstairs, Jewell, Sadie, and Mae were the only people I saw. They made me feel cushioned, as if none of the evils and pain from the past could ever touch me.

Little by little I told them my story. Just snippets at first—how my father had dreamed of coming out West. How beautiful and elegant my mother was. I made them smile with stories of my brother's exploits. Jewell said Chester sounded like he needed a good whipping. Mae smiled coyly and said she would have different plans for him entirely, at which point Sadie elbowed her so hard she nearly fell out of her chair. But when I told them about what I'd seen that last night in the barn, when Chester held Phoebe so tenderly, assuring her of her beauty and worth, all of us sighed, swept away with his promise.

I told them about Del too, though I kept the memory of his soft kiss to myself.

Of course they had to know the dark parts of my story too. My brother's disappearance. The murder of my parents. I tried to paint Laurent in some flattering light, befitting his redemption. How he clothed me, fed me, crafted rabbit-skin boots to keep my feet warm. I recounted the months of cold, dark hunger in Laurent's tiny cabin. They wept when I spoke of Phoebe, and I did too, having finally come to a place of safety and warmth that would allow such emotion.

But I couldn't tell them everything. Not about the end, or what happened that last day.

Until it was happening again. Not to me, but to someone in the house. It was late at night, and I was already asleep when the sound woke me. I didn't hear any screams, but then I hadn't screamed either, not after the first movement. Who could scream while your very life was being ripped away? Here, even with the sage green ruffle of my quilt pulled up to my nose, I could still feel him. Feel that awful weight. I closed my eyes and kicked off my covers. Then, both relieved and terrified to find myself alone, I grabbed up the quilt, wrapped it around myself, and ran downstairs.

Sadie was sitting on the sofa in the parlor; Jewell sat with a hand of solitaire dealt out on the little card table. Both women jumped when I ran into the room, and I must have looked like the face of fear itself, because Sadie immediately held her arms open for me. "Come, come, little one. What is the matter?"

I curled up beside her and laid my head on her breast. She wrapped her arms around me and drew me closer. Her breath held just a hint of whiskey, and after all her nights of nursing, the scent was now as familiar to me as my mother's perfume.

"There's a man. Upstairs. With Mae. Oh, Sadie, he's got Mae! You've got to help her."

"Hush, hush." Sadie rocked me just a little. "He is just a man. And he is not hurting Mae. He is just…visiting her."

Jewell gave a little chortle, and I felt Sadie stiffen.

"But it's awful," I said. "It's terrible. He shouldn't be allowed— You shouldn't allow—"

"You are safe here, you know," she said. "Nobody will touch you. Nobody will hurt you ever again."

"Aw, don't tell her that." Jewell licked her finger and turned over a card. "There ain't never a guarantee not to get hurt. Don't matter what you do. Only thing I can tell her for sure is that if the monster that did that to her ever stepped where I can get a whiff of him, he'll be lucky if he ever walks again, let alone—"

"Jewell, that is enough. You are going to frighten her."

I peeked up from behind my quilt and caught Jewell's deep-set, narrowed eyes looking at me like someone who'd just found the stash of Christmas candy. Suddenly I felt like a treasure, and as long as Sadie held me dear, I would have no reason to be frightened.

"Was it that Laurent fellow?" Jewell asked.

I shook my head.

"Friend of his?"

I nodded.

"Would you know him if you seen him again?"

How could I ever forget that face? I could see him now, twisted into unimaginable ugliness above me, disappearing as I closed my eyes, then disappearing as Laurent tore him away from me. Disappearing over that ledge, falling—silent—into the crevasse.

All of these visions, all of these memories filled my mind as I nodded again.

"Well then," Jewell gathered her cards in one swoop, "don't you worry. You ain't goin' nowhere till I know he ain't around to harm you."

I smiled at Jewell and snuggled deeper into Sadie's arms, determined to keep my secret for as long as it would keep me here.

Jewell considered everyone a suspect. As spring gave way to summer and more men came to Silver Peak—and, ultimately, to Jewell's—she brought every one of them to my attention and asked, "Is this one it?" Sometimes she was just that bold, and I would be in the clearing next to the house hanging out the wash and some poor fool would be dragged in front of me, his elbow gripped in Jewell's ring-

encrusted fist. After I shook my head and pronounced him innocent, he would slink away, tossing a suspicious look over his shoulder
at me. Other times I might be in the kitchen and Jewell would find
me, hold the door to the parlor open just an inch and direct me to
the tall fellow in the black hat standing by the fireplace. Once I was
in my room, tidying up, when her voice summoned me from the
yard below where she, with as much subtlety as Jewell could muster,
gestured to a handful of men standing around.

"Tell her no," I said to Sadie, who was helping me with my
afternoon chore. "In fact, I don't think he'll ever come here."

I did keep a constant vigilance for Chester and Del, even though
none of the women recognized them from my descriptions. On one
or two occasions I managed to find the courage to ask the men relaxing in Jewell's parlor if they had seen my brother, but based on the
reaction, it seemed Jewell had drilled an absolute fear of me into
them. One man held his hands up as if defending himself against me
and backed into a wall; another turned and ran out of the room.

By the end of June, I'd stopped asking. In July, I turned fifteen,
but I kept my new age to myself for fear that being one year older
would make me more suitable prey. Then came August, and it was
more than year since I'd left my home in Belleville. That anniver-
sary I did share with Sadie one afternoon as we sat on a blanket under
the summer sun.

"It is time to get you back home." Sadie picked a petal off a
pretty, pink wildflower and chewed it thoughtfully. "Away from here."

"Maybe I could just move into one of those." I gestured toward the two small cabins being constructed in the yard behind Jewell's larger, red-roofed house.

"Absolutely not! Those are for—well, never mind what they are for. Just know that Jewell is looking for other girls to live in those cabins."

I lay back flat on the blanket, loving the feel of the sun on my face. I would tan, I would freckle, and I didn't care one bit. The voices of the working men merged to a low, steady rumble. The faintest breeze carried the scent of newly cut lumber and fresh green growth. I wanted to open my eyes and stare straight into the sky, scan the endless blue heavens for a sign. This day marked, after all, a new year, and here I was reconnected with the sun. But to open my eyes, I'd need to lift my hand to shield them, and right now my arm was just too heavy.

"So what do you think?" Sadie was saying. "About going home."

"I am home." My words were slow and lazy, falling out of my mouth as I lolled my head to the side.

"This is not a home, Biddy."

"It's yours, isn't it?"

"Not by my choice."

I opened one eye to see her tying the flower's stem in and out of a little knot.

"You have a family, people waiting for you, who care about you."

"And just what should I do?" I rose up on my elbows and looked at her through squinted eyes. "Just show up back in Belleville all alone and say, 'Hello, everyone! Looks like I'm the only one who survived! Now, who's gonna be the lucky ones to take me in?' "

"Those are your people. They would be more than happy to—"

"No, they wouldn't." I sat up fully and drew my knees to my chest, wrapping my arms around them. "Not if they knew. Not if they knew everything I did."

"Oh, child."

She reached out for me, but I turned my shoulder to escape her embrace.

"I stole from my father. I wasn't there when he— Maybe I could have saved them."

"Surely they would understand. You cannot help what happened."

"You don't know that!" I spoke so loud, one of the men turned to look at me before doffing his hat to Sadie and returning to his work.

"I know that you cannot underestimate how much your family loves you. And how worried they must be about you."

"They won't care." I picked a flower and set upon ripping it apart. "They thought Daddy was a fool. They'll just think he got what he deserved, and I'll just be some charity case. For all I know, Chester's already there, whooping it up, laughing at all of us."

"And worrying about you. Tell me, Biddy, have you ever sent any word home? Does your family even know about this tragedy?"

I shook my head. "There hasn't been time."

"Well, there is time now."

Sadie stood, and I felt myself draped in shadow. I looked up and saw her standing over me, tall and strong. Her head blocked out the sun, creating something like a halo with thin strands of her blond

hair dancing within it. She reached down, and I took her hand, relying on her strength to pull me to my feet.

"You are going back into the house, young lady, and you are
going to write a letter. The next time the supply wagon comes, we
will send it off."

"All right." I fell into an easy step with her. "But I'm not going
to tell them I'm going back. God brought me here, and I'm going to
stay here until He decides to take me someplace else."

Sadie laughed. "And just how do you suppose He is going to do
that? Just pick you up and drop you?"

"Yes," I tossed my denuded flower stem to the ground. "Just like
He did when He brought me here."

Later that evening I sat on my bed with Jewell's little lap desk and
stared at a sheet of blank stationery. At the top I'd written the date,
August 11, 1862, and nothing else. My hand gripped the pen and
wafted it in circles, then tapped it on the corner of the desk, then
made circles again before I finally took a deep breath and touched
the tip to the paper.

   Dear Uncle Silas and Aunt Nadine,

      It is my sad duty to tell you that your lovely daughter,
   Phoebe, has gone to be with the Lord. She took ill in the
   harsh frontier winter and passed away quite peacefully after a
   bout of fever.

Take comfort in knowing that her final words were of her love for you and that she left this earth eager to see you again when you all gather in the presence of God in heaven.

Your loving niece,

Belinda

Of course, they would wonder why I and not Mother had written the letter. They would question why the letter contained no other news of our family. But I had lived with the loss—all of them gone with such bitter swiftness. I would give them the chance to mourn one life before losing another, the chance God hadn't given me.

I folded the letter and sealed it in an envelope, then printed the address in careful letters on the front, leaving them to wonder—perhaps forever—just where it had come from.

24

*I*t didn't take long—even with my limited knowledge—for me to realize that, brothel or not, Jewell's house was not nearly as packed with sin as she would have liked. She frequently complained to Sadie about the state of their business affairs, bemoaning that the clientele here was far more interested in playing cards than anything else, forever tainting my memories of Chester's late nights out at the poker tables.

"What we need to do is pack up and move on," Jewell would say.

"I am not going anywhere," Sadie would reply.

"Then maybe we just need to get some new blood workin' up there." At this point, Jewell would send a glance my way, and I would feel my very blood freeze within me.

"No, Jewell. Not her."

I'm not sure exactly when Jewell's attitude toward me changed. One day I was the weak little girl found in the forest; the next, an interloper not earning her keep. I used to catch her looking at me, her eyes wistful and sad. She would reach a tentative hand toward me and touch my hair, my shoulder, as if reassured that I was alive and whole. Then, almost overnight, her eyes narrowed to suspicious slits. When she touched my hair, she did so with an air of primping;

when she touched my shoulder, she told me what a pretty girl I was, with such a nice, slender figure.

"You know," she said on more than one occasion, "some of them young men workin' the mine ain't much older'n you. An' I know for a fact they think you're awful pretty."

Last summer, the idea of even one young man having eyes for me might have sent me into a swoon. Now it made the bile rise to the top of my throat as my nose burned with the memory of stinking, rotten breath.

Jewell never said such things if Sadie was nearby, so I worked whatever excuse I could to keep myself in Sadie's presence. Failing that, I tried to ingratiate myself by doing little chores—fetching, carrying—anything to make myself indispensable. Except in the evenings. Once supper dishes were cleared away and the men started trickling into the parlor, I took to my room and shut the door.

Until that crisp autumn day when Gloria arrived.

By far, my least favorite chore was hanging the freshly washed laundry on the line. The thin rope was suspended high above my head, requiring that I step back and launch each garment over it— rarely achieving success the first time. The wet fabric slapped my face until I was lost in a flapping sea of lace and linen. That's why I didn't see her coming up the path. If I had, I would have run to the main house to find Jewell and announce the fruition of her greatest dream. Instead, I was fighting a losing battle with one of

Mae's billowy petticoats when Jewell's deep voice summoned me to the kitchen door. When I got there she was grinning like the child who had just snagged the last piece of Christmas pie.

"Now you go on into the parlor an' tell that woman in there to make herself at home."

"What woman?"

She gave me a broad wink. "Oh, you'll see."

I walked into the parlor and was stopped speechless. Perhaps it was because there were so few of us, being the only ones within miles, that the women at Jewell's house tended toward extremes. Jewell was extremely fat, Sadie tremendously tall, Mae incredibly sweet. Now, here in the parlor, was perhaps the most beautiful woman I had ever seen. Despite the layer of dust covering her skirt and skin, she looked as if she had stepped straight out of a *Godey's Lady's Book*. Her figure was proud and perfect, even if her hair was not, as rebellious curls threatened escape from what was once a flawless chignon. Her skin was pale—perhaps pallid with exhaustion from an arduous journey—but flawless. Her nose, exquisitely shaped and slightly upturned, sat atop a mouth that seemed poised to break into a smile, and the cornflower blue eyes made it clear that she might be the only one who knew the joke.

All this I took in the minute I walked into the room. So struck was I that I could barely find my voice to ask, "Would you like to sit down, miss?"

"Some water would be nice." She plopped down on the sofa, obviously used to being obeyed.

"Nothing to eat?" Closer inspection showed a hollowness to her cheeks, and I offered her everything in the house, including the bounty of a migrating goose one of the men had brought down earlier in the day.

"Just the water, thanks."

The dismissive tone was unmistakable, so I spun on my heel to leave and collided with Jewell's ample bosom. For a moment the whole world was a mass of wine-colored velvet and black buttons before Jewell grabbed my arms and set me straight.

"Fetch a light supper for our guest, Biddy." She talked straight over my head to the stranger behind me.

"She says she just wants some water." The tension between the two women was palpable, and I added a weak, "ma'am" at the end of my statement.

"Nonsense. Boil some tea. Toast some bread, and open the last jar of marmalade."

Without any further argument, I ran out of the room to do Jewell's bidding. By now both Sadie and Mae were in the kitchen, and Mae had already put a kettle on.

"Who is she?" Mae was asking as I walked in.

"Her name is Gloria." Sadie had sliced the bread and was putting it on the toast forks to pop into the oven. "Jewell knows her from way back. In California."

"And she's beautiful," I added, measuring out the tea.

"Well, you just be careful of that," Sadie said. "Such beauty often comes with a price."

Once the bread was toasted, Mae spread it with generous swoops of marmalade, and I took the tray back out to the parlor. I had the impression that Jewell and Gloria called an immediate halt to their conversation as soon as I walked through the door. Both seemed poised like cats on ice, so I backed out of the room as soon as the tray was settled on the little table by the sofa and ran up to my room.

I was brushing my hair, wanting to clean up and make a good impression on our guest at supper, when Jewell walked in.

"I'm takin' my old friend into my room for a little chat. Her bag's down in the parlor."

"Do you want me to bring it up to you?"

Jewell chuckled. "Nah. I want you to do some lookin' for me."

"What kind of looking?"

"Pretty thing like that, travelin' like she does, she's bound to have some money on her. I want you to find it, count it, and let me know just what she's bringin' to the house. Better yet," she added before turning to leave, "just bring it to me. Don't want her to have a chance to hide it away."

She left me sitting, brush in hand, my mouth open in a protest I would never voice. My life had been torn apart once by the simple act of pilfering money from a suitcase, and as I looked down at my hands still clutching my hairbrush, I could almost see the taint of that past crime lingering on my flesh.

She asked me to do this because she knows I'm a thief. A thief and a killer. And if I am all of this, what small step would it be to become a—

I longed for Sadie's strength to defend me against Jewell's request, and when I finished plaiting my hair, I went back to the kitchen, where Sadie and Mae were preparing the evening meal.

"Biddy!" Mae handed me my favorite treat—a slice of salted, raw potato—the minute I walked through the door. "You look like you've just seen a ghost."

"Go on and tell us," Sadie said. "What did Jewell do to you?"

I told them about Jewell's suspicions of Gloria and her request of me, and by the end of my gloomy tale, Mae gave me another slice of potato.

"Well, do not do it," Sadie said. "Take the bag upstairs and tell Jewell you looked but found nothing."

"That would make me a liar," I said.

"Then I will do it myself." Sadie wiped her hands on a kitchen towel and walked toward the door. "I have no problem at all lying to that woman."

Although I would have been happy to move back into Sadie's room and give Gloria mine, Jewell decided to let her live in one of the new little cabins out back.

"It's not likely she'll be doin' any business for me anyway," Jewell had said with a scowl that night as the five of us ate supper together. "It's tough enough gettin' them excited over plump little Mae, here. Ain't nothin' gonna make them go upstairs with a pregnant woman."

At this announcement, Mae squealed and clapped her hands, and a look of absolute hunger came over Sadie's face.

"Ah, Jewell," Gloria said, "you're every bit the warm, nurturing woman I remember."

"I'm givin' you a free bed till next summer, ain't I? There's not a lot that would do that."

My servitude toward Jewell somehow transferred to Gloria, and the first morning she took the little path to the first cabin, I followed behind, my arms laden with clean linens. In the days since her arrival, one of the men had constructed a bed frame from the left-over lumber, and we had stuffed a ticking with what straw and goose feathers we could find. Jewell donated a bureau from her room, and Mae carried over a tiny three-legged table from the parlor. A tiny little stove had appeared out of nowhere—I fully suspected that Jewell had coerced its donation from a disgruntled miner who just wanted to go back to his farm—and I gave her the chair that had sat next to the window in my room.

"I wish it were a rocking chair." I laid the folded linens on the bureau. I could just imagine the cozy scene of Gloria in this tiny cabin, holding a newborn baby.

"I don't think a rocking chair quite suits me." She dropped her green satchel on the floor.

"Well, I think you'll like it here anyway."

Gloria seemed ready for me to leave, or at least to remain silent for as long as I stayed helping her get the cabin in order. But the spirit of conversation overtook me, and I found myself prattling on.

"The women here are so nice. I feel quite at home."

"Really." Gloria cocked an eyebrow at me—a feat I would

practice for endless hours with my mirror. "Well, I wouldn't put too much stock in any of them, especially Jewell. She's nothing but a big old snake waiting to pounce on you, little Biddy. You stay clear of her."

"How bad can she be? You came back to her."

"Not all of us are lucky enough to have choices in life. You listen to me. First chance you have to get out of here, you run. Fast and far."

"I wouldn't consider leaving." I unfolded the first sheet. "God brought me here, after all. He's got to have some purpose in it. Why do you think He brought you here?"

Gloria gave a little laugh that, coming from anyone less beautiful, would have seemed downright sinister. "For all I know, God and I don't even know each other exists. And I think we're both happier that way."

She and I continued puttering around, staying clear of each other. She hung a pair of simple yellow curtains over the window. Then, when the bed was made, she set her case on top of it, and I paused, certain I would see exotic treasures.

"Here," she said, handing a bundle of fabric to me. "Hang this up. From the shoulders, mind you. Not the back or you'll ruin the shape."

I unfolded it to find a beautiful green dress trimmed in black velvet. A series of wooden pegs protruded from one wall, and I draped the shoulders of the bodice over two of them. I stepped back to see that the garment was hanging straight, and was struck by the realization that the dress took on a perfect figure. A life of its own. Nothing I owned had ever looked this good *on* me, let alone hanging on a hook in a one-room cabin.

"My mother would have loved this." I allowed myself to finger the fine stitching at the gathering on the back of the skirt. "She always said a woman's most important ally is a good seamstress."

Gloria's smile turned warm. "She sounds like a wise woman, your mother."

"She is." Somehow the pride I felt at having Gloria's approval dulled the pain of talking about her. "Rather, she was."

"Oh." Gloria pulled out a handful of stockings and handed them to me, gesturing toward the top bureau drawer. "She died?"

I nodded. "About a year ago."

"Mine too. When I was about your age." Another dress. Three petticoats.

"My mother was"—I paused, waiting for the strength to say the word, momentarily fascinated by red lace—"murdered."

Gloria's eyes narrowed and something like a chuckle rumbled deep in her throat. "Mine too. Or she may just as well have been. Would've been quicker."

"What happened?"

I was fully prepared for her to tell me it was none of my business, but she was sitting on her new bed, staring into her empty suitcase wearing an expression of such tragic elegance that she could have been the heroine in one of the tales Phoebe and I used to concoct. If she refused to tell me, I would probably spend the rest of the evening making up my own details.

But she didn't refuse.

"She was killed," Gloria said, a wry turn to her lips. "This life killed her. She hated it so much she passed it on to me, then kept herself full of enough morphine to forget about what she did to us."

"I'm sorry," I said. The coldness in her voice was almost frightening, and I felt guilty at the twinge of fascination her story carried with it. "Do you miss her at all?"

Gloria snapped the case shut. "My mother was a whore. Before she died, she made sure that I was one too. So, no, I don't miss her. Not one day."

"I'm sorry," I said again, this time with sincerity. I closed the bureau drawers and ran my hand needlessly along its top before moving toward the door.

"Wait a minute. Let me tell you something. That 'kind woman' who wants you to think she's doing all of us a favor by taking us in was pounding the nails in my mother's coffin long before she took sick. She wants to destroy us, Biddy. She wants us all to be as mean and miserable as she is, make no mistake. You may have walked in here pure as a dove in snow, but you won't walk out that way. Not if she has anything to say about it."

"I'm hardly pure," I said, thinking how surprised Gloria might be if she knew all I had to hide.

"You're close enough, from what Jewell tells me. Get away while you have the chance."

ut of course I didn't get away. If my journey taught me nothing else, it's that nobody goes anywhere in a Wyoming winter. The best anybody can do is find a place, hunker down, and wait for the storms to pass.

But this winter was a far cry from the last. Jewell and the other women had nearly an army of willing men to see that they were well supplied with firewood, so at the very least we had a cozy fire burning in the kitchen for all those long evenings. We wrapped hot bricks and ran bedwarmers under our blankets, so I fell asleep every night feeling toasty warm. The same comfort awaited me downstairs each morning, along with a piping hot breakfast, courtesy of Mae.

The house was rarely silent. It was again a winter spent telling stories, but now it was I who sat enraptured, listening to lives I could hardly imagine. While my life had been confined to two sets of four walls—with a stagecoach in-between—these women seemed to have had most of the world under their feet. Sadie told stories of New York City, both terrible and wonderful. She'd sailed halfway around the world, seen exotic islands, and lived upon the vast, crashing ocean. Gloria had lived with celebrated beauty, telling stories of men literally showering her with gold dust.

"Don't see none of that money now," Jewell would say, lighting one of her thin cigarettes.

"You're just upset that you didn't get a piece of it," Gloria would reply, squinching her nose at Jewell and looking even more beautiful.

Of course, to hear Jewell speak, neither Sadie nor Gloria had done anything to compare with her own life of adventure. One time she said, "If it weren't for me, that whole city'd still be nothing but a mud strip with a dock."

"What city?" I asked.

She looked at me as if I'd just grown a third eye. "San Francisco, of course."

The other three women groaned.

"You can pooh-pooh it all you want," Jewell said. "But I'm tellin' you, I'm the one that brought class to that place. And you just watch. I'll do the same thing here."

Then they all laughed, giving Jewell mock reassurance.

During the hard months of winter, very few men came to enjoy the ladies' company. Many left the camp altogether, seeking warmer lodging until spring. Jewell complained it was because she didn't have anything to offer them besides Sadie and Mae, and if the men weren't keen on giraffes and elephants, they were just plumb out of luck. Some did, however, like to share our company and play cards in our warm parlor. The first time a man settled himself at the little table and asked, "Who's up for a game?" I felt a surge of excitement and sat down at the next chair.

"What do you know about playing cards, kid?" The man was older, maybe forty, with a graying beard and soft eyes.

"Deal them and see," I responded with a glint of my own. By the end of the evening, he was glad we were just playing for beans.

Gloria's warning that I should get away from here seemed as far removed as the home I would go to. In fact, there wasn't anything about this place that didn't feel like a home. I was safe, protected, warm, fed. The day I sent the letter to Aunt Nadine, I felt I was severing a tie between us rather than establishing one.

One night as we were sitting around the kitchen table, Gloria got the strangest look on her face, excused herself, and left. Sadie, Mae, and Jewell exchanged a knowing look, and Mae was almost beside herself with bubbling glee.

"What is it?" I asked, looking at each of them in turn.

"It's time for the baby! It's time for the baby!" Mae clapped her hands.

Seized with the same excitement, I was eager to go out to Gloria's cabin to help. I'd been watching Gloria's body expand for months and was thrilled every time she allowed me to put my hand on her stomach and feel the life within. But now Sadie put her steadying hand on mine and told me to wait.

"It might be morning before the child is here," she said. "You go and sleep. You can see the little one tomorrow."

Disappointed, I said my good nights and went to my room. It was late March, and soft, wet flakes were dropping lazily from the sky. I opened my window, still in love with the stinging scent of new snow, and took a deep breath before closing it again. The house was quiet except for the faintest hints of conversation coming up from the kitchen. Somehow I knew the other women wouldn't be banished to their rooms to wait for the arrival of the baby. Rather than feeling resentful, though, I felt a certain appreciation for my exile. For the first time in a long time I felt wonderful, like a carefree child.

I knelt beside my bed and felt the cool fabric of the quilt against my forehead as I asked God to keep Gloria and the baby safe through the night. I intended to stay there praying until somebody came upstairs with the news, but after a time I was half aroused from sleep when Mae came in.

"Is the baby here?" I remember asking.

"Not yet, dear." Mae helped me under my covers and tucked me in.

The next morning, though, I ran down the stairs and burst into the kitchen, only to find it empty. I called throughout the house before poking my head out the back door. Sadie was on her way in, coming from Gloria's cabin. She looked exhausted, her gray eyes rimmed in red, her skin pale. But she was smiling.

"Go and see the baby," she said.

I stopped midway to Gloria's cabin to give Sadie a quick hug, then tried to bring about some composure before walking in. Both Mae and Jewell were there, although Jewell was complaining loudly about never understanding why people pulled such a fuss over something as ordinary as a baby. She took one last look at the bundle in Mae's arms and left.

"It's a little boy." Mae held the child in front of her.

Gloria lay on her bed, sleeping, looking more beautiful than I think any woman has ever looked. Her face was soft and peaceful, her hair golden. To me, she was a princess, and Mae held in her arms the newest little prince.

"Would you like to see him?" Mae asked. "Here, sit down and hold out your arms."

I sat in the chair next to the stove and held out my arms for the squirming bundle. He was wrapped in a blanket, though one little arm had escaped, and he waved that fist to and fro until I caught it with my hand and let him curl his fist around my finger.

"Did she give him a name?"

"Danny," Mae said. "Isn't he perfect?"

He was, as far as I could tell. He let out an enormous yawn, closing one eye and scrunching up half of his face to do so. I thought about that little boy I'd seen in the foundling home in St. Louis, and I wondered how any woman could look at a child like this and then stick it in a turnstile box.

"Does she love him?" I asked.

"Does she— Well, of course she does, silly. What kind of a question is that?"

"A silly one, I guess," I said. "I wonder if I'll ever have a baby of my own."

"Now, Biddy, you're just a child. There's plenty of time for that later. Give that little one to me, and let's see if Auntie Mae can't get him to go to sleep."

I got up from the chair and handed Danny over to Mae as soon as she had settled into it. She took the baby and nestled him close to her, gently swaying back and forth, singing a soft lullaby.

I sat on the floor and—without any protest from her—rested my head on her knee. I couldn't help but think of all the horrible names the people back home would have for little Danny. And for Gloria. For Mae and me too. There was, of course, no husband to be Danny's father, and while there were plenty of men nearby, none seemed in any hurry to claim a bride.

Mae had told me once that she was just nineteen years old. "Not much older than you, dearie!" she'd enthused. Thinking of that now, I couldn't help but be afraid about how quickly time could pass. Only two years ago I was a sheltered child. In their stories, Gloria, Mae, and Sadie all told of losing their innocence—embarking on this life—when they were just my age. It seemed an inevitability.

Besides the birth of baby Danny, the spring thaw brought new life to Silver Peak. Every day new faces appeared around the camp, some of them coming into Jewell's parlor for a drink or a game of cards or a visit upstairs with Mae. Others took to congregating in her yard, setting up games of horseshoes and speculating—often loudly— about the pretty blonde hiding out in the back cabin.

None of them ever took much notice of me, perhaps because I was still so small. I hadn't grown even an inch since coming to Jewell's, and my body seemed determined to cling to the same gauntness

I'd acquired during my winter with Laurent. Jewell was adamant that I not wear my hair in braids, saying it made me look like I was about nine years old, so I left it to fall in its natural soft brown waves, securing it with a loose ribbon at the back of my neck. And though I'd long ago discarded the threadbare dress I'd worn all last winter, the new ones Mae had sewn for me were the same, childish style—high-necked, long-sleeved, and plain. Nothing like the more elegant styles the other women wore.

To be truthful, I was glad the men didn't pay me any attention. I often felt like I was awash in a sea of anonymous uncles, fetching their drinks and laughing at their jokes.

Then, one day, Buck came.

The first evening he came to Jewell's, I was up in my room, having decided to turn in early and rest. The night before, I had been in Gloria's cabin, tending to baby Danny so she could get some sleep, and I'd fought exhaustion all day. I hadn't even bothered to change into my nightgown but was plopped on my bed fully clothed when the noise from downstairs drew my attention. I was used to hearing loud conversations and laughter, but there was something different tonight. Music. Not the bawdy, raucous drinking songs that were often brought to a ragged, abrupt halt whenever I walked into the room, but a single pure voice beckoning me to listen.

I got up and slipped down the stairs, staying on the bottom step rather than walking into the parlor, lest I interrupt the song. It told the story of a soldier who lay dying in a foreign land, and with each verse, he was instructing his comrades to send his story home—to send love to his mother, to tell his brothers of his bravery, to comfort his dear sister, to tell his lover that his soul had been set free.

Slowly I turned my head to peek into the parlor, and while the singer himself was out of my vision, I did see the men gathered around. Most of them with tears flowing unchecked down their cheeks. Even Jewell was moved by the song.

Then, in that clear tenor voice, he sang the final verse:

> *His voice grew faint and hoarser, his grasp was*
> *childish weak.*
> *His eyes put on a dying look, he sighed and ceased*
> *to speak.*
> *His comrade bent to lift him, but the spark of life*
> *had fled.*
> *The soldier of the Legion in a foreign land was dead!*
> *And the soft moon rose up slowly and calmly she*
> *looked down*
> *On the red sand of the battle field, with bloody*
> *corpses strewn.*
> *Yea, calmly on that dreadful scene her pale light*
> *seemed to shine*
> *As it shone on distant Bingen, fair Bingen on the*
> *Rhine!*

The room exploded in thunderous applause, and I didn't think I'd ever heard anything more beautiful. I too felt the emotion of the song, but I waited until my tears were dry before walking into the parlor to see who had been the singer.

His name was Ben Danglars, but everybody called him Buck because he always wore a buckskin jacket with fringe along the sleeves and hem. He'd come from Virginia, and I think I could have fallen in love with his voice without ever seeing his face. That is, until I saw his face when I turned the corner and came into the room.

He towered above every other man there—would have even if he weren't the only one standing. His hair was the color of wet sand, cut short above his ears but longer on top. His lips were full, his smile wide; blue eyes looked at me from behind heavy, hooded lids, and a tiny cleft punctuated his square chin.

The men were urging him to sing another song—something fun and rollicking this time, but he held out a hand to me, saying, "I believe this next song will be the little lady's request."

All eyes turned to me, and my surprise at being singled out must have registered on my face, because there were more than a few chuckles in the room.

"Come on, Biddy," Jewell said, her voice thick with amusement. "What d'ya want to hear?"

At that moment I could just as easily name a song as sprout wings and fly. "Anything. Anything at all. I'm going back to my room."

That remark was followed by whoops and hollers, with more than one man saying that sounded like an invitation. But Sadie's voice hushed them all. I listened to it all from the stairwell, my face burning, but soon enough I was forgotten, and Buck's voice rang out again, this time leading the rest of the room in a robust singing of "Buffalo Gals."

I ran all the way up to my room and threw myself on my bed. Not even the day spent with Del could cause my heart to pound the way it was now, and while I loved to remember the kiss he gave me, the thoughts of Buck doing the same thing was too much to think about.

Suddenly, the comfort I'd felt at being thought of as a child disappeared. I hoped Buck would look at me one day and see a woman.

26

After that night, I was down in Jewell's parlor every evening. I had convinced Mae to add a bustle to one of the dresses she made for me, giving the illusion that I had more of a womanly figure than I did. I also spent nearly an hour each day fighting with Sadie's curling tongs to create ringlets to frame my face once I'd fastened the rest of my hair in a sophisticated twist. One evening I even snuck into Jewell's rouge pot and added just a hint of color to my cheeks and lips, but Sadie caught me in the hall.

"Go in and wash that off your face," she said, grabbing my arm and steering me none too gently back to my room. "What will people think?"

I knew exactly what they would think, living upstairs in this house as I did, and I didn't care. Buck would never talk to me if he thought I was just a child.

Not that he talked to me much anyway. He didn't come to Jewell's often, and on the evenings he did, he rarely said more than "Good evenin'" to me before falling into conversation with one of the other men. Each night I positioned myself somewhere in the room to make it easy for him to see me. I stood on the hearth, enjoying the higher perspective, thinking we might be close to eye level if he came to stand by the fire. But he didn't. I perched myself on the arm of the sofa, but Sadie sat on the end and threatened to topple me to the ground if I didn't find someplace more proper to sit.

On one of the nicer spring evenings, Jewell moved the party into her yard. Another supply wagon had visited earlier that week, bringing with it a keg of beer which, for this camp, was reason enough for a celebration. Jewell let the men build a big fire in the center of our gathering, and it warmed all of us as it popped and sparked long into the night.

Buck looked beautiful in the firelight. Irresistible, really. I made my way through the miners, who hoisted great mugs of beer amid much cheering over the lode to come and, braver than I ever could have been in the parlor, sidled right next to him.

"You don't have a drink," I said, thankful to have my hostess role to fall back on. "Would you like me to get you one?"

He looked down at me and smiled. "That'd be real nice."

Once I was out of his sight, I ran back to the house and into the kitchen, tearing through the cabinets looking for a cup. The only one I could find was a beat-up old tin thing, but it would have to do. The men had moved our kitchen table out into the yard and set the keg on it. I held the mug under the spigot and filled it nearly to the top, then made my way back to where Buck stood, hands in his pockets, looking into the fire.

"Here you are." I handed him his drink.

"Thanks." He lifted the cup to me as if making a toast, then took a long drink. "None for you?"

I shook my head. "My mother would never approve."

He raised one eyebrow and smiled. "Well, that's not something I ever thought I'd hear a—one of you ladies say."

"I'm not one of those ladies."

"Good to know. How old are you, Biddy?"

"You know my name?"

"There's only five women in this whole place—six if you count the one of us that has a wife. It's not hard to know all the names."

"Oh." I hated the battle between foolishness and disappointment. "I'm almost sixteen. But Jewell thinks I'm younger."

"That's probably smart. But you wouldn't lie to me, would you? Because you look a lot younger than almost sixteen."

"I wouldn't lie to you."

"Well, that's good to know too." He finished the rest of his drink with one deep swallow and handed his cup to a grizzled man who happened to walk by. "Miss Biddy," he bowed to me and offered his arm, "would you be so kind as to take a walk with me?"

My heart pounded, but I must have given some affirmation because he took my hand and led me away from the fire, into the dark woods just beyond the clearing.

"I can't get used to how cold it is here," he said once we were separated from the crowd.

"This is nothing," I said, though now that we were away from the fire, I was wishing I had my scarf and hat. "Wait until you live through a winter."

He laughed. "Don't know that I'll do that. I'm only here because

I don't want to fight in no war back home. Once that's blown over, it's back to the South for me."

"Oh," I said again, feeling that same ridiculous disappointment. "You don't like the mountains?"

"I'll tell you what I like."

We'd walked only a few yards into the forest; I could still see glimpses of the bonfire in the distance. There was a fallen log on the ground, and Buck sat down on it, pulling me down to sit next to him. He took my chin in his hand and turned my face toward his.

"I like a starry night, and a pretty girl to share it with."

I was sure he could feel the great gulp of my swallow.

"Have you ever been kissed before, Miss Biddy-who-is-almost-sixteen?"

I thought of Del's soft lips brushing my cheek, of Hiram's rancid mouth raking across mine. "No."

"Well then, I'd like to be your first, if that's all right with you."

Slowly, slowly he drew me closer, until his lips touched mine. They were warm and soft as they moved across my mouth, and he brought his hand to the back of my head, kissing me deeper until I could taste the beer on his breath. I reached for him too, wrapping my arms around his neck, combing my fingers through his sandy hair.

All I could hear was my blood rushing in my head. I opened my eyes for just a second and saw glimpses of him, sand-colored lashes dusting his cheek. My breath was full of him, my body drawn toward him, clinging to him, even as he pulled himself away.

"Are you sure you've never been kissed before?" He smiled in a way that made me feel as though I were being kissed again.

"Not like that," I said, feeling shy.

"Well then, I'll have to do it again."

He did, and we quickly reached the intensity of the first kiss. I could have stayed there all night, kissing him, but after a time I sensed a change, and his embrace took on a zealousness I couldn't begin to match, and his hand snaked its way from my waist to my thigh.

At once I was back in the snow, back on the ledge with Hiram writhing on top of me.

"Stop it!" I turned my head, summoning the courage I wish I'd had that afternoon.

"I'm sorry," Buck whispered. He took his hand away, but continued to lean toward me, seeking my mouth.

"No!" I pulled myself away.

I buried my head in my hands, surprised at how hot my cheeks were. For a minute I was glad we were in darkness, because I must have been flaming red. Beside me, Buck's breathing was as ragged as my own, and we sat, both of us staring at the ground, inhaling and exhaling in almost perfect unison.

"I'm sorry," I said.

"It's fine," he said, though I thought I heard a hint of disgust in his voice.

"It's just—I can't—"

"It's fine," Buck said, more sweetly than before. He stood up and offered me his hand, which I took, and helped me to my feet.

"Are you all right?" he asked, noting my slight stagger as I gained my balance.

I nodded.

"Good." He bent down to give me one more soft kiss on the top of my head. "I knew you were a nice girl. There aren't too many of them in these parts. Can I walk you back?"

"Please."

I didn't think anybody noticed when Buck and I walked back to the fire. As soon as we rejoined the crowd, he dropped my hand and I went inside.

"Biddy." Sadie's voice beckoned from the kitchen door, and I turned around. "You be careful. One charming man can ruin your life."

"I know." I took a candle from the shelf and held the wick in the lantern's flame before heading to my room where I stood, gazing at myself in the mirror on the wall.

I looked different. I put my hand to my lips; they were fuller, swollen and red, the same color they'd taken the day I dipped into Jewell's rouge pot. The flush had not left my cheeks, and as I took off my coat and unbuttoned my blouse, I saw that my chest was tinged with red. My heart was still pounding, and there was an unfamiliar queasiness in my stomach.

I took off my shoes and stripped down to my chemise, letting my dress pile on the floor, and fell to my knees.

Father God, forgive me, I prayed. *Oh, Lord God, take this temptation away from me. Lead me not to it. Deliver me from it.*

But I could not banish the memory. I tasted Buck's breath on my breath, heard his heart with my heart. When I closed my eyes I saw only his, and I felt his hand on the small of my back. I couldn't do any more than beg for forgiveness and trust that the Lord granted me that grace, despite my wayward thoughts.

I climbed into bed and burrowed under my covers. Sleep was a long time coming that night, but when it did, it was sweet and deep and full of dreams that became elusive in the light of morning.

27

*D*o you think I'll ever be beautiful?"

It was evening, and I was sitting with Gloria in her cabin. Outside a cold spring rain pounded the tiny roof, sounding just like I always imagined the ocean would.

"No," Gloria answered without hesitation.

Her reply couldn't have surprised me more if she'd delivered it with a slap to my face.

"Don't look so wounded," she said. "There's a lot more to life than being beautiful." When she spoke, she looked down at baby Danny nursing at her breast.

"I suppose," I said, though I didn't feel any better. "Do you think I'll ever have a family? I mean one of my own. With a home…and a baby."

"Not if you stay here. Trust me, Biddy. You want a life; get out of this place now. I didn't have that choice when I was your age."

"I don't think I could ever be…what you are."

"Referring to what, exactly? being beautiful? or a mother? or a whore?"

I tried to stammer a reply, but she interrupted me with a laugh, saying, "Don't worry about it, kid. It's not so easy to hurt my feelings. I know what I am. All I'm saying is that you still have a chance to live the kind of life you want, and there's not many women who have that. Go on back to Beetown—"

"Belleville."

"—wherever you came from. Start up your life there."

"I don't know what I'd do back home. It wouldn't be the same without my parents."

"So do something else. Get that sweet young boy to marry you."

I blushed at the thought of it. "Buck? What do you know about him?"

Gloria chuckled. "Honey, everybody knows you're sweet on him."

"Everybody?" Which probably meant he would never want to see me again.

"Just be careful. I don't know anything about courting and having a beau, but I know plenty about men and what they expect from a girl who lives in a whorehouse."

"But I'm not—"

"After a time it won't matter what you are and what you're not. Jewell has her eye set on making you earn your keep. I know that woman. Don't trust her."

"I don't have to trust her," I said. "I trust God, and I know He didn't bring me here to become a—to do anything wrong."

"That's what you think?" She practically snorted. "That God brought you here? Well, I know less about God than anything else, but if this is something He'd do to a person, I'm better off on my own."

There was a knock on the door, and Sadie stepped inside, nearly soaked through from the short walk from the main house.

"I am going to MacGregans' cabin," she told Gloria. "It is her time."

"What?" Gloria's outburst startled little Danny, whose arm flailed out in surprise. She lowered her voice and ran a soothing hand across Danny's soft, fuzz-covered head. "I can't believe you would help that woman."

"Who's MacGregan?"

"One of the men who lives outside of camp," Sadie said. "His wife is having a baby too. And she needs my help."

"That's not what she said before." Gloria made no attempt to soften her bitterness. "I believe she said she wouldn't have anything to do with a woman like you. See Biddy? That's what I mean. You stay around us long enough and you become 'that kind of woman.'"

"*Mrs.* MacGregan did not ask for my help," Sadie said. "It was the husband. I have to see what I can do."

"Because you're such a good person?" Gloria said.

"Because I am just another woman." Sadie reached for the door, but she turned back before leaving. "I almost forgot. Biddy, that young man was in the parlor tonight, and he was asking about you."

After that, nothing mattered but Buck. I woke up in the morning thinking about him and fell asleep ready to dream about him. I curled my hair hoping he would think it looked pretty and walked around slightly tiptoeing hoping it would make me look tall.

When Sadie came into the kitchen with the sad news that Mrs. MacGregan had died after giving birth to a little girl, I could barely bring myself to feel sad because my head was too full of the thought that Buck had asked about me. When the camp gathered together to give the poor woman a funeral, I chose to stay in my room, claiming I'd had more than my share of death and mourning. But when I heard his clear tenor voice singing the first few phrases of "Amazing Grace," I threw on my shoes and ran down the stairs, arriving breathless at the gravesite before the third stanza.

When MacGregan's little girl was brought to Gloria to nurse and be cared for, she called on me more than ever to help. Now, though, when I held either of the squirming infants, I imagined it might be mine. Something with his nose and my eyes named after one of my parents.

The second time he kissed me was an afternoon when I was hanging out the wash. After that there was an evening when our eyes met in Jewell's parlor. With a silent agreement, we met outside at the smoldering firepit and took another walk in the woods. I found myself constantly on the verge of smiling, and when I was alone, I'd say his name out loud, just to hear the sound of it.

I missed Phoebe terribly. We would have lain in bed at night, meticulously creating a future for me and Buck. How he would whisk me off to Virginia, where we'd live out our days on his grandfather's tobacco plantation or some such nonsense. As it was, I had to make up the vision myself, because he never spoke of anything beyond the moments we were together. Even then, he seemed far more interested in kissing me than anything else.

Things changed the day the piano arrived and with it, two new girls.

The piano itself had been long anticipated. Jewell had sent word back with the last supply wagon that she was looking for something to liven up her house, and the next month here it came, sounding out great crashing notes as it bounced over the rough trail in the back of the wagon. Right behind it was a sleek black carriage, and when it stopped in the clearing in front of Jewell's house, two women practically slithered out of it.

They were like nothing I'd ever seen—nothing I'd ever been allowed to see, anyway. Everything about them was dark—their hair, their skin, their eyes—which made the bright colors of their dresses all the more stunning. My mother would have been appalled enough at their brazen display of bare shoulders in the middle of the afternoon, but that their exposure continued halfway down their bosom would have sent her into an absolute fit.

"Jewell, darling!" one of them called out, waving a long, gloved hand. "We're here, sugar. It took a few years, but we found you!"

Jewell gave each of the girls a hearty kiss on the cheek and ushered them straight into the parlor.

"Girls," she said to all of us gathered in the room, "this here is Yolanda and that's Donna. They're gonna see if they can't get things stirred up a little around here."

And stir things up they did. Our quiet little parlor became a bona fide saloon, where every evening music poured from the piano and drinks were poured into glasses raised high to make loud toasts about almost anything. Gloria insisted they raised such a ruckus that the babies would never get any sleep, and with uncharacteristic generosity, Jewel agreed. Of course, that meant I was forced to move back into Sadie's room, where I cringed at the thought of the new girls' sinful antics in my pretty bed.

"Why can't they go out to Gloria's cabin?" I whined to Jewell when she announced the move.

"You think I want them babies in this house? Listen, girl, there's all kinds of noise I can put up with, but babies ain't one of 'em."

Just three nights after Yolanda and Donna arrived, I walked into the parlor only to see Buck sitting on the sofa with Yolanda perched on his lap.

"Sing me a song, *chico*," she said, her words thick with a Spanish accent.

"I don't think I know any Mexican songs," he said, his own southern accent more pronounced than it ever was when he talked to me.

"Maybe then we go upstairs and I teach you some?"

She was running her finger along the length of his nose, and though he showed no sign of backing away, he did have the decency to scramble to his feet once he saw me.

"Hey there, Biddy." He turned his hat in his hand. "You want to go for a walk with me?"

Something in the pit of my stomach told me if I didn't say yes, he'd soon be walking in the woods with someone else.

One day, Sadie came down to breakfast brimming with news. Mac-Gregan was leaving in less than a week, and he was taking Gloria and the babies to start a new life in Oregon.

The night before Gloria was to leave, we all gathered together in her cabin. The coziness of the kitchen had long disappeared with the introduction of loud music and wild girls. The sound of it carried across the clearing and through the windows open to the late spring breeze.

Even Jewell was drawn out to us, though at first she simply leaned in through the cabin window and berated us for ignoring the guests in the house.

"Oh, they are fine," Sadie said. "Let them drink and play cards."

"They don't *pay* to play cards," Jewell said.

We had all worked very hard to get Gloria ready to go, cutting up any spare garment we could find to make diapers for the babies. Mae had thrown herself into the task of making more suitable clothes for Gloria's new life as a pioneer, and we were all a bit amused to see her buttoned into a plain calico skirt and blouse. As much as we admired her new style, all Mae could see was an urgent need for alterations, so she gathered the garments and ran back to the house, promising to have them hemmed and pressed for the morning.

"All you need now is a sunbonnet and a hunched back." Sadie laughed through a mouthful of a molasses cookie Mae had baked.

"Don't think I'm going to turn into any farmer's wife," Gloria said.

"Oh now, ain't that every woman's dream?" Jewell had come inside the minute Mae left and immediately took up too much space. "You know," Jewell continued, taking a sip from her flask and speaking with a slight slur, "I sure ain't gonna miss listenin' to them kids wailin' at all hours."

"Not much of a mother type, are you?" Sadie said.

"No more'n you are. I'm the mama to all my girls. That's enough for me."

The thought of Jewell even knowing my mother made me shudder.

Jewell leaned forward in her chair and pointed with her flask. "And from what I know, your mamas weren't no different from me." With that, she sat back and took another triumphant swig.

"You're not like my mother," I said quietly. "You're not like her at all."

"Well, listen, little missy," Jewell said. "You're more than welcome to head on out and make a life on your own. Like our little friend here."

Gloria held Danny closer. "Stop it, Jewell."

"But Gloria really isn't on her own, is she? No ma'am. She's living every whore's dream."

"And just what dream is that?" Sadie asked. "Getting stuck with some man's baby? Or getting hauled off to some godforsaken wilderness to churn butter and tend crops?"

"I'm not going to churn butter," Gloria said.

"It's the dream," Jewell said, "of some man comin' along and takin' you to be the little wife."

"That is not everybody's dream, Jewell," Sadie said, though something in her eyes told me it might have been, a long time ago.

I didn't want to be like that. I didn't want to spend the rest of my life here, becoming one of Jewell's girls. Not as beautiful as Gloria, not as smart as Sadie. I didn't have Mae's fun, gentle spirit or the new girls' shameless air. Since Donna and Yolanda arrived, some of the men had been looking at me too. Not the way Buck did—he'd never been anything but chivalrous and kind—but the way Hiram did the minute he walked into Laurent's cabin.

"It's my dream," I said.

Jewell shot me a look that made me too terrified to elaborate.

"Well then," Gloria said, "if it will help with the cause…"

She took a dress from its hook on the wall and draped it over my lap. It was the green one trimmed with black velvet that I had admired so much.

"You'll have to get Mae to do some alterations, but I think the color would be lovely on you."

The conversation continued on around me, but it blurred behind my thoughts as I ran my finger over the soft velvet lining of the dress. It was beautiful, more stylish than anything I had ever owned. But it was a prostitute's dress. Not nearly as vulgar as the gowns Yolanda and

Donna wore, but rich in detail and cut to emphasize a womanly figure, which I despaired of ever having.

I stood up, still holding the dress, and went to the window.
Across the clearing I could see Buck standing at the door, as if deciding whether or not to go inside.

"Look!" I interrupted the other women. "Buck Danglars is coming to visit. I—I think he really fancies me."

All three of the women stopped to stare at me.

"Go talk to him," Sadie said softly, her voice full of protective
affection. "Just talk to him. Don't go upstairs."

Well, of course I wouldn't go upstairs; Buck had never even
hinted at such a thing. Just the question of it haunted me as I made
my way back to the house, my new dress draped over my arm.

Buck met me in the middle of the clearing and looked down at
me with that lanky, shy manner he always seemed to have.

"You ladies having a nice talk?" he asked, inclining his head
toward Gloria's cabin.

"Yes."

"Do you want to go out for a walk with me tonight?"

The moon was shining full and bright, and when I looked up I
could see his eyes as clear and blue as ever. His smile was broad; I
knew his lips would be warm and soft, and the thought of them set
my heart thudding with the same intensity it had the first time he
kissed me.

"Let me ask you something." I tore my eyes away from his face so I could gather my thoughts. "What do you think of me? Do you think that— Do you think I'm like the other girls here?"

He thrust his hands deep into his pockets and stared down at the ground where he was working his boot into a little hole.

"Well," he said finally, "you sure aren't like the girls back home."

"But that first night. You said I was a nice girl. You said you could tell I was a nice girl. Do you still think I am?"

"Compared with those others—"

"No. Not compared to the others. Just me."

He took my face in his hands and leaned down. "Well, you've always been real nice to me."

His lips were on mine, kissing me out in the moonlight, like a dozen other kisses we'd shared before, and I gave into him as we both knew I would. He pulled me close against him, crushing Gloria's dress between us, and for an instant I forgot all about it. Forgot about all my fears. It wasn't until he pulled away and said, "Now, how about taking that walk with me?" that they came crashing back.

I touched my hand to my lips. "I don't think so."

woke up early the morning Gloria left so I could tell her good-bye. I'd never had much to do with Mr. MacGregan, and when I saw him that morning I was struck by what a massive man he was. He lifted Gloria into his wagon as if she were a tiny, prized possession. The rest of us stood and stared. At that point even Jewell would have knocked Gloria clean out of the seat and jumped in that wagon herself had Mr. MacGregan given the slightest invitation.

Watching Gloria drive away put Jewell in a foul mood, and she imposed a state of sobriety for her house, even though the rest of the camp took it as a holiday. When Donna and Yolanda finally roused themselves at noon, Jewell informed them that if they wanted to spend a day carousing, they would have to take themselves to the mountains. They obeyed, gladly, taking more than an evening's supply of whiskey with them.

Once they were gone, the first order of business was to move them out to Gloria's vacated cabin, and I spent the afternoon reclaiming my room. I stripped the sheets, scoured them clean, and hung them out to dry on the wash line in the yard. I wiped off the traces of powder and paint left behind on my bureau, and I thought

I would never see the end to the colorful tufts of fur and feathers scattered in the corners.

As far as Jewell was concerned, we could have thrown the whole lot of their stuff in the yard. She stood on the porch, watching us parade their belongings, and shook her head muttering something about gettin' too old for this mess.

"Admit it, you old crank," Sadie said, "you are going to miss Gloria. And those babies."

"I ain't goin' to be missin' nothin'." But for all Jewell's bluster, there was a hint of sadness in her deep-set little eyes.

Mae and I worked together unpacking their things. It was a fascinating collection of stockings and perfume, jewels and paint. I'd never seen so much silk in my life, and the sheer number of hats could have stocked a small boutique back home. I ran my hands along everything, fascinated by the myriad textures. Everything was lush and rich; my fingers remembered the feel of the black velvet trimming on my new green dress. I wondered if this collection started with a single special garment.

"Well, it looks like it is just the four of us again, at least for tonight," Sadie said that evening as we sat around the kitchen table together.

"Just think," Mae said with the ever-present giggle in her voice, "it wasn't that long ago that it was just the three of us. And now we have our Biddy!"

I smiled at Mae, knowing her heart to be true despite the trepidation her words caused.

"Oh, I hope not for long," Sadie said. "Our next responsibility is to get Biddy home."

"But what about her young beau?" Mae winked.

"I wouldn't worry 'bout that if I was you," Jewell said. "Sadie's been talkin' 'bout goin' home since the day I met her. Ain't happened yet."

"We are not talking about me, Jewell. We are talking about Biddy."

"An' it seems the only one not talkin' is Biddy. Maybe we need to let her decide what she wants."

All eyes fell on me.

"I can't make that decision for myself." I chose to look at the grain in the tabletop. "God will take me where He wants me to go."

Jewell let out her deep, whiskey laugh. "Well, that just tears it then. Guess I'll just have to keep my eyes peeled to see you flyin' outta here someday."

Mae giggled, and even Sadie smiled. I just stared at my folded hands and said, "Unless He decides I should stay."

Although it was still early, we all decided to head for bed, and I was eager to be back in my own room. The sheets on my bed smelled like mountain sunshine, and the open window let in a cooling breeze that carried with it the scent of pine. I quickly changed into my nightgown before letting down my hair and brushing it, replaying the conversation from downstairs. *Just the four of us.* The wonderful sense of safety and protection I'd felt when I first arrived had turned, and now I had the distinct feeling that I was on the verge of drowning.

My Sunday school teacher was fond of saying that sin was a slippery slope. At the time it was just a silly phrase, something we used to mimic when his back was turned, scrunching up our faces and pinching imaginary glasses on our noses as we intoned, "Sin is a slippery slope." Phoebe was especially adept at imitation, and if she ever suspected I was on the verge of doing something wrong, she would come up behind me and sneer, "Sin is a slippery, slippery slope."

But now I knew it was true, like so many of the aphorisms and proverbs of my youth. How had I come to see this place as my home? When did I lose the desire to find my brother? The memory of my parents was fading, and every moment spent with Laurent seemed little more than a dream. Even my prayers had slipped in my zeal to ingratiate myself to this household. As it grew in bawdiness and transgression, I'd grown right along with it.

I picked up my candle and ventured out into the dark hallway. I knocked softly once, then opened the door to Sadie's room. It was dark—she was already in bed—but she sat up the minute I walked in.

"What are you doing here?" she asked, scooting over and patting the mattress beside her. "You have your own room now. Do not tell me you have grown afraid of the dark."

"No." I set the candle on the table by the bed and crawled under the covers. "I was just thinking; then I got a little sad."

"What were you thinking about?"

"Would you ever want to leave this place, Sadie?"

"Yes."

"Where would you go?"

"I have not given it that much thought, but I think I would like to go back to New York. I have a daughter there, you know."

"That sounds wonderful. I wish my mother could come back to me."

"I do not know if my daughter even knows that I am alive," Sadie said, "or what she thinks of me. But I need to find out."

"Do you want to get married?"

She laughed. "Not any time soon."

"Why did you become a prostitute?"

"Ha! That is a very good question. And one with a very long answer. Too long for this late hour."

"I'm not sleepy."

I looked at her in the candlelight, and the look on her face told me she was taking a journey back to a day she'd vowed never to revisit.

"I was not much older than you, dear. And I felt I didn't have any choice."

"Do you…do you think I'll have a choice?"

"Of course you will." Sadie grasped my hands. "Do not get into this life, Biddy. You will never be able to leave it behind if you do."

"There's that boy, Buck Danglars—"

"Be careful. My life was ruined by a boy like that."

My first instinct was to protest and tell her that he seemed to be a nice young man, but the charm of talking about him had worn thin. We talked late into the night, but I didn't leave with the reassurance I sought. I'd hoped Sadie would tell me that her life could never be mine, that because of some great right given at birth or rebirth, I could never become what she was. Instead, I learned how quickly one simple step could lead a girl to slide away from everything she'd ever known.

Once I was back in my room, I slipped off my nightgown and let it fall to the floor. Gloria's dress was lying across the foot of my bed; I picked it up and dropped it over my head. The skirt, of course, pooled around my feet, but I knew Mae's gifted hands would fix that. I reached in the back and pulled the bodice tight against me and stood in front of the mirror. The dress was a flawless wool serge, and the dark green complemented my features more than any I'd ever worn. The neckline fell in a gentle scoop, not deep enough to expose my shoulders, but wide enough to bring focus to my collarbones which, thanks to more than a year of Mae's good cooking, no longer looked as if I'd stolen them from a chicken. My hair was full of waves from the braiding and pinning I'd worn it in all day, and it fell loose around my face and shoulders.

I looked beautiful.

"You look real pretty there, Biddy."

I was too startled to scream, but my gasp was so violent I was just as likely to choke to death as ever breathe normally again. I spun around and saw Buck's smiling face framed by my bedroom window.

"What are you— How did you get up here?"

"What kind of a romantic would I be if I didn't have a ladder?"

"Lower your voice," I said, speaking in a hushed tone myself. "You'll get me into trouble."

Buck laughed. "Just look where you are, Biddy. Now come over here and give me a kiss."

I released my grip and let the bodice expand around me. Then I gathered the skirt so I could walk across the room to the window without tripping. After giving him a quick, chaste kiss on the cheek, I told him to go away.

"That sure is a pretty dress," he said.

"Gloria gave it to me. It doesn't fit."

He reached across the window sill and grabbed my hand. "Come on out and go for a walk with me."

"No, Buck. Not tonight."

He stroked the back of my hand and brought it to his lips, kissing each finger before saying, "Then let me come in there."

This request shocked me as much as hearing his voice in the window, and that same breathlessness overtook me. "How can you ask such a thing?" I finally managed to say.

"Don't worry." He looked straight into my eyes. "Jewell doesn't have to know. And if she finds out…well, I'll work something out with her later."

I felt myself growing smaller and smaller. "Is that how you think of me?"

"Oh, I don't mean any harm by it." He mustered up that smile again. "One more kiss and I'll go."

"I don't think so." I tugged my hands from his grip and reached for the window sash. "Good night."

I slid the window closed and nearly mashed his fingers. The last thing I saw before blowing out my candle was his scowling face behind the glass.

Once he was gone, I pulled the curtain closed and took off Gloria's dress. Feeling my way through the darkness, I found the peg on the wall and hung the dress up before gathering my nightgown from where I'd dropped it on the floor.

No sooner had the white cotton settled on my shoulders than there was a soft knock on my door. And then the door began to open.

Somehow I found a voice to say, "Get out of here, Buck Danglars! I swear I'll go get Jewell, and she'll kill you if I tell her to."

"Sshh! Biddy, it is me." Sadie's voice spoke from the shadows, and I ran into her arms, sobbing against her. "Hush now, *liebling*. What is this about that boy?"

"Oh, Sadie, he thinks I'm a— I don't want to be like you."

"Well now, of course you don't." She stroked my hair.

"I want to go away."

"Then away you shall go." Something in her voice told me she was not speaking mere platitudes.

"How?" I asked. "You're always talking about how much money it would take to leave this place. And I certainly don't have any. And Jewell would never give you—"

"No, Jewell would not. But Gloria would."

"But Gloria's gone." I pulled away from her at last.

Sadie went to the window and pulled the curtain aside. I worried for a moment that Buck's face might still be at the window, but he had vanished as quickly as he'd appeared, and there was nothing left to come into the room but a stream of gray moonlight.

"You are not the only person to receive a gift from Gloria."

Sadie settled on the edge of my bed and patted the mattress, inviting me to join her. Her face was softer than I ever remembered seeing it. Maybe the moonlight smoothed away the roughness, but there was a peacefulness about her that made her seem younger— infused with direction and hope.

"Do you remember the day Gloria arrived and Jewell asked you to search her bags to see if she had any money?"

"Of course."

"Well, Jewell was right to suspect. Gloria did have a lot of money, but she hid it. From Jewell, from all of us. Until now."

"What do you mean?" My own kernel of hope was growing within me.

"Gloria left you that beautiful dress. And to me she left the curtains that were hanging in her window."

"I know. I helped you hang them in your room this afternoon."

Sadie giggled like the long-lost child within her. "They are not ordinary curtains, Biddy. Tonight, after you left just a while ago, I went to my window. To pray, if you must know. I—I have not prayed in quite some time, but something about tonight. I feel like we all need—"

"I know. Seeing Gloria leave and start a new life—and just a while ago, Buck was here—"

"That is all behind you now, my darling. Because when I went to my window, I noticed something odd about the curtains. I found this stitched into the hem."

Sadie reached into the pocket of her dressing gown, pulled out a bundle of folded bills, and held them up in the moonlight. I hadn't seen anything like this since I reached into my father's case and took our modest family fortune.

"All of this was hers?"

"Yes," Sadie said, fanning the notes once before bundling them up again. "And she walked away from it. She left it all behind. If she can do that, Biddy, there is no reason why you and I cannot do the same."

"Do you think that's what she wanted?"

"I am not sure, but I do know she was insistent that I not tell Jewell about the curtains. And now I know why."

"Do you think Jewell will try to take it away?"

I knew the answer to that already. Jewell could be kind, almost motherly, but deep within that billowing breast of hers beat the cold heart of a businesswoman.

"She will not have the opportunity. We owe her nothing."

Sadie's eyes had grown cold, but the change in mood was only temporary, as the next minute she smiled again and clutched me to her in an affectionate embrace.

"Do you realize what this means?" She held me out at arm's length. "Within a week we could be on a stagecoach to anywhere we want to go. Or a train! I hear there are railroads halfway across the country now."

"Would you go back to New York?"

"Perhaps, though I do not know that anything is left for me there. But I could get on a ship there and go to Europe if I wanted to. Start a whole new life. Now we have a choice."

"We've always had a choice," I said softly.

"I know." Sadie's voice matched the softness of my own. "But can you not accept that this is a gift from God? Just as much as it is from Gloria? You have always said that He must have brought you here for a reason. Maybe this is the reason. Maybe you had to come here so that you could go home."

I looked at Sadie and remembered the first time I saw her, when, in my delirium, I thought she was the tallest woman I'd ever seen. Now she was also the strongest. Every part of her story, her life, was etched in her face, but somehow she bore it with grace. I leaned forward, wrapped my hands around her waist, and rested my head on one of her strong shoulders.

"I'm sorry I said I didn't want to be like you," I sobbed into the fabric of her gown.

"Oh, *liebling*. After tonight, I do not want to be like me, either."

That, when our life of faith is done,
In realms of clearer light
We may behold Thee as Thou art,
With full and endless sight.
Amen.

29

One week after finding the money in the curtains, our camp's faithful supply wagon—laden with beer, whiskey, and food—made its way up the pass. Jewell set up her usual impromptu party, laying planks across empty barrels to set up a bar and charging exorbitant prices for drinks and dinner. Music pounded out on the piano inside the parlor, drifting through the open window to accent the festivities.

In the midst of it all, Sadie was quietly talking to the driver, arranging a ride for us to South Pass.

"You should have seen his face when I told him what I was prepared to pay," Sadie whispered later that night as we packed our things. "I even convinced him to set back some of the supplies so we can have a nice supper when we camp."

All this she told me as I stood on the chair in my room while Mae put the final stitches in the hem of Gloria's green dress. She had done a masterful job remaking the dress, creating a cascading tier of fabric along the back of the skirt and lifting the neckline to a respectable level. She used the excess fabric to create a matching reticule embellished with shiny jet beads.

"Oh, I just can't believe you're both leaving." Mae managed to speak without dropping a single pin from her pouting lips. "It's going to be so lonely here without the two of you."

"Nonsense, Mae." Sadie draped an arm across Mae's shoulder. "You have Yolanda and Donna to keep you company."

"Why don't you come with us?" I asked. Her warmth would be the one thing I would truly miss about this home.

"Oh, I couldn't." She held the fabric away, admired her work, then brought it close to her squinted face and resumed her stitching. "Somebody has to keep Jewell in line."

Just then the door flew open, and Jewell stormed inside, startling Mae so much, she pricked her finger with the needle.

"Don't tell me you was plannin' to sneak off in the middle of the night without so much as a good-bye." She planted her hands on her ample hips and surveyed the scene in front of her. "Seems there oughta be a better way for me to find out I'm losin' my partner besides hearin' it from some drunken loon and his pack o' mules."

"I am hardly your partner, Jewell," Sadie said.

"You put up half the money to start this place."

"And I have not taken a dime since. It is yours, Jewell. I can walk away, leaving it all to you. But this cannot be a part of my life anymore."

"And the young one here?" Jewell leaned her head back to look up at me. "Give her another year or so and I could—"

"No, you could not, Jewell," Sadie said. "Not with her. And I think deep down inside you know that."

"Well, you won't be leavin' with my blessings." She turned to leave the room. "But you might as well take somethin'."

She disappeared for just a moment and returned carrying a small satchel covered in a lovely floral tapestry. The bag was open, and inside I could see that it was lined with a rich red silk. She tossed it on the bed.

"Now, Biddy, you come here with nothin', and you're leavin' without much more. But what you got, you need somethin' pretty to carry it in."

"Oh, Jewell…"

I hopped off the chair and ran to embrace this woman whose heart was hidden so far beneath such bluster. My arms would not quite encircle her girth, but I relished the softness of her and buried my face in her ample bosom, which always smelled of sweet powder and tobacco.

I heard the click of her rings as she patted my back. "That driver says he plans to leave before first light, so don't you get any ideas about wakin' me up. You know how I am without my beauty sleep."

"Of course." Sadie leaned over me to give Jewell a kiss on her cheek. "Good-bye, Jewell. I will write when I am settled."

"See that you do." Jewell pulled me closer and bent to kiss the top of my head before pushing me away. "Get on up and let Mae finish that dress."

I obeyed, and by the time I was standing steady, Jewell was gone.

"She didn't ask about where we got money for our trip." I tried to hold very still.

"Oh, she knew about the money." Mae wiped a tear before resuming her stitching. "She knew all along."

South Pass City was two days' drive from Silver Peak. Sadie and I rode in the back of Clem's wagon, bouncing on the hard wooden bed, sometimes unable to talk for fear of biting our tongues. There was, of course, room for one of us to sit next to Clem, but that would leave the other one to bounce alone, and we'd vowed—for the time being, at least—to stick together.

When night fell we made camp. We had sausages to roast on a stick, and we ate them wrapped in soft sourdough rolls that Mae baked the day before. Clem sat with us, drinking whiskey and talking, mostly about Mae, and it soon became clear why he regularly chose to take on this treacherous delivery route.

Sadie and I slept in the back of the wagon and woke up only because we were jostling along again.

When we arrived in South Pass City near dusk the next day, it was obvious *City* had been added to the town's name out of vanity. It was scattered across a wide valley with no attempt to arrange the buildings along a straight street. At least two of them had the familiar look of what we'd left behind, with their doors thrown open to the summer evening. Groups of men gathered around bars while fancily dressed women circulated throughout.

"Ladies," Clem said, after bringing the wagon to a halt, "I believe this is where I will say my farewell." He tipped his hat and disappeared inside the first saloon, receiving a boisterous welcome from the crowd within.

Sadie and I looked around, taking in all the town had to offer. A small stream ran straight through, and several small wooden bridges allowed passage from one side to the other.

"There it is." I pointed to a three-story building on the other side of the stream. "There's the hotel."

We took our bags out of the wagon and made our way across the nearest bridge, though there were plenty of hoots and hollers from the saloon urging us to turn back.

"What do you think, Biddy?" Sadie stepped gingerly on the wooden slats. "Do you want to try your hand at being a saloon girl?"

"No," I said, sharing her humor. "I don't look good in red."

The lobby of the Brasco Hotel was modest but clean, with a well-worn carpet and walls painted in a pleasant, peeling blue. The desk was manned by a tall gentleman with jet black hair and a small mouth surrounded by an equally black, well-groomed goatee. I assumed he was Mr. Brasco.

"We need a room, please," Sadie said.

On the desk sat an oversized guest ledger and a pen. She picked up the pen, dipped it in the inkwell, and signed the book with the poise and confidence of a world traveler.

"Now you." She handed the pen to me.

"Now listen here." The man held up his hands as if to ward off an attack. "I run a clean place here. You want that funny stuff, you need to go across the bridge."

"Do not worry," Sadie said. "We are clean girls. How soon can we expect a eastbound stage?"

"I can't tell you that. You'll have to check at the station in the morning, but I don't think it'll be more than three days."

"Then we will need the room for three days."

Sadie handed a bill across the desk, and Mr. Brasco smiled and offered to take our bags.

The room was like the lobby: serviceable, plain, and clean. We stripped off our dresses and stockings and shoes, and after splashing cool water from the washbasin on our faces and necks, we lay down on the bed wearing only our undergarments. The window was open, letting in the sounds of the town, and I felt tears gather in my eyes and spill over, falling into my ears.

"Biddy, *liebling*, why are you crying?"

"I'm just happy, I guess."

"I am happy too." Sadie squeezed my hand.

"To think how everything changes in just one night."

Mr. Brasco also owned a small restaurant next to the hotel, where Sadie and I went for breakfast after sleeping until midmorning. We each had a plate full of eggs and bacon, with stacks of fluffy hotcakes slathered in butter and gooseberry jam. Afterward we went to the station to inquire about the next stage and learned that one was due in that night, to leave first thing in the morning.

"Come back tonight to see if they have any seats," the station manager said.

That left us the afternoon free to explore the surrounding countryside within walking distance, which we did, enjoying a leisurely pace. We found a small dry goods store, and it felt like a homecoming to examine yards upon yards of ribbon before choosing a tartan pattern that complemented my green dress. We also bought sticks of horehound candy and two small notebooks and pencils so that we would have no excuse not to write to each other in the coming months. I gave her the address of Phoebe's parents in Belleville, and she promised to send word once she had decided on her own destination.

We walked past the edge of the last building in town and saw a crew of men hammering smooth boards into a large square platform raised one foot off the ground.

"What is this?" Sadie asked, boldly approaching one of the laborers, a big burly man with arms that looked like great hairy cannons.

"Independence Day celebration," he said without missing a strike. "This here's the dance floor. Wanna help?"

"I am afraid we are not the best carpenters," Sadie told him, coming as close to flirting as I had ever seen.

"The lady in charge wants two hundred paper stars." He pulled another nail out of the leather pouch attached to his belt and moved down the board. "We don't have time to cut out two hundred paper stars. Maybe you could do that."

"I do not think—"

"Of course we can," I said. "We don't have anything else to do this afternoon."

The man indicated a crate off to the side. "Paper's in there."

In the crate were sheets of red, white, and blue paper, a spool of twine, and a sharpened pair of scissors.

I clapped my hands and gave a little hop, looking like a miniature Mae. "I haven't been to a dance in years."

"You will have a lifetime to go to dances, *liebling*. When you get back home, they will probably have a dance in your honor."

We settled down in the shade of a lumber wagon and dug into our supplies. As there was only one pair of scissors, Sadie folded the papers to make the star pattern easier for me to cut, and then she threaded the twine through each one, creating a garland.

We worked silently as I mulled over the picture in my mind of a grand ball to celebrate my homecoming. There would be a lovely grand ballroom with marble floors and chandeliers and an orchestra assembled on the balcony overlooking the dance floor. The men would wear elegant suits; women, silk gowns; and young girls—like me—would be dressed in ivory satin with white lace gloves.

Who was I to deserve such a celebration? The daughter of a man who squandered away his business and a woman who valued her social position so much her husband would live a lie rather than tell her she didn't belong there. In the years I'd been gone, my companions had been thieves, rapists, murderers, and whores. They had become my family; I'd found refuge in their homes. How likely would it be that the society of Belleville would festoon themselves in satins and lace and command the musicians to strike up a waltz?

I sat with my back to the soft Wyoming summer wind and listened to the chorus of its whisper across the valley grasses. The staccato rhythm of the hammers and the sound of the scissor blades slicing through the paper combined to create the perfect symphony. I looked up at the endless blue sky and imagined what it would be like in a few nights, when all the paper stars Sadie and I created fluttered in the evening breeze beneath a stunning canvas of God's own creation. What would it be like to waltz underneath its vast expanse? to feel the evening breeze cooling the exuberance of the dance from my skin? to feel that God Himself was watching from the rafters, applauding the couples and anticipating the next song?

I snipped the final corner of a crisp red star and handed it over to Sadie.

"I'm not going with you on that stagecoach," I said, unable to look up at her.

"I understand if you want to stay a few days to go to the party."

"No. I mean I'm not going home."

"That, I do not understand."

"There's nothing left for me there, Sadie. I don't think I'd fit in."

"Well, this is out of the question," she said, sounding exactly like my mother. "I cannot simply leave you here alone."

"I'll be fine. I'm a strong girl, remember? I just don't feel like my journey here is over."

"You should pray about this," she said, and I smiled at her new-found faith. "I can stay longer with you, at least until you are sure."

"No, Sadie. I'm sure now, just as you are. You need to do what's right for you. And you need to let me do the same."

She handed me a folded blue paper, and I sliced the first straight line.

"Very well," she said. "But that does not mean I need to leave first thing tomorrow."

"Yes it does. If you don't, you never will."

It was late in the afternoon when we completed our paper star gar-land. The posts were not yet up to hang it, so we carefully layered it in the wooden crate and presented it to the laborer who assigned the task. When our efforts received little more than a grunt of acknowl-edgment, we took our aching hands back to the restaurant next to the Brasco Hotel for a late dinner.

As the manager had promised, the stagecoach arrived around seven that evening. Sadie and I sat on the hotel porch swing, watch-ing the passengers disembark. This was a much bigger rig than the one my family had traveled in, as I counted seven people slapping the dust off their clothes. The sight brought back bittersweet mem-ories, and I spent the rest of the evening telling Sadie the harrowing details of stagecoach travel, with tears choked at the back of my throat and a smile.

The passengers were all guests for the night at our hotel, and Sadie wanted to spend the rest of the evening making their acquaintance.

"Don't bother," I told her. "By tomorrow you'll know them better than you want to."

The next morning I got up early to see Sadie off. We had just enough time for a roll and coffee at the restaurant before walking over to the station to board with the other passengers. When we arrived, the horses were already hitched and the driver was loading bags into the boot.

"This it?" he asked when Sadie handed him her modest satchel.

"That is everything." She handed him a silver coin.

"You want to hurry and get in so you can get a seat by the window," I told her. "Trust me, you don't want to sit in the middle."

"I will fight them off if I have to." She assumed a boxer's stance before enveloping me in a final hug. "I will worry about you with every mile. Whatever will you do with yourself?"

"I don't know." I gave her a final squeeze and stepped away. "Maybe I'll be a scullery maid for Mr. Brasco."

"Well, you would do a wonderful job." She hugged me again, but this time she leaned down close to whisper in my ear. "I have left your half of the money in your bag. Be careful with it."

"So much? Sadie, I don't need—"

"I know it is what Gloria would have wanted. She was quite fond of you, I think. Make the life you want for yourself."

"I will," I whispered, choking back tears.

I remained on the platform even after Sadie was settled in the coach so that she could chat with me through the window. Until the moment the driver cracked his whip and the coach disappeared with the jangling of the traces and a cloud of dust, I think we both thought it possible that I might change my mind and jump inside.

However, before the dust had a chance to settle, I knew I had made the right decision. It was just past dawn, and I was faced with an entire day to myself and an entire town at my disposal. I could go back to my hotel room and sleep the morning away, or I could ask the restaurant to pack me a picnic lunch and I could go exploring. I could go back to the dry goods store and buy whatever my heart desired. I took my first step off the platform, utterly, deliciously independent and alone.

Until I heard my name.

"Lindy!"

I spun on my heel, looking back at the crowd still gathered at the station.

"Lindy!"

I walked away from the platform and around the edge of the building.

"Lindy! Over here!"

The station was behind a two-story building with double doors and a bell tower. It was obviously the town's schoolhouse, because yesterday morning Sadie and I had seen a handful of children pouring through its doors to play in the grassy yard beside it. Neither of us had seen children for so long, we stood and watched, remarking at how little childhood games had changed through the years.

Now I viewed that same building from the back, and to my surprise I saw that the windows were covered with iron bars. And behind those iron bars, yelling my name into this new morning, was my brother Chester.

30

*H*is thick brown curls fell below his eyes, and soft tufts of whiskers peppered his jaw. By the time I reached the window, both of his hands were thrust through the bars, and I caught them in mine. It was the nearest to an embrace that we could manage. Both of us wept great, rolling tears, and when we attempted to speak, our questions ran together.

"How did you—"

"Where have you—"

"When did you—"

At some point the deputy pounded on the inner door, suspicious of all the noise coming from Chester's cell.

"It's my sister." Chester looked over his shoulder.

"Well then," said a voice from within, "tell her to come on in and you two can visit proper."

I went around to the front of the building, arriving just as the doors were unlocked by a tall, thin man with a star pinned to his untucked shirt.

"Morning, miss." He tipped an imaginary hat. "This is a great day in here—you're about all this guy ever talks about. I'll even open his door and let you inside if you promise you won't try to sneak him away."

"I won't."

He led me into a large front room that looked just like the classroom of my childhood. A dozen desks were bolted to the floor, and a large teacher's desk sat at the front. Three of the walls were covered with blackboard paint with yesterday's arithmetic problems still visible in white chalk, and above them the alphabet was painted in perfect script.

"We use this as the courtroom when the judge is in town," the deputy told me as we walked past a small shelf holding half a dozen books.

To the left of the blackboard along the back wall was a door that led to a second room with three prison cells. Chester was in the first one on the far left, looking so much smaller than I remembered.

"You probably don't need to open the door, Lee," he said to the deputy. "Lindy here can probably squeeze right through the bars."

"Oh, shut up," I said, though his taunting pleased me in ways I couldn't begin to describe.

When Deputy Lee unlocked the door, I ran into my brother's arms and would have been content to have the door locked behind me forever.

"Come, sit down." Chester sat on the thin cot that took up nearly half the room, and I sat down beside him. "I've looked for you every day. We were supposed to meet you here, remember?"

I shook my head. "Everything went so wrong. You don't know…"

He pulled me to him, and I rested my head on his shoulder. "Yeah, I do, Lindy. I heard what happened. About Ma and Dad."

"It was so awful. I couldn't do— I couldn't stop him."

"Shh, shh." He rocked me back and forth as if I were a little girl. "Of course you couldn't. But when I heard about the family that had been…killed, and I knew it was my own, I asked everyone, 'What about the girls? My sister and our cousin?' But nobody knew."

"There's no way anybody could have."

"But you're here now, Sis." He held me away to look in my eyes. "Tell me. Everything."

"I can't. Not now, anyway. There's just too much. All that matters is that God has brought me here to you, and He's kept me safe until I could get here."

"And Phoebe?"

If Phoebe were watching from heaven, she would be dancing on the golden streets, because Chester's eyes grew mournful when I was finally able to say that she'd taken ill and died.

"You were so good to her that night," I said.

"Which night are you talking about?"

"In the barn—the night you and Del left."

"Oh yeah, that one. So how much did you see?"

"Everything."

He looked away, but I reached out and turned his face toward me again.

"A kiss can change a girl's whole world, Chester. It was the most generous thing you've ever done."

He held me close again, and this time it was I who broke away.

"Now," I said, "you tell me. What ever happened to Del?"

His face took on that mischievous grin. "I always thought you were a little sweet on him."

"Don't be stupid."

"Well, if it's any comfort, I have no doubt that he returns your affections."

"I couldn't care in the least, as a matter of fact," I said, but I felt my pulse quicken. "I just wondered where he is, that's all."

Chester stood up and walked to the cell door. "Believe it or not, he's probably still asleep. That guy could sleep through an earthquake."

"He's here?" I jumped up from the cot and started to smooth my skirt.

"Right next door." Chester held a finger to his lips and motioned the deputy to come near. "Do me a favor, Lee. Go open Saunders's cell and let her in it. Then bang on his foot or something until he wakes up."

Deputy Lee shrugged, let me out of Chester's cell, then opened the next door down.

"Go on," Chester urged.

While it seemed right to be a part of one of Chester's pranks, my stomach churned. Still, I walked into the middle cell behind Deputy Lee and kept my eyes to the floor.

"Hey, Saunders," Lee said, his voice so gruff it had to be part of the joke. "Wake up, son. There's somebody here to see you."

I looked up just in time to see the deputy give me a wink, and my eyes followed him as he slunk out of the cell. Then, I turned to face the form sleeping on the cot. I'd like to think that, had my brother known Del was not wearing a shirt, he would never have put me in this position. As it was, the first thing I saw was a strong, wide back and his hair—even longer than it had been—splayed out over his bare shoulders. Then he braced his hands against the mattress, slowly pushed himself up, and turned to face me.

I stood motionless. Proud of myself for remembering to breathe.

"Belinda?"

"Good morning, Del."

He swung his legs over the edge of his cot and sat there, clasping his hands in front of him, bowing his head so that his hair became a curtain obscuring his face. Then I heard his voice whispering, "Thank You, God, for bringing her home."

Later that morning I brought over a platter of pastries from the restaurant, and Deputy Lee allowed the three of us to gather in one cell for breakfast. In the time that I was gone, both Chester and Del cleaned up considerably, running a wet comb through their hair and donning relatively clean shirts. A small table was procured from somewhere in the courthouse and covered with a blue-checked cloth. Chester's cot was used as a bench—he and I sat on it together—and another chair was brought in for Del. We had a pot of good, strong tea, which I generously laced with honey, and a dish of strawberry preserves courtesy of the deputy's wife.

It wasn't until we were all in place and Del had asked a blessing on the food that I finally had the chance to ask the question that had been plaguing me all morning.

"Who is going to tell me why you are both in jail?"

They exchanged a sheepish look before Chester said, "It's my fault."

"No argument there," Del said.

"We were at Celine's," Chester began.

"Oh," I said. "The place with the piano music and fancy ladies?"

"And card tables," Del said. "Don't forget card tables."

"The man accused me of cheating," Chester said. "Not only have I never cheated in a card game in my life, what proof would he have, seeing that I was twenty bucks in the hole?"

"It's the age-old mystery." Del held up his hands.

"There I am, hardly winning a hand all night, and he has the nerve to call me a cheater."

"So your brother threw a table," Del said.

"I did not! I tripped as I was standing to leave the game, and the man got the wrong idea."

"And you got into a fight," I said.

"I had my honor to protect, Sis."

"And just how did you get involved in this?" I asked Del.

"Just happened to be walking by, heard the ruckus, and realized this boy needed saving. He was—"

"Doing fine."

"—pinned to the floor. I pulled the guy off him, and the next thing you know, all three of us are being hauled in for drunken and disorderly conduct."

"Which is another lie." Chester gestured with his pastry. "Neither of us were drunk. Del here doesn't touch the stuff."

"So, why isn't this other man in here with you two?" I said.

"The circuit judge was here about a week after we were arrested," Del said. "That guy paid his fine and got out."

"Paid it with the money he won from me," Chester said. "Tell me where the justice is in that."

"How much is the fine?" I asked

"Twenty dollars," Del said.

"For each of you?"

"Yes."

Neither he nor Chester would look at me.

"And you don't have it?" I trained my eyes on Chester. "It's gone? All of it?"

"I'm so sorry, Lindy."

"That was everything we had. Our parents died for that."

"I know," Chester was whispering now. "I'm so sorry. I just—"

"It's not all gone," Del said. "There's a bit of it here in the bank. But I can think of better things to spend forty dollars on. Plus," his broad, smooth face broke into a smile, "it's six months we don't have to pay room and board."

"You've been here for six months?"

"Just two so far."

"When does the judge come back around?" I asked.

They looked at each other and shrugged.

"Because I have money."

"Well then, you're in luck." Deputy Lee stood in the cell door-way, twirling his keys. "Judge'll be here in a week."

I visited the boys often during the intervening days, bringing them breakfast and dinner. It was over these meals that I told them, as much as I could, the stories of all that had happened to me after the murder of our parents. Once again we were all silent and sad as I recounted Phoebe's illness and passing, but Del beamed when I told them of Laurent's redemption. Chester said nothing, and I knew he hadn't found it in his heart yet to forgive. When I told them of Hiram's demise, I said only that he seemed bent on attacking me, letting them fill in any missing details for themselves. I described my time at Jewell's as a year of friendship, restoration, and healing.

When I was not at the jail, I spent my time back at the site for the Independence Day celebration. I'd established a friendship with Lars, the carpenter in charge, and he relegated all the decorating to me. A ten-foot pole was set up at each corner of the dance floor, and I wrapped red, white, and blue streamers around each one before hanging tiny lanterns on the ropes strung between them. When the floor was complete, I took my place among all the workers on my hands and knees, sanding it smooth. I suggested that they erect a framework behind the band's stage on which we could display the flag. Finally, the day before the celebration, I pulled out the garland of paper stars and directed the men who had somehow become my crew in stringing them high above the dance floor.

Then it was time to go to court.

The proceedings were informal and brief. Perhaps it was because of the holiday, but the circuit judge did little more than doff his hat, take my money, and pronounce my brother and Del to be free men. They each had their few belongings in a drawstring canvas bag that the deputy handed over upon their release.

Before their arrest, Chester and Del had shared a room over the town's post office, but I reserved a room for them down the hall from me at the Brasco Hotel. On the ground floor behind the lobby was a washroom with running water where the boys could each get a bath in Mr. Brasco's porcelain, claw-foot tub before heading off to the celebration. I had taken one the night before and highly recommended Mrs. Brasco's aloe-caked soap.

While I waited for Chester and Del to finish their baths, I pressed Gloria's green dress, curled and pinned my hair in a complicated, fetching style, and fashioned the tartan ribbon into a bow around my neck. A long oval mirror hung behind my hotel room door, and I turned slowly in front of it to see that I looked passably attractive from all angles. After all, I would be dancing.

There was a knock on my door, and I opened it to see Chester, his hair neatly trimmed and his face clean-shaven.

"You look beautiful, Lindy," he said as he walked in.

"Thank you, dear brother." I offered a curtsy.

"I worry about you staying in this room all by yourself."

"I'll be fine. I've been in worse places. Besides, I think Mr. Brasco sees me as a long-lost daughter. He takes very good care of me."

"Well, that's good to know." He had a handkerchief in his pocket that he took out now and refolded. "I don't think it's such a good idea for you to have all that money in here with you, though. That can't be safe."

"I know." I used my foot to slide my satchel under the bed. "But I made a tiny rip in the lining, and I keep it in there."

Chester continued to fidget with his handkerchief. "That's probably a good idea. You're the smart one."

"Always have been."

"Come on." He offered me his arm. "We're meeting Del in the lobby."

I dropped my comb and handkerchief in my reticule and looped it over my wrist. Together, Chester and I walked down the stairs to where Del sat in one of the threadbare lobby chairs. The minute he saw us, he stood up. He wore a starched blue shirt with a sprigged pattern of tiny green leaves and a clean pair of brown wool pants. He'd combed his hair back off his face, though I much preferred it loose, with tendrils draped in front of his eyes. But his most striking feature was the slight smile that came to his face the minute he saw me and the soft green eyes that never looked away.

"Shall we?" He opened the front doors wide.

We could hear the slightest strains of the band even from here, and my toes tapped in anticipation. But when I heard Del's heavy step drag across the hotel porch, both my toes and my heart became still.

We made our way toward the music, walking companionably at Del's pace. The sun was setting behind us, casting three long shadows.

"You know what?" Chester clapped one hand on my shoulder and the other on Del's. "I forgot something back in the room. Why don't you both go on without me, and I'll catch up."

"What'd you forget?" Del said.

"Just some extra nickels for lemonade. Or whatever other goodies they might have."

"I have money." I held up my reticule.

"Now, Sis, there might be some pretty ladies—excuse me, some *other* pretty ladies—there tonight. What would I look like if I had to ask my little sister for a nickel to buy a lemonade?"

Without pausing for a response, he started jogging back to the hotel, leaving Del and me to walk alone.

"It's a nice breeze," he said after a few minutes.

"It is," I said. "Del, I haven't had a chance to say this yet, but thank you."

"For what?"

"For taking care of Chester. He needs looking after sometimes."

"Glad to do it," he said.

Even though I'd contributed many of the details myself, the vision of the dance floor took my breath away. There had to be more than a hundred people milling about, all dressed in their finest. I even scanned the crowd for Jewell or any of the men from Silver Peak, though I knew she would be throwing her own festivities there.

"This looks nice, don't it?" Del said.

"Yes, it does. You know, I cut out every one of those paper stars."

He stepped back to get the fullest effect. "Very impressive."

"And just what did you do to bring this all together?"

He turned to me. "I prayed for you, Belinda. Every day I prayed that God would bring you back safe to your brother. And," he added softly, "to me."

"Oh. Well, thank you."

We made our way through the crowd washing down sausages and corn pone with cold lemonade. One long table full of pies had been judged earlier, and they were available for ten cents a slice. Since we couldn't decide on a flavor, we shared pieces of cherry, apple, and pumpkin between us.

"Shouldn't we wait for Chester to join us?" I was licking my lips after eating a stick of sugar-encrusted fried bread.

"When he gets here, we'll go for seconds." Del fished in his pocket for another nickel to buy us each a cup of spiced cider.

I craned my neck looking for my brother, but it was getting harder to see as the clearing turned to twilight. Finally, I caught his face in the crowd and grabbed Del's hand to bring us to him.

"Where have you been?" I hollered in Chester's ear to make myself heard over the band of three fiddles, a snare drum, a banjo, and an accordion. "Come dance with your sister!"

Chester looked at me, his eyes dark pools of shame and sadness. "You lied to me, Lindy."

"What are you talking about?" Del said.

"This." Chester reached into his pocket, pulled out a slip of paper, and thrust it at Del. "Read it."

I couldn't hear the words Del mouthed as he read out loud. But I didn't have to. I'd written them myself earlier that morning.

" 'Better is little with the fear of the LORD than great treasure and trouble therewith.' Proverbs 15:16."

At first, Del was the only one laughing, but soon enough Chester's crooked smile appeared, and I allowed myself to relax and smile too.

"I'm sorry I lied to you." I uncinched the string of my reticule and drew out a couple of bills and a handful of coins. "We're family, Chester. What's mine is yours. You have only to ask." I pressed the money into his hand. "Now, please, dance with me."

Chester pulled me to him and planted a kiss on top of my head. "Sorry, Sis, I've been detained. Maybe later?" He held me close so close I could hear him whisper, "Stay here with Del, Lindy. Dance with him. He's as good a man as I've ever known."

He was turning to walk away when Del grabbed his arm. "Don't do this, brother."

Chester pulled his arm away. "It's fine. I'm fine," he said, before disappearing into the crowd.

The song ended, and Del and I stood in the middle of soft, rippling applause.

"You shouldn't have done that, Belinda."

"He's my brother."

"He's just going to—"

"That's between Chester and God then, isn't it?"

"I guess it is at that," Del said. "Want to take a walk?"

I nodded and slipped my hand through the crook of his offered arm. His steps faltered as usual, but I matched mine to his as we wove through the crowd.

"You know, Miss Belinda," he said, "there's lots of other verses in the Bible about treasures."

"I know."

"Do you know the one that says wherever your treasure is, that's where your heart is too?"

"Yes," I said.

He stopped walking and put his hands on my shoulders, turning me to face him.

"I never cared about the money. Didn't care much about that brother of yours at first, but I figured if I stuck with him, I'd get myself back to you. What I'm sayin' is, my heart is with you tonight, Belinda. It's been yours since the first night I saw you."

"Is that why you kissed me?"

He smiled. "I apologize for my boldness. I just couldn't take a chance on not seein' you again."

"I'm glad."

"So," he leaned down so close that he blocked out every other image, "can I kiss you again?"

"That depends. Are you planning to ride off in the middle of the night with all my money?"

"Never. I'm never letting you out of my sight again."

"Then you may kiss me. But see that you make it a good one, in case it needs to last for another year."

Del burst into laughter, picked me right off my feet, and twirled me in circle after circle until I was breathless with protest.

"Then we'll wait until later." He looked up into my face. "For now, just dance with me."

My expression must have registered my misgiving, because he squeezed me tighter and gave me a little shake.

"Come on! You have to trust me. Do you trust me?"

Deciding I had answered yes, he carried me through the crowd and onto the dance floor just as the band struck up a waltz. Del lowered me to the ground and we stood, motionless, as the music swirled around us. His hands were on my waist, and mine almost on his shoulders. I'd never felt so small. Or so safe.

"I know my steps aren't perfect when I walk," he said, "but somehow I think it'll be different when we dance."

He held me so close, I could feel his heart beating beneath my touch. I tried to focus on the pattern of leaves on his shirt, but they blurred between my fingers. I closed my eyes and waited to be afraid, waited for the nightmare of Hiram to close around my throat, for the memory of my lurid behavior with Buck to fill me with shame. Instead, I saw only darkness, as complete and profound as the night I walked backward down the cellar stairs.

I had seen my future after all.

Now when I open my eyes, I look up and see paper stars fluttering above us, and God's own twinkling above those. Del clasps one hand in his and brings it to his lips. We stand for just a minute until the next downbeat. Then, with a smoothness I could never have predicted, he leads me in our first step together. And I follow. He leads, I follow, effortlessly, through the next and the next and the next.

Reader's Guide

1. *With Endless Sight* opens with a childhood game to "predict" a future love. Do you remember any such games from your childhood? Why is this such an appealing game for little girls?

2. Belinda and her mother have a strained relationship. What are some things that often cause friction between mothers and daughters?

3. As brother and sister, Belinda and Chester are equally at each other's throats and in each other's hearts. What are some of the unique qualities of the brother/sister relationship? How does this translate to the fact that, as Christians, we are brothers and sisters in Christ?

4. Belinda confronts Chester with this verse: "Better a little with the fear of the LORD than great wealth with turmoil" (Proverbs 15:16, NIV). How does this verse hold true throughout the story? Was there ever a time in your life when great wealth or the possibility of great wealth held the threat of great turmoil?

5. What do you think motivates Chester in the tender scene between Phoebe and him in Chapter 11?

6. Why is Belinda able to forgive Laurent? What are some situations in your life where you've found it difficult to forgive someone?

7. Belinda forms relationships with four very different young men in this book: Chester, Laurent, Buck, and Del. What does she gain from each? How do different people fulfill different needs in our lives?

8. Belinda is quite young—only fifteen by the end of the story. In what ways is she like a typical, modern teenager? In what ways is she different? Have the changes that have occurred in the last one hundred fifty years made our society safer for young women?

9. The characters Sadie, Jewell, and Gloria all appear in the first two Crossroads of Grace novels: *Ten Thousand Charms* and *Speak Through the Wind*. What new insights do you have about those characters, having read *With Endless Sight*?

10. Revisit the first chapter of the book. In what way is it a snapshot of all that is to come?

11. The title *With Endless Sight* comes from a line in the hymn "We Walk by Faith and Not by Sight," which is printed at the front of the story with stanzas throughout. Having read the hymn, in what way are its lyrics significant to you? What other hymns or worship songs do you think might relate to this story?

12. Psalm 31:14 (NIV) says, "But I trust in you, O LORD; I say, 'You are my God.'" Where in the story do you see Belinda wholly putting her trust in God? Was there ever a time when you were so depleted you could rely only on Him?

13. *With Endless Sight* begins with an awakening. What role does the idea of "awakening" play throughout the story?

Author's Note

WITH ENDLESS SIGHT concludes in South Pass City, Wyoming, a little town that factors into all three books in the Crossroads of Grace series. South Pass City is a real place, a ghost town located just two miles off Highway 28, thirty-five miles south of Lander, Wyoming. I admit I had to play with some of the dates since much of the town didn't exist until several years after the Crossroads stories take place.

But if you have a chance to go, you'll see that the buildings are perfectly restored. There really is a schoolhouse combined with a jail where you can still see the alphabet painted high on the walls and step back into one of the three tiny cells. There is also a hotel (though I supplied the name) with a tall, narrow staircase and bright green walls. And, of course, there are several colorful entertainment establishments.

On a warm summer day in South Pass City, you can sit and refresh your feet in the cool stream that runs through the town. If you close your eyes and listen, the wind will speak. If you are very still, it will feel like the embrace of our Savior. If you look out over the horizon, you'll get just a tiny glimpse of the endless sight of our Creator.

DISCOVER THE FIRST TWO BOOKS IN
THE CROSSROAD OF GRACE SERIES!

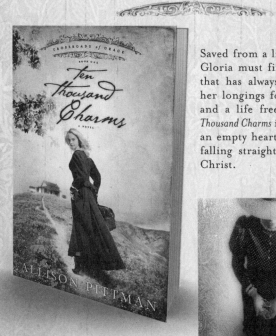

Saved from a life of prostitution, Gloria must finally face the pain that has always plagued her and her longings for home, a family, and a life free from shame. *Ten Thousand Charms* is a beautiful tale of an empty heart floundering...and falling straight into the arms of Christ.

Life in a tiny room above a brothel, the loss of a child, a lover's rejection, and finally, life as a prostitute. Feeling as though she has nothing left to lose and nowhere to go, Kassandra leaves behind her hopes of redemption and heads west to California, where she is transformed into the woman known as Sadie. Unfortunately, nothing in her life is pointing to a happy ending, and Sadie is forced to grapple with the question: Once you've passed the point of no return, can you ever go back?